"You're a Woman of Many Talents, Is That It?"

"You might say that. At least I haven't had any complaints," Leslie was goaded into saying.

His slow, insolent gaze traveled up her body. "I can believe that. In fact, I wouldn't be averse to finding out myself."

"You flatter yourself, Mr. Mackenzie. You don't happen to be my type."

His smile was slow and confident. "Are you sure about that?" He sauntered lazily over to her and trapped her in her chair. "That's a challenge no man could refuse."

TRACY SINCLAIR
has traveled extensively throughout the continental United States as well as Alaska, the Hawaiian Islands and Canada. She currently resides in San Francisco.

Dear Reader,

Silhouette Special Editions are an exciting new line of contemporary romances from Silhouette Books. Special Editions are written specifically for our readers who want a story with heightened romantic tension.

Special Editions have all the elements you've enjoyed in Silhouette Romances and *more.* These stories concentrate on romance in a longer, more realistic and sophisticated way, and they feature greater sensual detail.

I hope you enjoy this book and all the wonderful romances from Silhouette. We welcome any suggestions or comments and invite you to write to us at the address below.

Karen Solem
Editor-in-Chief
Silhouette Books
P.O. Box 769
New York, N. Y. 10019

TRACY SINCLAIR

Fair Exchange

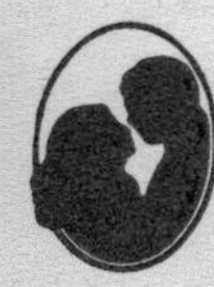

SILHOUETTE BOOKS, a Division of Simon & Schuster, Inc.
1230 Avenue of the Americas, New York, N.Y. 10020

Distributed by Pocket Books

ISBN: 0-671-53605-2

First Silhouette Books printing July, 1983

10 9 8 7 6 5 4 3 2 1

Map by Ray Lundgren

America's Publisher of Contemporary Romance

Printed in the U.S.A.

To Ed and Jeff,
the two men in my life

Other Silhouette Books by Tracy Sinclair

Paradise Island
Holiday in Jamaica
Never Give Your Heart
Mixed Blessing
Flight to Romance
Designed for Love
Castles in the Air

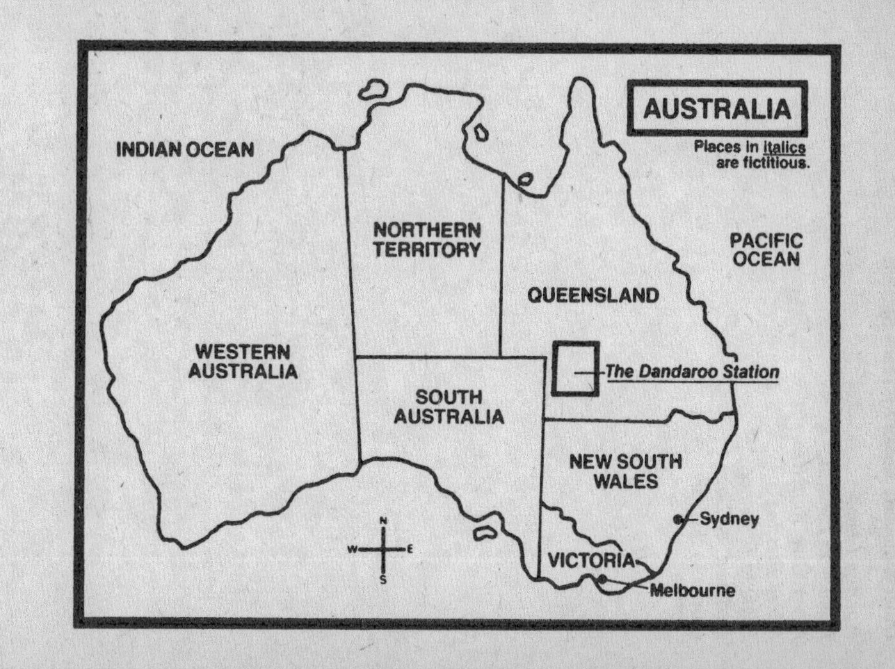
AUSTRALIA
Places in italics are fictitious.
INDIAN OCEAN
PACIFIC OCEAN
NORTHERN TERRITORY
QUEENSLAND
WESTERN AUSTRALIA
SOUTH AUSTRALIA
The Dandaroo Station
NEW SOUTH WALES
Sydney
VICTORIA
Melbourne
N
W
E
S

Chapter One

Leslie Farraday flexed her tired neck muscles, wearily pushing slim fingers through the cloud of red-gold hair that framed her delicate face.

Well, everything eventually comes to an end, she thought wryly, even though there were times when her trip hadn't seemed like it ever would. The flight from Los Angeles to Sydney had been bad enough—fourteen hours in the air. Then she had had to get on another plane to fly to Broken Hill in the Australian outback, the wilderness area given over to wild animals, huge cattle ranches, called stations, and not much else. Even then her journey hadn't been over. In Broken Hill she had had to rent a car to take her the final distance to her destination, the Danduroo Station.

Driving in this wide-open country was a sobering experience. There were no other cars on the road or any signs of human life. And although this was supposed to be cattle and sheep country, there wasn't an animal in sight. The rolling plains were bare except for occasional groves of pungent-smelling eucalyptus trees and clumps of feathery acacias. Not even an isolated farmhouse was to be seen.

The only evidence of civilization was the narrow road and the barbed wire protecting the land on both sides of it. Bold signs posted at intervals warned off intruders. *Scarcely a welcoming touch,* Leslie thought, anxiously looking for some kind of entrance. The man at the car rental agency had told her that the Danduroo covered fifteen thousand acres, but surely there must be some way to get inside.

Her tense body relaxed slightly when she spied a narrow lane to the left. After a long bumpy ride along what was little more than a dusty trail, the way was barred by a gate. As she got out to open it, a sudden burst of hysterical laughter shattered the silence, making the hair rise on the back of her neck. There was a flash of blue and white in the dense bordering trees, and Leslie started to breathe again. It must have been one of the kookaburras she had read about. The Australians called this largest member of the kingfisher family the "laughing jackass." With good reason, she decided. Peering fruitlessly into the dense foliage after it, Leslie slowly got back into the car and continued up the road, uneasiness accompanying her.

What kind of reception awaited her when Raider Mackenzie, whoever he was, discovered she was here under false pretenses? Well, it wasn't her fault, Leslie told herself defensively. Heaven knows she had done everything she could to convince him that she wasn't who he thought she was. Everything except refuse to use the free ticket he had sent, the small voice of conscience reminded her.

The first letter from him had been waiting when she and her roommate, Kay Borden, arrived back at their small apartment on the last day of school. Kay was filled with euphoria at the thought of the two and a half months of summer vacation that lay ahead, but Leslie was feeling rather forlorn.

"It's just because this is your first teaching job," Kay assured her. "Plus the fact that you teach kindergarten. If you had to handle my sixth graders, you'd be singing hallelujah just like I am."

"You're a big faker." Leslie smiled. "You know you're going to miss them."

"Not this summer. I'm going to be too busy." Kay reached into their slot in the bank of mailboxes. "I do wish you were coming with me. Are you sure there's no way you can swing it?"

Leslie's deep blue eyes were regretful. The white water rafting trip down the Colorado River that Kay was planning sounded wonderful. "I wish I could, but you know the problem—money. I still owe part of what I borrowed from Aunt Laura to move down here. If I'd known how expensive it was to live in Los Angeles, I might have stayed in San Francisco."

"You went to college here," Kay pointed out. "It shouldn't have come as such a shock to you."

"That was different. For one thing, I didn't need a car. Westwood Village was within walking distance," she said, naming the college town tucked like an oasis in the sprawling environs of Los Angeles. "And if I needed to go anywhere else, there was always some accommodating soul with wheels."

"I don't doubt it," Kay said dryly, eyeing her roommate's curved figure and the exquisite face framed by its cloud of copper-colored hair. "You must have had half the males at UCLA dancing attendance on you.

I'm just surprised that you made it to graduation without getting hauled to the altar."

Leslie unlocked the front door and pushed it open. "My mother married young," she said shortly, as though that explained it.

Kay was silent. She knew the tensions that existed between Leslie and her father, a spare, silent man with a bitter face. In the ten months that Kay and Leslie had shared an apartment, he had never been to visit his daughter, nor had they corresponded. Kay had met him in San Francisco when she was helping Leslie move, and she had been puzzled at the hostility he couldn't conceal. It was especially noticeable since Leslie was so close to her younger brother, Bart, and her beloved Aunt Laura, her father's sister.

Seeking a way to change the subject, Kay glanced down at the mail in her hand. "Well, this is a switch. Instead of our usual tasteful collection of bills and circulars, there's an interesting-looking letter for you." She held it closer to look at the foreign stamp. "Who do you know in Australia?"

"Not a soul." Leslie examined the letter. "I knew it had to be a mistake. Look, it's addressed to *Mr.* Leslie Farraday."

"They probably just hit the *r* instead of the *s*. Open it."

"Do you think I should?" Leslie asked doubtfully.

"Of course. It's your name and address."

It was all the urging Leslie needed, since her curiosity equaled Kay's. Once she read the contents Leslie said, "I knew I shouldn't have opened it."

"What does it say?"

Kay looked over her friend's shoulder while together they read, "Dear Mr. Farraday: This is to inform you that you have been named sole beneficiary in the will of Lester Eames, who died on May 20th of this year. Your inheritance consists of ten acres, including a house, on the Danduroo Station in the outback region of Australia. Since you have never expressed an interest in visiting this area, I assume that you will expect to sell the property, in which case I am prepared to offer you a fair price. If you will contact me by return mail, we can consummate the deal with all due haste, which I am sure will please you greatly." It was signed "Raider Mackenzie."

"Well, somebody's an heiress—or I guess I should say an heir," Kay said.

"Yes, but whoever this Raider Mackenzie is, he sounds like a very angry man," Leslie said slowly. "I wonder why?"

"Who knows? Maybe he expected to inherit the property himself."

"I guess so. Anyway, it doesn't concern me."

Leslie sent the letter back with an explanation that it had been opened by mistake, thinking that would be the end of it. But another letter came by return mail, even testier in tone, informing her that there had been no mistake and asking her to name her terms. Leslie again attempted to set things straight, with the same result. After that, things got even more complicated, until the final letter arrived with a ticket to Australia and what almost amounted to an order for Leslie to come in person and resolve the matter.

"Take it," Kay advised. "What do you have to lose? You've done everything you can to convince this character he's wrong. The worst thing that can happen is that you get a marvelous free vacation out of it."

"Do you know how much it costs to fly to Australia?" Leslie gasped.

"All the more reason. You could never afford it yourself, and this guy seems to have more money than brains. You've explained it to him enough times, heaven knows. Now grab the opportunity. You're in the clear. *He* is the one who's insisting."

It had seemed reasonable when Kay was explaining it, yet now that the confrontation was near, Leslie felt her nerves tightening. Raider Mackenzie hadn't sounded very pleasant in his letters. What would he be like in person? She conjured up an image of a stout, red-faced man who was apt to become abusive—verbally only, she hoped.

Suddenly a rather dilapidated house appeared out of the uncharted wilderness. It was badly in need of paint, and the windows looked as if they hadn't been washed in a year, but to Leslie it looked like a palace. Every bone and muscle in her body ached. She wanted a bath and something to eat, after which she planned on sleeping for hours on end.

Getting stiffly out of the car, she approached the front door. Total silence came from the house, but a peculiar sound permeated the countryside—men's voices punctuated by strange low animal noises. As she punched the front doorbell impatiently, the sound increased in volume, setting her already jangled nerves on edge.

When no one answered her ring, Leslie felt her patience giving out. She had come halfway around the world, she was tired and hungry and she wanted to get out of the clothes she had been wearing for twenty-four hours. Was this the great Australian hospitality she had been hearing so much about? Marching to her car, she leaned on the horn, filling the countryside with raucous sound. The events that followed were a frightening blur.

For a moment she thought no one had heard her urgent summons, then the volume of noise increased. A cloud of dust was her first warning. Leslie stood by her car and watched in disbelief as the swirling dust of a herd of stampeding cattle headed straight for her. They were running amuck, heedless of the frenzied shouts of the mounted cowboys who sought to alter their course. The solid wall of rampaging animals was deaf to anything but their own panic. With rolling eyes, they thundered straight ahead, trampling everything in their path.

Leslie could only stare in horror as they came so close that she could see their gaping red mouths. She was frozen with fear, facing certain death yet unable to save herself, when salvation appeared miraculously. Out of nowhere, a man on a rearing black horse appeared.

At first he seemed like part of the nightmare: a satanic figure on a beast straight out of hell. If Leslie could have run, this would have given her the impetus, but she was powerless to move. She remained rooted to the spot, gazing mutely at the fearsome apparition as he leaned down and lifted her roughly into the saddle, almost under the hooves of the galloping cattle. The terrifying animals were almost upon them when, at the last instant, they parted and charged past, re-forming in a mindless race to nowhere as she clung to her savior, devil or no.

One strong arm held her to a hard-muscled chest while he tried to control the plunging horse with the other. She hung on for dear life, burying her face in his neck and wrapping her arms convulsively around his lean waist.

In a matter of minutes that seemed like hours, the herd thundered off into the distance, leaving a pool of blessed silence. Still Leslie didn't relinquish her death grip or raise her head, even when the man swore savagely.

"You bloody idiot! Are you the one who left the gate open?" A long shudder ran through her as he rasped, "Don't you know you could have been killed? What kind of half-wit would lean on a horn and spook a whole herd?"

When she remained silent, being incapable of speech, he grabbed a handful of her hair and pulled her head back roughly. Leslie found herself looking into a pair of the angriest gray eyes she had ever encountered. They were surrounded by thick, spiky black lashes and were set in a lean face distinguished by high cheekbones and a firm mouth with a sensuous lower lip, which was thinned now with rage.

Angrily raking a big, capable hand through the thick dark hair that fell across his wide forehead, he demanded, "Who the hell are you, and what are you doing here?"

Leslie's trembling mouth opened, but she couldn't make a sound, just as she couldn't force herself to remove her arms from around his waist. The strength of that sinewy body provided the security she badly needed. His warmth was the only thing she had to cling to.

Some of the anger left his face as he recognized that she was in shock. Folding her close, he pressed her head against his shoulder, holding her quietly while he waited for her to calm down. When she couldn't seem to stop shaking, he stroked her hair gently, murmuring soothing words.

At last her quivering subsided somewhat and he tucked a strand of bright hair behind her ear. "Feel better now?" he asked softly.

She nodded her head, still without lifting her face. For the first time since she had come to this strange land, Leslie felt safe. This man had demonstrated that he could protect her from anything, and she was reluctant to leave the haven of his arms.

He lifted her chin, forcing her to look at him. "I didn't mean to yell at you, but that was a very foolish thing you did."

"I'm sorry," she whispered, her eyes wide with remembered terror.

His arms tightened for a moment as he looked at her soft mouth. "Yes, well, I don't think you'll do it again."

"Oh, I won't, I promise!" Leslie suddenly became aware of the fact that she was locked in the embrace of a strange man and was resisting his efforts to free himself. Color stained her pale cheeks as she self-consciously removed her arms from around his waist. Her long eyelashes fluttered down. "I'm sorry," she murmured again.

Laughter softened the man's arrogant face. "Don't apologize for that. It was the only nice thing about this near tragedy." He looked at her curiously. "Who are you, anyway, and how did you stray onto the Danduroo?"

"I was looking for a man named Raider Mackenzie."

"At your service." He smiled.

"Oh, no!" This was turning out to be even worse than she had imagined. How could he be the man who had fired off those irritable letters to her? If she had had any idea that Raider Mackenzie was a man like this, she never would have let Kay talk her into this insane adventure. Explaining matters to a testy old country squire was one thing. Justifying herself to this dominant male, who looked perfectly capable of doing something about his displeasure, was quite another.

He raised a sardonic eyebrow. "I'm sorry I don't measure up to whatever preconceived notion you had, but I assure you I am Raider Mackenzie."

"I didn't mean . . . it's just that I thought . . ."

"Why is the idea so frightening? In spite of what you might have been told, I don't devour little girls for breakfast." His amused smile changed to a puzzled frown. "What did you want to see me about? You haven't told me yet who you are."

"My . . . my name is Leslie Farraday, and I—"

The halting words stopped as his fingers bit into her shoulder. He was looking at her with open hostility. "You're not Leslie Farraday. What are you trying to pull?"

"Nothing. I . . . I really am."

The gray eyes that had been so warmly teasing were now like chips of ice. "I don't know what your game is, but you didn't do your homework very well. Leslie Farraday is a man."

"No, I tried to tell you. I wrote to you over and over again, but you wouldn't believe me. And then Kay said—well, I know it was wrong but it didn't seem—I mean, you *did* insist." The lame words came to a halt, shriveled by his black fury.

"It couldn't be!" A fierce scowl of concentration drew his dark brows together as he stared at her. "I guess it could at that," he said slowly. "He didn't actually say. I just assumed." Suddenly his gaze sharpened. After examining her frightened face minutely, his eyes moved to the glowing red-gold hair. A muscle jumped briefly in his rigid jaw. "Yes, I guess there isn't any doubt."

"I'm sorry. I know I shouldn't have come, but I did try to convince you and you wouldn't . . . I'll leave right away."

He stared at her for a long moment in silence. Then he slid out of the saddle.

"I think we'd better go inside and have a talk," he said ominously, holding up his arms to help her down.

Leslie put her hands on his shoulders, uneasily noting their muscular width. His big hands almost spanned her slim waist, and when she was standing on the ground he towered over her by half a foot. It put her at an immediate disadvantage to have to look up so far.

"In here," he ordered, unlocking the door of the little house.

It had a musty smell, and there was dust on the odds and ends of nondescript furniture. If this man had a wife, she wasn't a very good housekeeper.

"It seems I've made an error," Raider Mackenzie said. "I gathered from Lester that you were a boy. A man," he amended.

"*Your* Leslie Farraday probably is. These unisex names are confusing." Her manner was anxiously conciliatory.

The smile he gave her held no mirth. "No, the confusion was all in my mind."

"Do you mean you still don't believe me?" she asked in disbelief. "I couldn't possibly be the person you're looking for. I've never heard of Lester Eames, and I've never been in Australia before in my life!"

"I'm certainly aware of that." He looked at her with a contempt that completely bewildered Leslie. "But Lester knew you, or I should say he knew about you."

"How could he possibly?"

The lines around Raider's nose deepened. "He was a . . . friend of your mother's. Caroline was her name, wasn't it?"

Leslie was startled. How could he know that? Nevertheless, she said firmly, "You must be mistaken. My mother never mentioned anyone named Lester Eames."

"That isn't too surprising," he said sardonically.

Leslie's eyes sparkled angrily. "Just what are you implying, Mr. Mackenzie? That my mother was some kind of a snob? Well, you couldn't be more wrong! I'm sure she didn't know him either."

There was disbelief—and something else—on his strong face. "Why don't you ask her?"

"My mother is dead," she said flatly.

"I didn't know." Although he didn't express sympathy, his voice was less stern. "Was it recent?"

"About a year ago." The pain of it was still with Leslie. It had been just before her graduation from college. That was what had hurt so much. Without her, the ceremony had been diminished.

"I'm sorry," Raider said finally, noticing the shimmer of unshed tears.

Leslie squared her shoulders. She didn't want sympathy from this huge, brawny stranger, who seemed to be casting vague aspersions on her mother—the dearest, sweetest woman who had ever lived. "It can't possibly matter to you. You never met her," she said rudely.

He shrugged. "If I did, I wouldn't remember. I was only eight when she was here."

Leslie looked at him with the first stirrings of doubt. Her mother *had* been in Australia. Was it possible? No, that was too absurd. She had been only eighteen years old at the time, just graduated from high school. Leslie's grandfather had been in the meat packing business, and since his daughter's graduation coincided with one of his semiannual trips to Australia, he had taken her and her best friend, Laura Farraday, as a graduation present. It was possible, of course, that her mother had met this Lester Eames at some point, but to suppose that his passion for a teenage girl had been durable enough for him to make her daughter his sole heir twenty-three years later was merely laughable.

"I still say you've made a mistake, Mr. Mackenzie. The fact that my mother visited here once doesn't prove anything. That's ancient history."

"How about the fact that Lester asked to see you before he died?"

"Not *me*. Someone by the same name, unfortunately."

His gray eyes glittered with dislike. "All right, if that's the way you want it. Just answer one question for me. Why did you ignore the letter that told you he was dying and wanted to see you, yet you responded to the one that said you were his heir?"

None of this made any sense. "You wrote to me before?"

"Please don't insult my intelligence by trying to tell me you didn't receive it, Miss Farraday," he said contemptuously. "The letter was never returned."

Leslie felt physically bruised by his animosity. Adding to her distress was a terrible feeling that he was telling the truth. The letter informing Leslie of her supposed inheritance had been forwarded by her brother, who was home from Stanford for the summer vacation. If a previous letter addressed to her had arrived, her father would have directed it to the dead letter office.

Leslie's relationship with her father was the great tragedy of her life. She had been aware of his preference for her brother all the years that she was growing up. It was so obvious that even her mother noticed, although there was nothing she could do about it except suffer along with her daughter. It took a long while for Leslie to realize that it was more than that.

In the beginning she had run to her father with small triumphs, only to be rejected coldly. He was too busy, or he wasn't interested, or he disparaged what she considered to be accomplishments. It had hurt a great deal. Only gradually did Leslie come to accept it and stop trying to win his approval. After her mother died, things had worsened to the extent that Leslie knew she had to leave home. The break with her father was now quite final, although her relationships with her brother and aunt were warm enough to make up for it.

The trouble was that there was no way she was going to air her dirty linen in public. This man would never believe she hadn't received the first letter anyway.

"I can't tell you how sorry I am about this whole mix-up. Was Mr. Eames . . . was he sick long?"

"He had an accident on the station," Raider said tersely. "It might interest you to know that you were in his thoughts at the end."

She spread her hands helplessly. "Is there no way that I can convince you that you're wrong?"

"Lester himself gave me your address in San Francisco. Does that sound like there is any doubt?"

Fatigue enveloped Leslie and she sank into a chair. What had seemed like a relatively harmless lark was turning into a nightmare. A man she had never heard of had called for her on his deathbed, and she hadn't responded. The fact that she hadn't known about it didn't lessen her feeling of guilt.

"I don't understand any of this," she said wearily. "Could you tell me something about this Lester Eames?"

"I wondered when you'd get around to asking that." He moved to stand over her, looking down from a great height with his arms folded as though in judgment. "Lester was one of the finest men I've ever known. He had a generous, giving nature. Too bad you—" Raider stopped abruptly.

When he didn't continue, Leslie said diffidently, "I gather that he didn't have any family, if he left his property to me."

"I believe there were some distant relatives back in England, but he had lost touch with them. Lester came to Australia when he was a young man. His first and only job was working for my father."

"Even though he had his own ranch?" she asked. When Raider looked at her blankly, Leslie said, "The . . . the ten acres he left to me."

Raider's face relaxed in a completely natural smile for the first time. The transformation was startling. This was a man who clearly had considerable charm when he cared to exercise it. Leslie could only guess at the countless women who had been bowled over by his male magnetism.

"Ten acres in the outback constitutes a rather roomy yard, Miss Farraday."

Remembering belatedly that Danduroo Station consisted of fifteen *thousand* acres, Leslie understood his mirth. "It would be a sizable estate in California," she said defensively.

His momentary goodwill dissipated. "I'm sorry if your anticipation of being an heiress was premature."

"That wasn't what I—oh, what's the use! Why do you dislike me so much, Mr. Mackenzie?" she cried.

He looked at her impassively. "How I feel about you personally doesn't enter into it. You have something to sell, and I'm prepared to buy. I think that covers it."

Leslie felt chilled by his disapproval. She wasn't used to this treatment by men, and it angered her. Seeking to strike back at him, she said, "You're only half-right."

"What do you mean?"

"You're obviously very anxious to buy my paltry ten acres, but I'm not sure I want to sell."

His eyes narrowed dangerously. "What do you plan to do with them?"

"I haven't decided yet. Maybe I'll just keep them for a summer place," she said airily.

"Your summer or ours? As you can see, it's quite chilly here. July is one of our winter months."

"So what? Cold weather doesn't bother me."

"How much of it do you have in California?" he asked mockingly.

"I'm sure Australia isn't so backward that you don't have heat in your houses."

"We have heat," he agreed. "But sometimes it's different from what you're used to. This house of Lester's, for instance—"

"This isn't where you live?" she interrupted.

Something was affording Raider a great deal of amusement, which he tried unsuccessfully to conceal. "No, this is part of your inheritance, Miss Farraday."

"Oh, I . . . I didn't realize."

"Well, now you do. Perhaps I'd better explain how you—"

His insufferable superiority stiffened Leslie's resolve not to let this man patronize her. "You don't have to explain anything to me," she interrupted again. "I'll get along just fine without any help from you."

"I was only going to say that the heat is not what you're accustomed to."

"Very kind of you, but completely unnecessary. I'm sure you have a great deal to do, Mr. Mackenzie, and I wouldn't want to keep you from it."

"You're right, I do have a lot to do." His manner suggested that he had already wasted more time than he cared to. "But you and I have some unfinished business," he said flatly.

"I told you. I haven't made up my mind yet."

He restrained himself with an effort. "How long do you think it will take?"

"I'm not certain. However, when I do decide, you'll be the first to know," she told him, delighted to see the muscle that bunched at the point of his strong jaw.

He didn't storm out of the house in a rage as she had half expected. To her dismay, he sank into a chair instead, his long legs stretched indolently. He had evidently decided on a new tack. "The outback isn't exactly jumping with excitement. The nights especially can be pretty deadly if you're all alone." His gaze swept over her insolently, pausing at the rounded breasts that thrust upward against her white sweater.

Leslie felt her whole body heat with what she assured herself was rage. Springing to her feet, she cried, "I don't know if your low opinion encompasses all women or just me, but let me assure you, Mr. Mackenzie, that I don't need a man to keep me happy, if that's what you're implying."

He rose to his feet with a fluid grace that reminded her uncomfortably of a panther's leashed power. "I can hardly believe that, Miss Farraday." His big hand caressed her slender neck, sliding up to tangle in the glowing mass of her hair. Bringing her head forward, he said, "Surely more than one man has had the pleasure of . . . your company."

He was so close that she could feel the heat of his body and smell the pungent male odor of leather and horseflesh that clung to his tight jeans and sheepskin jacket. The tiny pinpoints of light in his gray eyes as they fastened on her full mouth lit answering flames in Leslie's suddenly taut body.

"How dare you?" she raged. "You don't know anything about me. How *dare* you make such an accusation?"

His expression was enigmatic. "Perhaps I know more about you than you think."

"I doubt it. You've formed a very derogatory opinion of me for some reason, but how about yourself? What makes you so high-and-mighty? I don't notice you bristling with scruples. You're willing to do whatever is necessary to get my poor little ten acres. Tell me, Mr. Mackenzie, were you going to get me to sign the papers before, during or after the seduction?"

"Certainly not during," he chuckled.

Leslie's cheeks flamed. "You're disgusting!"

"I thought I was being very considerate," he said mockingly. "Regardless of how we feel about each other, I can assure you that I would see to it that you got a great deal of pleasure out of the . . . transaction."

Leslie's hands curled into little fists. "Get out of my house!" she commanded through clenched teeth.

"My, my, how fast we've taken possession."

"I want you out of here this instant!" she exploded.

"And supposing I don't choose to go?" He folded his arms, lounging against the doorframe while he regarded her with considerable amusement. "What do you propose to do about it?"

There was nothing she *could* do; they both knew that. A very strong man would have trouble evicting him if he didn't want to go. Suddenly Leslie was quiveringly aware of the fact that they were completely alone in his domain. No one even knew she was here. This huge stranger, who had taken such an inexplicable dislike to her, could do anything he wanted, even do away with her if it pleased his purpose. No, she mustn't let her imagination run riot. Raider Mackenzie was undoubtedly a man to be wary of, but not in that way.

Taking a deep breath to still her racing heart, Leslie tried a new approach. "Obviously I can't put you out bodily, if that's what you mean. I can't imagine why you would want to remain, though. You don't like me, and I don't like you," she said bluntly, "so why don't you just go?"

His face hardened. "As soon as we come to an agreement."

"It seems to me that you're making a big doggone deal out of ten measly acres when you already have fifteen thousand," she cried in exasperation.

He shrugged to show that it was a matter of no importance, yet his eyes were watchful. "They aren't any use to you."

"So you're really doing me a favor by taking them off my hands, is that it?" she asked sarcastically.

"No, I'm offering you a fair price." He named a sum that made her eyes widen. Taking in her startled expression, Raider smiled sardonically. "I thought that would change your mind."

"I didn't say I had changed my mind," she flared. "As a matter of fact, my land isn't for sale, Mr. Mackenzie!" Even as she said it, Leslie was dismayed. The amount of money involved would pay all her bills and give her a comfortable nest egg for the first time in her life. But this man made her so *angry!*

"Oh, you'll sell, Miss Farraday. Make no mistake about that," he said softly, yet the menace in that quiet voice made a shiver run up Leslie's spine.

"Don't count on it," she said with a scorn that covered growing trepidation. "I'm beginning to think you're trying to put something over on me. I don't even know where my acreage is."

"You're standing on part of it." Amusement cut lines in the tanned cheeks once more. "Did you think I was trying to fleece you out of an opal mine, perhaps? Sorry to disappoint you, but your ten acres are the ones directly surrounding this house."

Leslie thought about it. "The ones those crazy cows of yours stormed across? Then you were trespassing," she cried triumphantly. "I had every right to honk my own horn on my own property."

He covered the distance between them in two swift steps, his fingers biting into the tender skin of her upper arms. "If you ever do that again, you little idiot, I swear I'll let them trample you like a blade of grass!"

Leslie recoiled from the fury in his blazing eyes. "Well, I . . . of course I wouldn't. I only meant . . . why don't you drive your cattle on your own land?" she finished petulantly.

A strange expression came over his face, and he released her abruptly. "Your property, as you call it, is indistinguishable from mine."

"I don't understand."

"My father gave Lester that parcel in payment for a wager. It was a joke, really. Although it was deeded to him legally, there was never any question of its going to a stranger. It was always understood that we would buy it from him if he ever needed money." Raider raked annoyed fingers through his thick hair. "That ten acres is part of Danduroo Station."

"But it belongs to me," Leslie said gleefully.

He looked at her with contempt. "All right, what's your price?"

"Oh, it isn't the money. As I told you, I just might keep the place." She looked around the shabby living room. "With a little paint and some new curtains, I think this house could be quite charming."

"You're planning to stay?" he asked ominously.

"At least for the summer."

"Which is our winter, remember."

"No problem." She smiled. "I knew about that, so I brought warm clothes."

A vein throbbed at his temple. "What do you expect to do with yourself all alone out here in the wilderness?"

She surveyed the dusty room. "For one thing, make this place habitable. Lester wasn't great shakes as a housekeeper."

"He wasn't here very much," Raider said tersely.

It had such a rootless sound. Suddenly Leslie was overwhelmed by compassion for a man she had never met—a man who inspired respect and admiration in Raider Mackenzie, whose standards seemed to be very high indeed, yet who was so alone in the world that he left all his worldly goods to a complete stranger.

"I wish I had known him," she said wistfully.

Raider's expression was impassive. "Maybe it's better this way."

Once more she was up against the hard wall of his enmity without the strength to combat it. Fatigue overwhelmed her. "Can't we please talk tomorrow?" she pleaded. "It's been such a long trip."

His expression softened somewhat as he noticed her pale face and the circles under the wide blue eyes. "Right. You look like you could use some rest. Before I go, though, I'd better explain about the generator and the butane."

"Not now. Whatever it is can wait till tomorrow."

"But you have to know how to switch over when one tank gets empty."

She put her hands over her ears. "Don't you understand? I've been through as much as I can possibly take today. Please leave me alone!"

His mouth was a grim line in the rugged face. "You strain the bonds of hospitality pretty far, lady."

"I don't want you to be hospitable," she cried. "All I want to do is take a hot bath and go to bed."

The peaked eyebrow he raised was derisive. "For your sake, I hope the cylinder holds out."

With that cryptic remark, he was gone. Leslie hadn't the slightest idea what he was talking about, and she didn't care. The long journey plus the change in hours was catching up with her. She needed some time alone, away from this big man's disturbing presence.

Leslie dragged her suitcase into the one bedroom of the small house. Like everything else, it had a film of dust over it, but she decided that house cleaning would have to wait till tomorrow. Locating a linen closet, she was thankful to find clean sheets and blankets. After stripping the bed, she made it up with fresh linen. Then she ran a tub of steaming water and soaked her tired body.

When her eyes started to close, Leslie knew it was time to get out. Toweling herself dry with one of the big fluffy towels she had found in a cabinet, she pinned her hair on top of her head and put on the only robe she had brought. Unfortunately it was a pink silk caftan that was remarkable more for its beauty—and the fact that it didn't take up much room in her suitcase—than for its warmth.

In spite of the hot bath, she was starting to shiver slightly. How did one turn up the heat? Maybe she should have listened to Raider when he wanted to explain the workings of the house. Oh, well, there were blankets, and she would be going to bed soon.

The trouble was that she was hungry. Leslie had to think hard to remember the last time she had eaten. Was it on the plane? This trip had been so fraught with problems that mundane things like food had taken a back seat. Her body was now starting to rebel.

Going into the kitchen for the first time, Leslie inspected the contents of the refrigerator. It didn't take long. There was beer, some slightly moldy cheese and a few covered containers, the contents of which she didn't have the nerve to explore.

The cupboards weren't much better. They consisted mainly of sardines and a couple of cans of chili and beans.

A desolate feeling of being alone, deserted and unloved assailed Leslie. While she was trying to convince herself that going without dinner wasn't the worst thing that could happen, there was a pounding on the door.

She opened it to find Raider Mackenzie there, holding a large cardboard carton. Delicious odors were wafting from it. Shouldering past her as she looked at him blankly, he carried the carton into the kitchen.

"I figured there wasn't anything in the house to eat, so I brought you some dinner," he said.

"You didn't have—I mean, that was very nice of you," she mumbled.

"We don't let anyone starve on the Danduroo." His eyes traveled from the spill of bright curls piled on top of her head, down over the slim, provocatively revealed body.

Leslie's breathing quickened as she realized how little the semitransparent robe concealed. Folding her arms over her breasts, she said, "Thank you for the food. It was very thoughtful of you, but I don't want to impose any further on your time."

"I'm in no hurry." He lounged against the sink, inspecting her with the frank appreciation of a man with a hearty sexual appetite. "Is there anything else I can do for you?"

"Nothing," she gasped, backing away, although he made no move toward her. "I'll be just fine now."

"Will you? I wonder." His smile was mocking. "If you hear any noises in the night, don't worry. It's probably just wild dingoes. They hardly ever get in the house."

After he had gone, Leslie's breathing gradually returned to normal. Dingoes indeed! If he only knew he was a heck of a lot more frightening than a bunch of wild dogs!

The dinner he brought was delicious: chicken pie with baby carrots and new peas swimming in a rich gravy under a flaky crust. For dessert there was a gorgeous chocolate concoction stuffed with nuts and topped with whipped cream. Leslie ate every crumb while puzzling over this strange man.

Who had cooked this marvelous dinner? Certainly not he! His wife, then? He didn't act like a married man, but you never could tell. And why had he bothered to bring it to her? It was a singular act of kindness that didn't jibe with his earlier treatment. Which brought up another point. Why had he been prepared to dislike her even before they met?

It was all tied up somehow with Lester Eames, and that was another puzzle. Leslie was forced to concede, in the face of all the evidence, that she was Lester's designated heir. But why? Had he been in love with her mother? If so, the affection hadn't been returned. Even granting that they had met somewhere, he hadn't made much of an impression. Her mother had clearly forgotten him immediately, since she had married soon after returning home.

Leslie had only found out by accident about her mother's visit to Australia in the first place. And it wasn't even from her. Aunt Laura had mentioned it casually once. She was the one who had given Leslie the rather sketchy details.

The two young girls had evidently had a marvelous time exploring Sydney before spending some time on a cattle station. As it turned out, it was a last fling for Caroline. Leslie was always happy that her mother had at least had that brief period of carefree gaiety. Maybe that was the reason she never spoke about it. When her marriage turned out to be so joyless, perhaps the memory of those last days of freedom became too precious to talk about.

Leslie sighed and carried her plate to the sink. She would have to try and untangle everything tomorrow. Tonight she was much too tired.

Chapter Two

The sun was already climbing to its zenith when Leslie languidly opened her eyes the next morning. The unfamiliar surroundings recalled the events of the previous day, and a quick look at the clock brought her upright in bed. Almost noon! She never slept that late. It must be the tremendous change in time that had completely confused her sleep patterns. It was hopeless even to try to calculate what time it was in California.

One thing that registered was that she had better get up and dressed. If Raider Mackenzie returned to renew his campaign to get her out, Leslie didn't want him to find her in bed. The look he gave her the previous night when he surprised her in a robe had been altogether too masculine.

After a quick shower she scrambled into her clothes, breathing a sigh of relief that there was no sign of him. At least she was ready now. As the minutes ticked by,

Leslie became annoyed. Did he intend to wage a war of nerves, keeping her off balance wondering when he would turn up? Well, it wouldn't work! There were any number of things she had to do. Her bags weren't even unpacked yet, and the house could certainly stand a thorough cleaning, for starters.

The afternoon flew by as Leslie attacked the accumulated grime of weeks of neglect. Responding to her determined efforts, the windows sparkled, the kitchen floor displayed a charming blue and white pattern and dust motes no longer danced in the bright sunshine illuminating the shabby but comfortable living room.

It took all day. When the light started to fade, Leslie looked around the snug little house with a feeling of satisfaction mixed with regret. Of course she was going to sell to the Mackenzie man. What choice did she have? It would have been nice to keep the place, though—the first house she had ever owned. The following day she would inspect the ten acres that came with it, Leslie promised herself.

The large carton of food Raider had brought contained extensive provisions in addition to the cooked food, so dinner was no problem. Besides dairy goods, there were meat, fresh vegetables and a loaf of homemade bread. It didn't seem worthwhile to make dinner just for herself, so Leslie contented herself with some scrambled eggs and a glass of milk. Since that took no time at all, a very long evening stretched ahead of her.

What was Raider doing right now? That he was with a woman, she had no doubt. Even without the evidence of that well-cooked food, Leslie knew there had to be a woman in the picture somewhere. He was definitely not the lonesome cowboy type, content with the sole company of his horse.

An unexpected quiver passed over Leslie as she relived the experience of being in his arms. After clinging to him so tightly, she knew every whipcord muscle in that hard chest, knew there hadn't been an ounce of fat to cushion the impact on her own yielding body.

Leslie grew warm with embarrassment as she remembered the way her lips had inadvertently pressed against the smooth skin of his neck, feeling the cords that stood out as he struggled to master the rearing horse. Even in the midst of her terror, his raw masculinity had inspired confidence.

Leslie suddenly experienced a funny sensation in the pit of her stomach. What would it be like to lie in his arms for a different reason? She had seen laughter warm those icy gray eyes, transforming him into the kind of wickedly charming man that mothers warned their daughters about. That sensuous mouth alone would draw women like a magnet.

Leslie gave a little shiver, pulling herself up short. She was letting her imagination run away with her. Okay, so he was rugged and tall and intensely masculine. He was also rude and threatening, and worst of all, he had jumped to some wild conclusion about her without bothering with facts. Their dislike was mutual. Although she would have to give him what he wanted, she didn't have to make it easy for him. Leslie was sure he wasn't often thwarted, certainly not by a woman, so it would be good for his character to be kept dangling for a bit, she decided with satisfaction.

Putting him firmly out of her mind, she settled down to read for a while, but she found it difficult to concentrate. For one thing, the night was filled with strange noises. Leslie couldn't help thinking about

Raider's reference to wild dingo dogs. Just how wild were they? she wondered uneasily. Surely he was only trying to frighten her, she assured herself. What else was out there, though? What kind of . . . thing . . . made those alarming sounds?

Thoroughly disgusted with herself for playing into Raider's hands, Leslie turned up the volume on her little transistor radio.

By the next morning she was over her attack of nerves and ready to go exploring. After pulling on a heavy sweater and a jacket, she went outside.

It was a glorious day, crisp yet sunny. The uninhabited countryside stretched out in all directions, slightly chilling in its magnitude. The grassland was dotted with groves of trees, and the only living things were butterflies and birds, both of which were enchanting. Some of them were to be found nowhere else in the world.

Leslie had done some reading on Australia in preparation for the trip, so she was able to identify a willie wagtail right away. Even if she hadn't recognized him, his amusing habit of bobbing his head and wagging his tail every time he landed on a branch would have given him away. The swarms of green and yellow parrakeets, or budgies, were familiar, as were the tiny zebra finches with their white-barred tails and brilliant red beaks. It was strange, though, to see them flying free in great flocks, when at home they were kept confined, one or two to a cage. Strange and wonderful.

Leslie wandered over the pastureland, enjoying the fresh air and the exercise. The thought that she was treading her own ground was very heady indeed. How much was ten acres? she wondered.

Time passed unnoticed as she strayed farther and

farther from the house. Sounds in the distance were the first indication that she wasn't the only person abroad on this beautiful day. Climbing a small knoll, she came upon a fascinating sight. Mounted cowboys were rounding up hundreds of cattle, funneling them into a chute that led to a fenced corral. The animals were making a terrible din, which was augmented by the shouting men and barking dogs that expertly circled the herd, rounding up strays.

Mindful of her last encounter with these beasts, Leslie prudently made for a large tree and leaned against it to watch, keeping very still. Gradually she realized that what looked like chaos was in reality a very professional, smoothly running operation, whatever they were doing.

Suddenly another sound was added to the melee: the strident clang of metal striking on metal. Several of the cowboys jumped down from their horses as Leslie noticed a chuck wagon standing to one side. A man who must have been the cook was beating on a steel triangle. A quick look at her watch told Leslie it was lunchtime, a fact her stomach verified.

Why hadn't she thought to bring along a sandwich? Or why hadn't she at least eaten breakfast instead of having just a cup of coffee? Leslie realized that she was far from home and ravenous. Was it worthwhile going all the way back? As she paused undecided, one of the men spotted her. Raising his arm, he shouted something she couldn't hear.

Leslie was smitten with instant apprehension. Had she done something wrong again? This must be Raider's property she was now on, and he undoubtedly had strict rules against trespassing. As she hurriedly turned to go, the mounted man came cantering up to her.

"I'm sorry. I didn't realize I was on private property," she said breathlessly. "I was just leaving."

"Did your horse bolt?" he asked sympathetically. He was young and good-looking, with curly blond hair and a friendly face.

"No, I . . . I don't have a horse."

A puzzled look crossed his face. "How did you get way out here?"

"I walked."

This was clearly erratic behavior as far as he was concerned. "From where?"

"I'm staying at Lester Eames's house," Leslie explained. "I didn't realize I had strayed off his property. I'll go right away."

"What's the hurry?" he smiled. "As long as you're here, why don't you come down and have some tucker with us?"

"I beg your pardon?"

"Tucker. Food." He grinned. "You're a Yank, aren't you? What part of the States?"

"California." She smiled back.

"I hear that's beautiful country."

"Yes, it is, but so is this." Leslie looked over the broad expanse. "I never knew there were such wide-open spaces left in the world."

He nodded in agreement. "You can ride for days and not be off Danduroo property."

Shouts from the men below interrupted them, and Leslie said, "I'm keeping you from your lunch."

"Come and join us," he invited again.

Leslie was torn between hunger and the sure knowledge that Raider wouldn't approve. "Maybe there isn't enough," she said tentatively.

"You sure don't know cattle country, lady," he

laughed. Sliding down from his horse, he wiped his hand on his jeans before extending it. "It's about time I introduced myself. I'm Marty Lanson."

Leslie shook hands, supplying her own name and allowing herself to be persuaded to join him. As they were walking toward the chuck wagon she said, "I've been watching you, and whatever you're doing looks fascinating. Could you tell me what it is?"

"I'll give you a crash course in cattle ranching over lunch," he promised.

The other cowboys were mostly young like Marty. Out of all the names that were thrown at her, Leslie managed to remember that the cook was named Hank, and some of the other men were Ed, Russell and Spike. They greeted her with the appreciative look that she was used to seeing in men's eyes. In addition, they were all polite and anxious to welcome her. It was a pleasant change from Raider's reception, Leslie thought dryly.

"This is awfully nice of you," she told Hank.

"It's our pleasure," he told her gallantly. "We don't usually have such lovely company."

"Make that never," Marty joked. "Our usual company is heifers and steers."

"You were going to tell me what you're doing with them," Leslie prompted.

"We're cutting the young bulls out of the herd," he explained. "It's time to put the two-year-olds into a separate pasture to get them ready to breed."

Hank's frown told that he considered this too indelicate a subject for a lady. Leslie was amused when he handed her a steaming plate of food and sought to change the subject. "I'm afraid this isn't very fancy, Miss Farraday, but at least you won't starve to death."

"Please call me Leslie, all of you, and it looks marvelous."

The beef stew lived up to its appetizing aroma. It was made out of tender meat and succulent vegetables cooked just right. To go with it were the flakiest biscuits she had ever tasted. There were no tables or chairs. Everyone sat on the ground, which made it seem like a picnic. That, and the companionship and laughter they shared with her.

"What made you turn up at Danduroo Station, Leslie?" Ed asked. "Most tourists go to Sydney or one of the other cities."

"Well, I . . ." She hesitated. "I was invited to stay at Lester's house for a while."

At mention of his name the laughter died. "We sure miss him," Marty said soberly. "He was a great guy, wasn't he?"

"I never knew him," Leslie answered without thinking. At their look of surprise, she said hastily, "He was a friend of my . . . my family. What was he like?" she asked impulsively. "I really have such a sketchy picture."

"Lester was the finest man I've ever met," Ed said. "He fit in with the cowboys just as easily as he fit in with the swells."

"That's right," Hank agreed. "You'd never know he had a fancy college education."

Leslie was startled. "I didn't know that."

"It was in England before he ever came to Australia."

"I remember when Lester first started at the Danduroo," Hank, who was older than the rest, said. "My father was the cook here then."

"Too bad he didn't teach you anything," one of the others joked.

Hank sent him a quelling glance before continuing. "I was just a little nipper. I followed him around like a sheepdog pup, always under his feet, but he never lost patience. He was the one who taught me how to rope and ride. Nobody else had time to bother with a small lad."

"My little brother thought he was Father Christmas and the Easter Bunny all rolled into one," Spike said. "Took it just terrible when Lester died."

"I gather he never married," Leslie said tentatively. "Do you . . . that is, it seems kind of strange considering how much he liked children."

Hank lit a cigarette, cupping his hands around the match for a moment before answering. "I think he had an unhappy love affair way back. Not that he ever talked about it. Lester never did talk about himself, or anybody else for that matter. It wasn't his style."

Their faces were somber as they paid silent tribute to a man they all respected and missed. Marty jumped up and reached into the chuck wagon, bringing out a guitar. "The one thing Lester would purely hate is having everyone sit around with long faces mourning him. Let's liven things up a little." Sitting cross-legged in front of Leslie, he told her, "This was one of his favorites."

Marty struck up the rollicking chords of "Waltzing Matilda," and all the men joined in singing:

> Once a jolly swagman camped by a billabong,
> Under the shade of a coolabah tree;
> And he sang as he watched and waited 'til his billy
> boiled,
> "Who'll come a waltzing Matilda with me?"

Leslie's blue eyes sparkled with pleasure. "I've heard that song so many times, but it didn't mean anything to me," she said. "Now whenever I hear it I'll be able to picture a handsome couple dancing together in this beautiful grass."

They disconcerted her by bursting into laughter. "Sorry to spoil your pretty picture, Leslie, but waltzing Matilda isn't frolicking around with a pretty girl. It means carrying a bedroll like the swagmen do."

"I didn't know that!" she exclaimed. "What on earth is a swagman?"

"A vagabond or wanderer."

"And a billabong?" she asked.

"That's a water hole." Anticipating her next question, Marty said, "A coolabah tree is a kind of eucalyptus."

Leslie digested this for a moment in silence. Then she said, "Well, at least I bet I know what billy is. Coffee?"

"Wrong again, luv. A billy is a tin can used for boiling water to make tea."

"I can't believe it," she marveled. "It's a whole different language. Sing some more and let me see if I can figure it out."

They obliged her with the second chorus, and when she heard the line that goes "And he sang as he stowed that jumbuck in his tucker bag," Leslie raised her hand like one of her pupils. "At least I know what part of it means. Tucker is food, but what's a jumbuck?"

She was not to find out. The laughter faded from their faces as they caught sight of something over her shoulder.

Before Leslie could turn to see what had caused this reaction, there was the sound of hooves. Raider cantered down the knoll and was in their midst, dominating the whole group by his mere presence. The big black horse tossed his head and wheeled around as though anxious to continue his ride, flaring his nostrils as Raider subdued him easily.

Surveying the group of men relaxing on the grass, his cold glance slid over Leslie. He pointedly pushed back the sleeve of his jacket and looked at the watch nestled among springing black hairs. "I didn't know today was a holiday. What are we celebrating?"

As though his voice had released them from a spell, they jumped to their feet. "We were just showing Miss Farraday here a little Australian hospitality," Hank said placatingly.

Leslie got up too, dusting off the seat of her jeans. "It was my fault. I'm afraid I was—"

"It's *always* your fault, Miss Farraday," Raider interrupted harshly. "Did you come here for the express purpose of disrupting my station?"

Leslie's temper flared to match her flaming hair, which looked in the brilliant light as though a piece of the sun had become tangled in it. She threw her head back to look up at him, her cheeks flushed a delicate pink. "I came here because you *insisted,* Mr. Mackenzie. Or perhaps you have conveniently forgotten that?"

His eyes narrowed on her lovely face for a moment before his wide mouth curved mockingly. "Anybody is entitled to one mistake." Becoming aware of the men regarding him disapprovingly, Raider scowled. "Do you intend going back to work today, or should I send the bulls a written invitation to meet you in the north pasture?"

The set of their shoulders indicated their opinion of Raider's sarcasm, but there was no open grumbling. Leslie was outraged. Who did he think he was, mounted on his horse high above them like some feudal lord of the manor? The traitorous thought surfaced that he certainly looked the part, even in work clothes. Satin breeches might have been more elegant, yet they couldn't have enhanced his manhood any more than the tight jeans. And the arrogant set of his head with that lock of dark hair falling over it would have done justice to some robber baron of old.

Leslie refused to allow any of this to intimidate her. Casting Raider a defiant glance, she ran after the men. "I want to thank you for the lunch. It was the best I ever had," she told Hank. Turning to Marty she added, "And for the music, too."

"Glad you enjoyed it," Marty said. "We'll have to do it again. Maybe I could come by one night and take you into town."

"I'd like that." She smiled.

"I'll see you then." Marty lifted his hand in a farewell salute before vaulting onto his horse.

Leslie was very conscious of Raider sitting in silent disapproval. Ignoring him pointedly, she tilted her nose in the air and started to walk back in the direction of Lester's house. He soon put a stop to that.

"Where do you think you're going now?" Raider asked.

"I don't think that's any concern of yours."

"Well, think again, lady. You've been nothing but trouble ever since you turned up here. The first day you spooked my cattle; today you disrupted my men. I want to know what you have planned next."

It was so unfair that Leslie's temper heated. "All I did was have lunch with them, for which I'll gladly pay you."

Raider's jaw set grimly. "Are you also going to pay me for the time they spent goofing off because they couldn't resist when you fluttered those long eyelashes at them?"

"I did no such thing!" she cried indignantly. "Unlike

you, those men were trying to make me feel welcome. The only thing I feel guilty about is that I got them into so much trouble."

"I wouldn't go that far," he said dryly.

"I'm just wondering how far you *do* go," she replied angrily. "Those poor souls were terrified when you swooped down on us."

Unexpectedly, Raider threw back his dark head and laughed aloud, even white teeth gleaming in his bronzed face. "You have a lot to learn about Australians," he chuckled. "They're the most independent people in the world. The only reason those men hopped to it was because they knew they were wrong. If I had ever tried to pull rank on them for no good reason, they would have told me what I could do with my job."

Leslie looked at him uncertainly. "Well, you didn't have to be so sarcastic about it."

His imperiousness returned. "I don't have time for a lesson in manners right now; I have a station to run. You ride, don't you?" he asked abruptly.

She gazed up at him blankly. "What do you mean?"

"Horseback," he said impatiently. "I'll borrow a mount for you."

This man never ceased to amaze her. "Why would you do that for me?"

"It isn't altruism," he assured her grimly. "I'm thinking about my men. I don't want them charging into each other because they have their minds on what's inside those tight jeans of yours."

Leslie gasped, unconsciously pulling her jacket down over her hips. "You are the most boorish man I ever—"

"Not now, Miss Farraday," he interrupted. "You can give me a list of my shortcomings some other time. The first order of business is to get you a horse."

She ran after him as he wheeled and started toward

the corral. "You needn't do that. I can walk back," she said urgently.

"No way! I'm taking you back myself, just to make sure you don't get into any mischief along the way. And if you think I'm going to walk, you're mighty mistaken. You're getting out of here pronto, so don't bother to think up any more excuses to hang around my men."

Leslie was too upset to be indignant. The truth was that she was terrified of horses, although she would sooner have been stretched on a rack than admit it to this overbearing man who would no doubt be contemptuous.

It was all mixed up in her mind with the disastrous time her father had put her on a horse for the first time. The mount he had chosen looked as big as a dinosaur to the five-year-old Leslie, who had started to cry. Instead of reassuring her, he had picked her up bodily and put her in the saddle, where she clung in terror, looking down from a great height. It was the source of one of the very few arguments Leslie had ever seen between her parents.

"I thought you of all people would want her to learn how to ride," her father had sneered.

Leslie still remembered how her mother's face had paled. Usually she gave in quietly, but this time she had insisted that Leslie not be coerced. Unfortunately, while they were arguing, the horse, which was much too spirited for any but an experienced rider, brushed Leslie off against a tree.

The whole incident—the traumatic argument between her parents; her father's callousness; and the fall, which hadn't actually hurt her—had left Leslie with an unreasoning terror of all horses.

Faced with the likelihood of being forced onto one again, her eyes darkened with distress. Without realizing it, she was twisting her fingers together as she gazed up at Raider.

Those all-seeing gray eyes surveyed her apprehensive face. "You don't know how to ride, do you?"

"Well, I've never . . . but I guess I . . ." Her voice trailed off.

Raider gave a deep sigh. "I might have known."

There he went, putting her in the wrong again. "You make it sound like a crime," Leslie said indignantly.

He eyed her dispassionately. "Not a crime—a necessity in this country."

"Not for me. I don't live in your country."

One dark eyebrow lifted sardonically. "Thank the Lord for small favors."

Leslie raised her chin, looking at him truculently. "Don't be too speedy. I might change my mind."

If she had thought to disconcert him, she was mistaken. Raider gave her a tigerlike smile. "In that case you'd better have your first riding lesson."

"Not from you," she scowled. "You'd probably put a burr under its saddle, or whatever it is you do to make a horse bolt. It would facilitate matters greatly if I broke my neck, wouldn't it?"

"Now why didn't I think of that?" He grinned.

"Are you sure you didn't?"

He eyed her slim, defiant figure thoughtfully. "No, but now that you mention it, there's any number of accidents that could happen to an inexperienced person in the outback."

"If you're trying to frighten me, you're not succeeding," Leslie told him. "I can take care of myself. And when you're around, I'm going to be extra cautious."

Amusement softened the hard lines of his face. "You don't honestly think I'd try to do away with you?"

Looking up at him as he lounged negligently in the

saddle, Leslie had a moment of doubt. It was crazy, of course. Raider was a civilized man. Yet there was something very basic about the way he sat that devil of a horse, looking with a jaundiced eye at anyone who didn't measure up to his impossible standards. A cold shiver ran up Leslie's spine as she realized how fragile her defenses were against this powerful man. Resolutely ignoring it, she turned without answering and started back in the direction of the house.

Raider followed her, the black horse tossing his head in displeasure at the slow pace. "Of course there are any number of places on the spread where I could dispose of you without a trace." He looked at her slender body. "You wouldn't take up any space at all. Or I could take you out to the far reaches and leave you without food or water," he mused.

She stopped walking and faced him angrily. "Before you go any further with your nefarious plans, I'd better warn you that there are a lot of people who expect to hear from me regularly. My roommate, for one, and . . . and . . ." Leslie suddenly realized that there was actually no one who would miss her. Kay was incommunicado in the wilds of Colorado, her brother Bart was crewing on a sailing vessel and Aunt Laura was on a year's sabbatical from her professorship at the university, poking around old ruins in Egypt.

Raider accurately read the dismay depicted on her expressive face. "I could always tell them that you decided to go exploring Australia. By the time they decided to come looking for you, the trail would be very cold indeed."

He had to be joking, Leslie told herself, trying to penetrate his unreadable expression. As she gazed at him uncertainly, Raider leaned forward and circled her slim waist with his arm, lifting her lightly into the saddle. Leslie struggled wildly, which turned out to be a futile exercise. He held on to her easily, turning her so that she was astride, his arm around her waist holding her body firmly against his hard chest. At first she tried to break his grip, but when he dug his heels lightly into the great horse's flanks and it gave a sudden leap forward, Leslie shrank back into his embrace.

Her fingers dug into his forearms. "Stop this thing. Stop him this minute! I want to get off."

Raider's mouth was close to her ear. "Satan wouldn't appreciate being called a 'thing,' " he chuckled.

"That's a good name for him . . . and for you, too!" she gasped, not daring to release her death grip to brush the long coppery hair from her eyes. "What are you going to do to me?"

His arm tightened around her. "I'm deciding between several alternatives."

Satan came to a small stream, which he took in one mighty leap like the legendary flying horse, Pegasus. Leslie huddled into Raider's arms, burying her face in his shoulder.

He held her close. "Are you ready to make a deal?" he asked softly.

Suddenly Leslie realized what a fool she was being. Her unreasoning terror was of the horse, not the man. She sensed that Raider would never harm her physically. It was all an act calculated to scare her, and she had played right into his hands. She was so angry that she sat up straight, giving him a furious glance from flashing blue eyes.

"No, I'm not!" she snapped. "I'm not afraid of you, so you're just wasting your threats."

For the first time he looked at her with an expression akin to respect. "Maybe there is something in heredity after all," he murmured.

Leslie was being shaken up unmercifully. "Couldn't you at least slow him down?" she begged.

"I didn't know you wanted to prolong our ride."

"I don't!" she gasped.

"You confuse me, Miss Farraday," he said mockingly.

The one thing Leslie was sure of was that this man was never confused, certainly not by a woman. "Haven't you had your fun?" she asked through clenched teeth.

The hand resting on her waist slid up her rib cage, stopping just short of the swelling breast. "Not yet," he murmured in her ear.

"Take your hands off me," she stormed.

To her dismay, he did just that. Leslie hadn't realized until it was removed just how comforting that sinewy arm was around her waist. She was almost resigned to a swift death beneath the horse's hooves, too distraught to notice that, although both Raider's hands held the reins, his arms formed protective barriers around her.

"Please stop him," she begged.

"Your wish is my command," he said, reining in the big animal.

The words of gratitude died on her lips as she discovered that they were back at Lester's house. Giving him a look of outrage, Leslie tried to scramble down by herself. In her haste she caught her foot in one of the stirrups and would have fallen headfirst if Raider hadn't caught her deftly. He dismounted with fluid grace, then extricated her foot and lifted her down, his big hands holding her firmly by the waist.

"I wasn't far wrong when I said you could meet with an accident." He grinned. "Are you always this clumsy?"

"Oh! You . . . you . . ." she sputtered. "I was right

about you the first time I laid eyes on you. You're a fiend straight out of hell!"

"Compliments will get you nowhere," he mocked.

"Yes, you *would* take that as a compliment. Do you get a lot of pleasure out of insulting innocent women?"

His gaze traveled insolently over her, making her aware that her clothes had become disarranged during the wild ride. After a disconcerting survey, his eyes returned to the tantalizing glimpse of curving breast revealed by her partially open shirt. Color rushed to Leslie's face as she hurriedly rebuttoned it.

He watched her efforts with broad amusement. "Is that what you are? An innocent woman?"

"*You* will never find out," she answered hotly.

"What makes you think I would be interested in trying?"

Leslie longed to wipe the smug smile off his face—by force, preferably. "I never know your intentions, nor am I interested in discovering them."

She turned haughtily toward the house, only to find her progress halted by steely fingers like a handcuff around her wrist.

"Not so fast," he said. "We still have a little unfinished business to clear up."

Leslie had had about as much of this man as she could take. He made her feel helpless and vulnerable—and rejected. She was furious at herself for being so aware of his virility when he viewed her with less interest than one of his precious bulls.

Setting her small chin, she said, "You have made it clear that I'm not welcome on your property, Mr. Mackenzie. Well, I'm sending you the same message. This is my property and you're trespassing."

Her barb hit the target she had intended. His fingers

tightened, almost cutting off her circulation. "You don't belong here," he grated.

"I have a piece of paper that says differently."

The amusement was effectively obliterated from his face, to be replaced by menacing hostility. "How much longer are we going to play out this charade?" he asked harshly. "We both know I want to buy your property, and we both know you want to sell. I offered a fair price, but knowing how the thought of money brings you running, I'm prepared to sweeten the pot." Before Leslie could burst into angry denials, he named an amount that left her with her mouth open. "I thought that would do the trick," he said cynically.

Leslie stared at him. He must be terribly rich or just plain crazy. The house was modest by anyone's standards, and ten acres of land was only a window box to a man who had fifteen thousand acres. Surely the amount he was offering was out of all proportion to the value. Then his insulting words penetrated and she saw red.

"Well, you thought wrong! If I ever did consider selling, you've just changed my mind. This is my property and I'm staying!"

"Think carefully, Miss Farraday." He took a step forward, the leashed power in that lean body meant to threaten. "I'm not a patient man. Every day you remain here my offer goes down."

Leslie refused to be intimidated. "If I weren't a lady, I'd tell you what you can do with your money!" she raged. "Now get off my land."

For a moment she thought he was going to refuse. Then, with an imperceptible shrug, Raider vaulted lightly onto Satan. "You'll come around," he said sardonically. "You won't let all that cash slip through those greedy little fingers."

Leslie was so furious that for once speech was beyond her. Stooping, she picked up a small oval rock and hurled it at him with all her might. It glanced harmlessly off his heavy leather jacket, but it spooked Satan, who reared up on his hind legs, snorting loudly.

Raider dug his knees into the plunging horse, pulling on the reins and turning him toward the open plains. They cantered off in a cloud of dust, Raider's mocking laugh floating back over his shoulder. "Enjoy your stay, Miss Farraday. Just remember that every day will cost you a bundle."

Chapter Three

After Raider had galloped off, leaving her trembling with fury, Leslie knew she had to blow off steam someway. Since the little house was already sparkling clean, she decided to attack the garden.

It needed it badly. There were some neglected rose bushes in rankly overgrown flower beds, flanked by a few shrubs that were struggling to peek over the weeds. In a small shed in back of the house Leslie found some gardening tools. She hacked at the undergrowth with all her pent-up anger, discovering how therapeutic it was to uproot things. Anger gave way to satisfaction a short time later when she began to see the fruits of her labor.

Hidden from view by the choking weeds were little bushes covered with delicate blooms. Leslie was to find out later that the pink flowers, like small hibiscus with raspberry red centers, were called Stuart's desert roses, the floral emblem of the Northern Territory. The tangle also disclosed a quantity of lovely amber flowers shaped something like irises with the delightful name of fairy lantern.

The hours slipped by as she weeded and hoed, returning the garden to its former beauty. There was still much to do when Leslie realized that it was getting dark. The time had flown by, but now the chill night air was seeping through her jacket and she was suddenly conscious of aching muscles.

A long soak in a hot tub chased away the fatigue. After that she washed her hair, blowing it dry until it framed her face in shining waves that looked like molten copper. The blue wool dress she chose was the color of her eyes, its square-cut neckline displaying her creamy skin to advantage.

Glancing in the mirror, Leslie had a momentary feeling of satisfaction which quickly vanished. What difference did it make what she looked like? There was no one to see her. The long, lonely evening stretched out like the one before and the one ahead. Was she being foolish to stick it out here alone?

Leslie set her round chin firmly. That was exactly the kind of thinking Raider was counting on. Without even knowing her, he had leapt to the conclusion that she spent all her time in one disco or another, which was far from the truth. Leslie couldn't care less about nightclubs. It was just that she felt so alone. If only she had someone to talk to, someone to tell her about this fascinating country that held a surprise around every corner. There were so many questions she wanted to ask. If only Raider weren't so hostile, she thought wistfully, how exciting he could make everything.

She banished the errant thought with disgust. Yes, it would be nice to be with someone—anyone except him.

He was an annoying, aggravating man. She didn't want his company any more than he wanted hers.

The sound of the doorbell surprised her, since she hadn't heard it before. Raider had chosen to announce his presence with thunderous knocks on the door. Leslie wondered why he had adopted the more formal approach now. She sighed, not relishing another skirmish so soon after the last one.

It never entered her mind that the visitor could be anyone else. It was a surprise, therefore, to see Marty Lanson's smiling face when she opened the door. For a moment Leslie could only stare at him blankly.

"You haven't forgotten me so soon, have you?" He grinned.

"No . . . no, of course not. I just didn't expect to see you."

"There's no phone in Lester's house, so I took a chance and came over, hoping you wouldn't be busy." He eyed the softly clinging dress and high-heeled sling pumps. "You aren't expecting anyone, are you?" he asked tentatively.

Leslie shook her head. "Not a soul. I can't tell you how happy I am to see you."

Marty looked dubious. "I thought maybe you and Raider . . ." The sentence trailed off.

Her soft mouth compressed. "Mr. Mackenzie and I are by no means friends. We happen to have some business dealings together, that's all."

"You have my sympathies. Raider is a great guy, but I wouldn't want to tangle with him. He'd be a tough man to get the best of."

"I don't want the best or any other part of him," Leslie said succinctly.

"That isn't the usual female reaction," Marty chuckled. "Raider's pretty hot stuff around these parts. But maybe he doesn't measure up to those big-city fellows where you come from."

Leslie thought about the men she knew at home. They all paled by comparison. She tried and failed to imagine them sitting tall in the saddle astride a huge black stallion like some reigning monarch. Raider radiated strength and competence. The men she knew had trouble refolding a road map.

Shaking her head in annoyance at herself, Leslie said, "I'm not being very hospitable. Won't you come in and sit down?"

"Thanks, but I thought maybe you'd like to see something of the town. There's a place called the Rose and Thistle that's popular around these parts. I hope you haven't had dinner yet?"

"No, and I was dreading having to eat alone. I'd love to go," she said.

The Rose and Thistle was the Australian version of an English pub, although, like everything in this country, it was bigger—a huge L-shaped room with a long polished mahogany bar along the wall. There was a dart board in one corner and round wooden tables and chairs scattered about. The place was crowded, and everyone seemed to know one another. Marty was hailed on all sides when they entered.

He led Leslie to the bar, where a big heavyset man with a florid complexion was dispensing drinks. "Leslie, I'd like you to meet Gordon, everybody's friend. Miss Farraday is visiting all the way from California."

The other man smiled, engulfing her small hand in his huge one. "A pleasure, Miss Farraday. We don't get many visitors in these parts. Certainly not such pretty ones, anyway. What brings you way out here?"

"Business and pleasure combined," she told him, which was actually the truth.

Gordon nodded. "There's some beautiful country around here. Have you been to Cutter Springs or Shelby's Rock?"

Leslie shook her head. "I haven't really seen anything yet. This is the first time I've been off the Danduroo."

"Leslie is staying at Lester Eames's house," Marty explained.

The big bartender took a sharp look at her. "I thought Lester's place was closed up after the accident."

"I guess it has been," Leslie said. "It was awfully dusty, and the weeds had just about taken over the garden. I got the house in pretty good shape, but I still haven't finished in the yard."

"Do you mean that Raider rented the place out?" Gordon demanded incredulously.

"Not exactly," she said. "Mr. Eames . . . that is . . . I was invited here, sort of."

Marty looked puzzled. "I thought you said you never met Lester."

"I didn't. It was . . . well, in a way it was Mr. Mackenzie who invited me." She was reluctant to go into it since she couldn't explain Lester's strange bequest. Leslie wasn't proud of her own trickery in taking advantage of the invitation, either.

Marty seemed to accept her stumbling explanation, but Gordon was staring at her intently, his enigmatic scrutiny going from her wide blue eyes to the glowing mass of coppery hair that framed her lovely oval face. "Of course," he murmured, almost under his breath. "You must be—"

At the same time Marty said, "Gordon was a good friend of Lester's. He knew him longer than anyone, didn't you, Gordon?"

"I guess so," the older man said absently, continuing to examine Leslie minutely.

"They worked on the Danduroo together. Isn't that how you met?" Marty asked.

Gordon came back to the present with an effort, still watching Leslie. "We were jackeroos together, apprentice ranch hands. It was right after Lester came out from England."

"That was when they were carefree young blades." Marty chuckled. "It wasn't till years later that Gordon got married and left to open this place. You and Lester always stayed in touch though, isn't that right?"

"Aye, he was a dinkum gent," Gordon said soberly.

The expression was incomprehensible, like much of the Aussie language she had heard, yet Leslie gathered from the respectful expression on his face that it meant a genuine person. These men evidently had been close friends.

"What was he like?" she asked impulsively.

The trip that had begun so lightheartedly was rapidly turning into an odyssey, a search for an illusive figure whose life at some point had become inexplicably intertwined with her own. What the connection could be she couldn't imagine, yet it was suddenly important to know what kind of man he had been.

"He was the finest bloke I ever knew," Gordon said slowly. "A man you could count on in a pinch. He never let anyone down in his life. It's just too bad that . . ."

Leslie waited in vain for him to continue. The big man was lost in visions of the past.

"In a way he reminded me of Raider," Marty said thoughtfully. "They might have been father and son except for coloring. They were almost that close, too, especially after old man Mackenzie died."

"Raider?" Leslie was incredulous. How could the two men have been anything alike? From all she had heard, Lester was a man in a million, while Raider was downright disagreeable.

Marty nodded, misunderstanding her exclamation. "Lester was like one of the family. Molly used to run to him with her troubles, even when her dad was alive."

Leslie looked blank. "Who is Molly?"

"Raider's kid sister."

"I didn't know he had a sister!"

"If you saw them together you might make that mistake over again," Marty chuckled. "Sometimes he acts more like her father. Drives the poor kid wild."

"Well, she's almost fifteen years younger than he is," Gordon said. "Let's see." He paused to figure. "That would make her about seventeen now. Doesn't seem possible."

Leslie hesitated for a moment before asking carelessly, "Does he also have a wife?"

"Who, Raider? No way." Marty grinned. "Although it isn't for lack of trying by the females for miles around. What a trophy he would be to hang over the mantel!" He turned to Gordon. "Do you think Allison will be the one to land him, or is your money on Marlene?"

"I don't think he'll marry anyone until he sees Molly safely launched," Gordon said decisively. "Too bad. It would be the best thing that ever happened to the girl. Their mother died when she was just a baby," he explained to Leslie. "The poor child's been brought up with a bunch of men. She needs another woman around. Raider does his darndest to be both mother and father to her, I'll give him that; but it just isn't the same thing."

This was a facet of Raider's personality that Leslie

had never seen and could hardly credit. She could have sworn there wasn't an ounce of tenderness in his makeup. Still, even a crocodile takes care of its young. If Molly had his personality, they were a formidable pair.

"Are they anything alike?" Leslie asked.

Both men laughed. "Couldn't be any different if they tried," Gordon said. "Molly is a little whirlwind, always jumping into situations that Raider has to pull her out of."

"She has a hankering for bright lights," Marty explained. "Wants to go off to Sydney to college."

"I suppose that's natural," Leslie commented. "Most young people want to go away to college."

"I think Raider's girlfriends would pay her way," Marty said, laughing. "They're hoping he'll get lonely rattling around in that big house all alone. Who knows? Maybe he will."

Several people came into the pub. When Gordon went to wait on them, Marty led Leslie to one of the tables. A pretty young waitress brought them menus.

"I'm afraid it isn't anything fancy," Marty warned. "Nothing like you're used to."

"Please don't say that. There isn't any place I'd rather be. Or anyone I'd rather be with," she added.

Marty beamed at her. "I take back all the bad things I used to think about city people."

"You really like this life, don't you?" she asked.

"I wouldn't trade it for anything," he said simply.

Leslie looked at him curiously. He appeared to be in his late twenties, a time when the men she knew were possessed with acquiring things: cars, a small sailboat if possible, clothes. Marty was personable enough to handle almost any kind of position dealing with the public, yet he seemed perfectly content to work at a job that involved hard labor. He was probably paid exceedingly well, but that obviously wasn't the motivating force.

"Tell me what it is you like about it," she urged.

"That's a tall order." He laughed. "It would be easier to tell you what I *don't* like." Then the smile faded. "This country gets into your blood. The air is clean and the people are real. I'll grant you it's no place for someone who has to be entertained every minute of the day. There are compensations, though. I'd feel like I was in jail if I had to work in an office from nine to five, having a boss tell me what to do."

"You do work for someone, though," Leslie said delicately.

"Raider?" Marty grinned. "Let's say I work *with* him—we all do. If he needed to tell me when to wean the calves or round up the mavericks for branding, I wouldn't be worth a jackeroo's pay. We all have a stake in this station. It's our home. You take pride in where you live, don't you? Isn't that why you cleaned up Lester's place?"

She was beginning to understand what Raider meant. These were fiercely independent people. They were friendly and outgoing, with a sense of their own worth that gave them supreme confidence. What a fine line Raider must walk, and how extremely well he did it.

Their food arrived as the place started to fill up. Each newcomer drew loud welcomes, and there was much good-natured joking between the cattle and sheep hands. The Rose and Thistle appeared to be the equivalent of country club, pub and disco all rolled into one. Some couples were dancing to a jukebox, while others played darts in a far corner, the rest visiting back and forth between the tables.

Leslie was enjoying herself tremendously until she

glanced up and saw Raider watching her from the bar with a distinctly displeased expression. He was wearing jeans like most of the others, with a blue work shirt unbuttoned halfway down his broad chest in spite of the weather outside. He should have looked like just another cowhand. Instead, he managed to look like a prince in disguise. Perhaps it was the fact that he towered over the group around him, although they were all big men. More likely it was the unconsciously arrogant tilt of his dark head plus the confident air of being in charge, even on someone else's turf.

As their eyes met he raised his schooner in a mock salute. Leslie nodded distantly. Her cool dismissal changed to apprehension when Raider made his way to their table.

"It didn't take you long to find our local bright lights," he said with a sardonic smile, looking down from his advantage.

Marty glanced up in pleased surprise, unaware that Leslie didn't share it. "Good to see you, mate. Come join us."

To Leslie's dismay, Raider did just that. To add to her discomfort, someone at the bar called to Marty, who excused himself and left them alone. A small silence descended as Leslie found herself unaccountably tongue-tied, a condition that unhappily didn't afflict Raider.

"Are you enjoying our limited rustic pleasures?" he asked mockingly.

Her soft mouth thinned with impatience. "Why should you assume that I'm not?"

"You mean it will make an amusing little story to take home with you?"

"No, that's *not* what I meant!" she said angrily.

"Until you walked in the door, I was having a very good time."

"Don't worry, I didn't drive your boyfriend away permanently. Marty will be back. You did your work well this afternoon."

"All I did was go for a walk," she cried indignantly. "It was the purest accident that I happened on their camp."

"You didn't lose any time putting it to good use."

"Marty asked me to join them for lunch and I was hungry. Was that such a crime?"

Raider's mouth was a grim line. "Not if you'd left it at that."

"Why does it bother you that he asked me out? You can hardly accuse me of wasting his time tonight," she said. It was Leslie's opinion that Raider was making a big deal over a slightly prolonged lunch hour.

His smile was unpleasant. "No, I'm sure it won't be wasted. What bothers me is who you have picked out for tomorrow night." Raider's tone left no doubt about his meaning.

His suspicions were not only insulting, they were unfounded, but Leslie refused to allow her hurt to show. "I don't believe that concerns you," she said coolly. "They are all grown men. You can hardly expect to control their free time."

His eyes held hers. "Understand this, lady. I'm not going to let you set my men at each other's throats. When a dingo skulks the herd it's a potential danger that's better dealt with sooner than later," he said softly.

"More threats, Mr. Mackenzie?"

"Call it a friendly warning." He leaned back in his chair, the denim shirt widening to disclose a bigger triangle of his powerful chest as he slung one muscular arm carelessly over the seat back.

Leslie tried to ignore the blatant display of masculinity that sent a funny shiver up her spine. Raising a skeptical eyebrow, she murmured, "Beware the Greeks bearing gifts."

The smile he gave her was wolflike. "At least we understand each other."

The hostility emanating from him destroyed Leslie's resolve to remain calm. "I don't understand you at all!" she cried. "Why do you dislike me so much? It has to be more than Lester's property. You had something against me before I ever got here."

"And you don't know what that could be," he commented cynically.

"No, I don't." Unconsciously Leslie leaned toward him, her soft lips slightly parted. The blue eyes were like unflawed sapphires as she widened them in an effort to comprehend, waiting for his answer in innocent expectation. With her defenses completely down, she was like a lovely doe, utterly vulnerable.

Raider drew a sharp breath, his attention riveted on her beautiful face. "Either you're a damn good actress, or . . ."

When he failed to continue, she pleaded, "If you'll just tell me what I'm supposed to have done, maybe we can clear this all up."

His gaze was intently devouring her face, moving from the short, straight nose to the incandescent mass of glowing hair that grazed her shoulders. Something flamed briefly in his eyes, thawing the ice. Then he frowned, the harshness returning. "I couldn't be wrong about you," he muttered.

Leslie felt a crushing sense of disappointment sweep

over her. For just a moment the bruising force of Raider's enmity had wavered. It seemed she had been about to pierce the curtain of mystery and misapprehension that lay between them. Then, like a door closing in her face, his attitude hardened. The realization of just how much she wanted to break down the wall between them made her furious—as much at herself as at him.

"You are without a doubt the most pigheaded, opinionated, overbearing man I've ever come across," she stormed. "It's people like you who start wars! You're so doggone sure you're right about everything. Well, for your information, I couldn't care less what you think of me!"

He was leaning comfortably back in his chair, amusement curling his mobile mouth. "I was wondering if there was a temper to match that flaming hair."

"You'd better believe it!" Leslie's eyes glittered like blue glass. "You're just lucky I'm showing restraint."

"I wouldn't exactly call that little speech restrained," he taunted.

"Count your blessings," she answered shortly. "When I was little I used to throw things."

"At whom?"

"At my brother, for one."

"I hope he threw them back at you," Raider said mockingly. "Does he have your red hair and fiery temper too?"

Leslie took a deep breath, annoyed at herself for letting this man get to her. "No, as a matter of fact. I'm the only one in my family with red hair—if it's of any interest to you," she said coldly.

His expression was unreadable. "It not only interests me, I could almost have predicted it."

Before she could respond, Marty returned with excuses. "Sorry, luv," he told Leslie. "I had to settle a bet. Has Raider been taking care of you?"

"I'm afraid Mr. Mackenzie felt compelled to stay with me. Luckily, now that you're back he can leave," she said, giving Raider an explicit look.

Raider leaned back more comfortably in his chair. "I believe Miss Farraday misunderstood," he said derisively. "I found our conversation most enlightening."

"Then I must have missed something," Leslie answered acidly, "because I didn't understand a word you said."

"Was he boring you with the Arabian horses we're breeding? You have to go easy on Raider," Marty chuckled. "I guess we all get carried away when we start to talk about them."

"It isn't a subject that's dear to Miss Farraday's heart." Raider was openly laughing at her.

"Why all the formality?" Marty complained. "Since when do we stand on ceremony in these parts? You two ought to be on a first-name basis by now."

Raider's eyes were dancing. "I hesitated to take liberties."

"I would have thought you'd take anything you thought you could get away with . . . Raider," Leslie said sweetly.

"She's sure got your number," Marty hooted, mistaking their edged exchange for friendly banter.

"Let's say we have each other's numbers. Isn't that right . . . Leslie?"

The tension between them stretched uncomfortably, for her if not for Raider. He was like a wolf circling a lamb, looking for the most vulnerable spot before he closed in. Well, it wasn't going to work, Leslie told herself angrily. No matter how unpleasant he tried to make things, he wasn't going to force her out until she was darn well ready to go.

At least tonight she had Marty as a buffer, although the subject he chose to dwell on was unfortunate. Marty was as carried away with the Arabian horses as he imagined Raider had been.

"There's never been anything like it in the outback," he enthused. "The little foal that's due any day now is going to have a hundred godfathers."

Wicked amusement shone in Raider's eyes. "Maybe Leslie would like to be its godmother." He turned to her as though just remembering something. "Oh, that's right, you're afraid of horses, aren't you?"

Marty looked at him blankly. "That's silly. Who could be afraid of a horse? You ride, don't you?" he asked Leslie.

"Well, I . . . that is . . . in a big city there isn't much opportunity."

"No wonder you picked the outback for a vacation." Marty nodded in understanding. "Up here you'll have plenty of chances."

"Why don't you set up a date?" Raider prodded.

"That's a good idea," Marty agreed. "How about tomorrow at lunchtime? I'll get Hank to pack us some sandwiches and we can have a picnic out by Spartan Creek. It's only about five miles, but it's better than nothing."

Leslie shot Raider a look of pure hatred. "No, not tomorrow. I . . . um . . . I have something to do."

"No problem, we'll make it the day after."

"We'll talk about it," Leslie said hastily. She got to her feet. "If you'll excuse me for a few minutes."

Leslie beat a speedy retreat to the ladies' room, cherishing murderous thoughts of Raider. His sense of humor left much to be desired, or was it really a joke?

Was he counting on her stubborn pride forcing her to get on one of those wild beasts? Surely they couldn't all be as spirited as that great demon he rode. But what difference did it make? The horses on this station wouldn't be placid little ponies, either, she'd wager. It would be terribly convenient if she broke her neck. Even an arm or a leg would force her to remove her unwelcome presence from the Danduroo.

Leslie decided the only course open to her was a delaying action. There was no way she was going to admit her deficiencies in front of that arrogant man! Setting her small chin determinedly, she went back to the table prepared to do battle, only to find her adversary had left.

"Raider said to say good night," Marty told her. "He had to leave."

"Oh, that's too bad," she commented with false regret.

Marty shrugged. "I'm surprised he hung around this long. I hear Allison Trent is back from Melbourne."

"Is she the girlfriend with the inside track?" Leslie asked, carefully straightening a spoon.

"Could be. She's quite a fluff." Realizing belatedly that Leslie might feel slighted, Marty said winningly, "Of course she's not a patch on you, luv."

She smiled to show no offense was taken. Unable to leave it alone, Leslie asked after a short pause, "What does she look like?"

"Oh, long black hair and brown eyes," Marty said carelessly. The male look in his eyes supplied the details he left out.

Raider's girlfriend was evidently something special, as Leslie had somehow known she would be. She shrugged off the vaguely unpleasant thought. It didn't make any difference to her, Leslie assured herself emphatically.

The rest of the evening passed pleasantly with laughter and conversation. Everyone welcomed her with the hospitality Australia was famous for, their warm, uncritical friendship enveloping her like a down comforter. It was surprising how much at home she felt here in such a short time. Surprising and faintly disquieting.

Leslie had a premonition that the longer she stayed, the more she would regret having to leave.

Chapter Four

Leslie awoke early the next morning, eager to go exploring. She decided that today would be a good time to investigate the forested area, well away from Raider and his men.

Hopping out of the warm bed, she started to shiver. Her short baby doll nightie, with its wide lace shoulder straps instead of sleeves, was definitely not winter attire. Leslie had packed sweaters and jackets, but warm nightwear was something she hadn't thought of—didn't even possess, for that matter. Had the house been this cold yesterday morning?

She tested the register with an outstretched hand, frowning at the small amount of heat coming up. She really must find out how to work the heating system. Wouldn't Raider be pleased if he could see her standing here shivering? His superior attitude was infuriating, wanting to make a big deal with all that gobbledegook about cylinders and tanks! She didn't need *him* to explain it. It couldn't be that hard to figure out.

Leslie washed quickly, getting into jeans and a warm wool sweater as fast as possible. Sitting on the end of the bed, she pulled on a pair of soft leather boots, admiring them as she did so. They had been much too expensive. She couldn't really afford such a frivolous expenditure, but she hadn't been able to resist. She had salved her conscience by telling herself they would last for a long time.

Even after she was fully clothed Leslie was aware of the cold. She would definitely have to take a look at the furnace or whatever it was when she came back this afternoon, but right now she was in a hurry to get going.

Part of her haste was due to the fact that she didn't relish another encounter with Raider so soon after last night. He was a very disturbing man. She didn't want Marty coming by either with more plans for a five-mile horseback ride.

The one thing Leslie took time to do was pack herself a lunch. There would be no one to share with her today except squirrels and chipmunks—she hoped. The thought of those wild dingoes nudged her consciousness, making her swear briefly at Raider. He had put them in her mind and they refused to go away. That's another thing he would be pleased about.

In the kitchen she assembled her lunch, wrapping a sandwich in waxed paper and putting it in a paper bag along with an apple and an orange. On the way through the living room she picked up a fascinating illustrated book on Australia, taking it along to identify any flora or fauna that might be unusual.

It was a glorious day. Leslie raised her face appreciatively, enjoying the warmth of the sun after being in the uncomfortably chilly house. Butterflies glided through the clear air in an erratic dance, like multicolored bits of paper caught in an updraught. Their jewel tones were unbelievably vibrant: glowing blues marked with yellow or crimson in geometric patterns. She had never seen anything like them. Promising herself that she would try to identify them later, Leslie went down the path and entered the woods.

It was cooler in the shade of the giant eucalyptus grove. Sunlight filtered with difficulty through the canopy of leaves that topped the woodland giants. A series of rustlings, both at her feet and up in the branches, told Leslie she wasn't alone. The forest denizens were going about their business heedless of an intruder.

It made her slightly uneasy, wondering exactly what was out there, until the sight of two strange-looking trees drove all apprehension from her mind. One had an immensely swollen trunk. It was roughly the shape of a giant vase with conventional branches spreading out from its tapered neck.

Sitting down on a convenient rock, Leslie leafed through her book until she identified it as the boab, or bottle tree, aptly nicknamed because of the gallons of water stored inside its trunk. The aborigines knew how to tap this convenient cache if they were caught without water, but early explorers had died of thirst under its shade, not knowing that salvation was at hand.

A loud squawk and a sudden whoosh of movement almost made Leslie drop the book. Two large parrots brilliantly marked in green and red chased each other directly over her head, their rapid progress creating a vivid splash of color through the dappled greenery.

After watching them until they were out of sight,

Leslie's attention returned to the book. Her other weird discovery was called a grass tree. Its rounded crown resembled a collection of giant paper pom-poms with drooping streamers. Rising grotesquely above them were twisted seed pods being sampled by a rainbow lorikeet.

It was like strolling through an enchanted forest with a discovery around every curve. Leslie wandered for hours, unaware of the time. The sun was past its peak and starting down the other way when she finally remembered to eat her lunch.

It felt good to rest. She was leaning back against a tree when a feeling of being watched made the short hairs on her neck prickle. A quick glance around disclosed nothing, yet the sensation persisted. Finally she investigated the trees above, discovering a plump koala bear watching her out of sleepy, unblinking eyes.

Leslie jumped to her feet with a delighted cry. The small creature looked like a fluffy teddy bear, draped around a branch and left there by a forgetful child. His tufted ears stood out as though they were wired on, his leathery black nose forming a contrast to the soft tan fur that covered his chubby face and body. When she approached close enough to see the long, curving black nails on his furry paws the koala became uneasy.

At first he merely climbed to another branch with slow, obviously reluctant movements. When that didn't discourage Leslie's pursuit, he took an unexpected leap to another tree, scrambling out of sight into the thick foliage.

"Hey, wait!" Leslie cried aloud.

She dodged around the big trunk, running toward the tree he had taken refuge in. With her head in the air craning to get another glimpse of the adorable creature Leslie didn't see the thick exposed root that was directly in her path. Her foot caught in the wicketlike curve and she went down with a thud, streaks of pain shooting up her leg. The humus-covered ground cushioned her fall, so she was merely shaken up, but the stiff boot had held her foot rigid. Judging by the agony in her ankle, Leslie was sure it was broken.

For a moment panic swept over her. She was all alone in the woods with no help to be expected. No one even knew she was here. For that matter, no one cared. Raider's words echoed unpleasantly in her ears: "There's any number of accidents that could happen to an inexperienced person in the outback." She gritted her teeth, as much against the memory as the pain. There wasn't any way she could blame Raider for her present predicament, yet it galled her knowing that he was right again.

In a way, that helped to steady her. If she kept her cool, everything would be all right. She would show him that she could take care of herself. Tiny beads of perspiration dewed her forehead in spite of the chill. The light slanting through the trees was definitely at a lower angle now. Soon it would be dark. Leslie's heart started to pound, confounding all her good intentions.

She pushed herself into a sitting position, carefully removing her foot from the tree root. Waves of nausea swept over her when she touched her ankle. Should she remove the boot because it was so constricting or leave it on for protection? Leslie hadn't the faintest notion. It was academic at any rate because her foot was starting to swell.

At first she had some wild notion that maybe she could crawl back on all fours. After a short distance this proved clearly unfeasible. Her injured foot kept bumping the ground, causing unbelievable pain. There was a long crooked tree branch lying on the path, and after catching her labored breath Leslie used it and the trunk of a tree to pull herself upright. A wave of dizziness assailed her. She waited for it to pass, then took a deep breath and started out once more, using the stick as a crutch.

Leslie often wondered afterward how long it had taken her to reach Lester's house. Time had ceased to have any meaning. Gritting her teeth, she stumbled on endlessly, falling frequently and laboriously picking herself up again, ignoring the fiery spasms that made her cry out against her will.

I'm going to make it, she vowed fiercely. I won't let him get the best of me. Somehow, in her dazed mind, this had become a contest of wills between Raider and herself.

Hours later she came out on the clearing. It was more difficult now without the trees to cling to, but eventually Leslie reached the house. The last act of turning the doorknob seemed an impossible feat. Her numbed fingers fumbled with the handle, and then, incredibly, she was safe inside.

Once the door was shut, Leslie started to shudder uncontrollably. It was all she could do to drag herself to the bedroom and collapse on the bed. It's just nerves, she assured herself when the shivering refused to stop. It will go away. When it didn't, an unpleasant realization was forced upon her. The house that had been merely uncomfortably chilly this morning was now freezing cold. There wasn't any heat at all, and night was coming on.

Tears of weakness flooded Leslie's eyes. Was there anything more that could happen to her? Dragging the blankets over her trembling body, she tried to ignore the throbbing pain, drifting into an exhausted state somewhere between sleep and wakefulness. The sound of determined pounding roused her.

"Leslie! Are you in there?"

"Raider," she tried to shout, except that it emerged in a whisper.

"Don't play games with me, damn it!" His angry voice came from the other side of the front door.

"Come in," she called in a slightly stronger voice. "Oh, *please* come in!" With a sinking sensation she realized that her words didn't carry. Although the house was small, it was sturdily built, with thick walls to withstand the winter's cold and the summer's heat.

"I know you're in there. Your car is outside," he stated implacably.

There was nothing for it but to try to get to the door, even if it did seem like the distance to the moon. Leslie started to unwind herself from the blankets, gasping with the effort.

"Okay, that's it. I'm coming in," he said grimly. "We're going to get this thing settled whether you like it or not."

With a sense of relief Leslie heard the front door open. "I'm in here," she called.

Raider appeared in the doorway, almost filling it with his height. His caustic glance swept over the huddled figure on the bed. "What's that supposed to be, an invitation?"

Instant anger stiffened her spine. "Don't flatter yourself!"

"What makes you think I'd be flattered? You look like you just went three rounds with a kangaroo—and lost."

Without having to see herself in a mirror, Leslie

knew what she must have looked like. Her long hair was tangled after catching on a dozen branches, and her face had to be dirty and scratched. Still, he didn't have to be so blasted uncomplimentary!

"I'm sorry if I don't measure up to your impossibly high standards of beauty," she stormed.

His eyes were flinty. "That isn't what I came here to discuss. Will you kindly get out of bed and come in the other room? And while you're at it, you can explain why the house is so cold."

"I . . . I don't know," she faltered.

"It couldn't be because you let the tank get empty?" he asked unpleasantly.

"Well, I . . . I haven't had a chance to tend to it yet." Leslie's long eyelashes fluttered down before his derisive smile of comprehension.

"Would you know what to do about it, anyway?"

His sarcasm made her defensive. "Probably," she said, raising her chin.

A disgusted sigh rumbled in his deep chest. "I don't have your confidence. Come with me and I'll explain it to you."

Leslie started to oblige, pausing when the slightest movement sent anguish through her whole body. Her knuckles whitened as she clutched the blanket, gathering courage for the ordeal.

"I don't have all night, Miss Farraday," he grated. "Although it seems that's what you had in mind."

Fury swept over Leslie, driving out common sense. She vowed to die sooner than ask for Raider's help. "Get out of my house this instant! Get out and don't come back—ever!"

With a muttered oath Raider strode to the bed. Grasping her by the shoulders he jerked her roughly to her feet. Leslie gave a high, thin scream, collapsing like a rag doll.

He caught her before she fell, easing her back on the bed and looking at her with a changed expression. "What's wrong?"

Tears filled her blue eyes, overflowing and running down her pale cheeks. She bit her trembling lower lip, looking up at him piteously.

Raider took a clean white handkerchief out of his pocket and wiped her face gently. "What's the matter, Leslie, did I scare you?"

His unexpected gentleness was a surprise. It took all the fight out of her. Shaking her head, she said, "I had an accident."

Raider frowned. "What kind of accident?"

She explained about falling over a tree root, feeling like an idiot for her clumsiness. "I'm afraid I broke my ankle," she ended diffidently.

He swept the blankets aside, sitting on the bed next to her. She stifled a cry of pain when he barely touched her foot, and Raider looked grim. He took a hunting knife out of his pocket.

"What are you going to do?" she cried apprehensively.

"I'll have to cut your boot off. The ankle is too swollen to get it off any other way. It would be too painful."

"You can't do that!" she gasped. "Do you know what I paid for these boots?"

He looked at her in disgust. "Don't you ever think about anything except money?"

"It isn't that," she protested. "It's just that I never spent—"

Everything was forgotten in the agony of the next

few minutes, although Raider was as gentle as possible. When her ankle was removed from its confinement, Leslie drew a deep breath, collapsing against the pillows. Raider's long fingers probed lightly, causing discomfort but not the torment of a few seconds ago.

"Does that hurt?" he asked, watching her closely as he turned her foot slowly from side to side.

"Of course it hurts," she said indignantly, pulling away from him. "What do you expect a broken ankle to do?"

"It isn't broken." His gray eyes warmed with amusement. "You'll live to chase koalas another day."

"How can you be so sure?"

"Knowing your inquisitive nature and your penchant for being where you shouldn't be, I can almost make book on it." He smiled.

"I mean how can you be sure it isn't broken?" she asked with dignity, ignoring his bantering tone.

"You'd be howling your head off if I moved it like that. The intense pain came from the swelling inside the tight boot."

"You mean I can walk now?" she asked dubiously.

"Not for a while. You have a bad sprain there."

"Oh." She wondered what you did for *that.* Hot packs or cold? Not wanting to give him the satisfaction of asking, she remained silent.

Raider didn't oblige her by offering any information. He stripped a blanket off the bed and deftly wrapped it around her.

"What are you doing?" she asked.

"The only thing I can at the present. I'm taking you up to my house."

"What on earth for?"

He slid an arm under her legs, cradling her against

his hard chest. "Because somebody has to take care of you, and, God help me, it looks like I'm elected."

She struggled in his grasp. "You don't have to do anything of the kind. I can take care of myself."

"So you keep telling me, but you haven't done a very good job of it so far. If I don't keep an eye on you, there's no predicting what you'll do next. Burn Lester's house down, probably."

So his concern was for his property! Leslie was indignant. It was true that she'd gotten into a certain amount of trouble since she'd arrived here, but that didn't mean he had to treat her like a menace.

"Put me down," she ordered. "I'm not going anywhere with you."

"Stop acting like a little idiot." He scowled. "Even if you could manage to hobble around on your own, you can't stay in this cold house."

Her struggles diminished. "Couldn't you . . . I mean . . . couldn't you fix the heat?"

Raider smiled broadly. "Don't tell me little Miss Independence is asking for help?"

Leslie swallowed her pride; it was either that or freeze to death. "Yes," she managed in a small voice.

"I'll remember that in case it never happens again." He continued toward the front door.

"Is the furnace outside?" she asked, wide-eyed.

"No."

"Then where are we going?" she persisted.

Raider opened the door of a pickup truck parked in front, dumping her unceremoniously on the front seat. "I told you, to my place." When Leslie started to protest again he slammed the passenger door. "You can't stay here. The house won't warm up for hours. Besides, you need someone to look after you for a few days. If you don't stay off of that ankle, you'll be laid up here for a long time." He gave her a level stare. "That's something neither of us wants, right?"

I might have known, Leslie thought bitterly. For just a moment she had actually felt grateful, when all the while he had only been worried about how long she was going to stick around.

Leslie sat up stiffly in her seat, extending her injured leg and putting her small straight nose in the air as Raider slipped behind the wheel. It was galling to have to accept this man's charity, and she wanted him to be aware of her reluctance. Raider merely chuckled. Having gotten his own way as usual, he was once more in a good mood.

It was too dark to see anything as they jounced along the rutted road. At one point Raider swerved to avoid hitting a small animal that ran across their path. When he inadvertently caught one wheel in a pothole, Leslie's foot banged against the floor with a thud. She bit her lip to keep from crying out, and Raider looked at her, his expression unreadable in the dark.

"Sorry," he murmured softly.

If Leslie hadn't known better, she would almost have believed he meant it.

After the pitch-black countryside it was a relief to see lights ahead. The atmosphere in the truck had an uncomfortable air of intimacy about it with Raider's long leg stretched out so close to her own, his wide shoulder in the heavy sheepskin jacket almost brushing hers.

She stole a look at his profile, dimly lit by the dashboard lights. It was an arrogant face, from the high cheekbones to the firm mouth and strong jaw line. Or would you call it arrogant? Perhaps confident was the word, or self-sufficient—but not completely so. That sensuous lower lip indicated a taste for female companionship. He wouldn't have any trouble satisfying his male needs, Leslie thought suddenly, then was grateful that the darkness hid her warm cheeks.

Raider turned his head. "Are you all right?"

"Yes, thank you," she murmured, assuring herself that she was trembling because of the cold.

She glanced out of the window when he stopped the truck, doing a startled double take. The house before them was a large and gracious two-story colonial with a curving brick walk that led up to a wide veranda. Light was streaming out of the windows, and there was a faint sound of music coming from somewhere.

"Here we are," Raider said, coming around to open her door.

"You live *here?"* she gasped.

He paused with his arms around her waist. "What were you envisioning, a stable?" He grinned.

"No, I . . . of course not," she said sharply, aware that he was laughing at her.

She should have realized that the owner of a spread this size would live well, but Raider had never seemed rich. He wore jeans like the other men and ran around in a battered pickup truck. Only that demon horse of his showed his pride of possession. What a strange man!

As he was about to pick her up, Leslie said, "You don't have to carry me. I can walk."

Ignoring her firm statement, he swept her into his arms, looking down with an arched eyebrow. "Let's get one thing straight. As long as you're under my roof, you'll do as I say."

"I didn't ask to come here," she told him mutinously.

"We've been through all that. Now behave yourself." When she scowled up at him with her lower lip thrust out Raider laughed. "You look like someone just took away your lollipop. Cheer up. If we're both lucky, you won't be here too long."

"You can't hope for that any more than I," she said furiously, feeling a pang nonetheless that this man found her so unattractive.

Raider didn't bother to answer. Shouldering the door open, he shouted, "Clara! Molly! Where is everybody?"

They were in a large entry hall with rooms opening on both sides. Next to the graceful staircase that rose to the second floor, a wide hall ran through to the back of the house. A woman came down the hall, wiping her hands on a dish towel. She was somewhere in her middle forties, small and slim, with short, curly light brown hair and hazel eyes that were now snapping with annoyance.

"Do you always have to *erupt* into a house, Raider? Can't you ever come in like—" The words broke off as the woman came into the entry and saw Leslie in his arms. "Great bashful budgies, what's going on?"

"This is Leslie Farraday. She sprained her ankle and I had to bring her here for a few days," Raider explained laconically.

The woman eyed them speculatively. "For a minute there I thought maybe you ran off and got married. It looked like you were carrying her over the threshold."

He gave a hard laugh. "Not likely."

"Will you kindly put me down?" Leslie demanded, her cheeks very pink.

Ignoring her as though she were a bale of hay he was delivering, Raider asked the woman, "Is the bed in the guest room made up?"

"It's always made up." As he started toward the stairs, she said tartly, "Don't you think it would be nice if you introduced us?" Not trusting Raider to perform the amenities, she said, "I'm Clara Brandt, the housekeeper. You're the one who's been staying down at Lester's, aren't you?"

"Yes, I am. I really didn't want to come here, Miss Brandt, I—"

"It's Mrs., but call me Clara."

The faint music Leslie had heard became louder as a door upstairs opened. There were light footsteps above, and then a lilting voice called, "Is that you, Raider?"

A tall, slender young girl appeared at the head of the steps. Her long dark hair was swept into a ponytail, secured at her crown with a barrette. Gray eyes the color of Raider's examined the little group curiously. "Well, hello," she said, starting down the stairs toward them.

"Meet Leslie Farraday," Raider said with a wry look at the housekeeper. "This is my sister, Molly. Now that I've made the introductions, would any of you mind if I put her in the guest room?"

When Molly looked blankly at the housekeeper, she relayed the small amount of information Raider had parted with. Molly whirled around, pounding up the stairs after them.

"I'm so glad to finally meet you, Leslie," she cried. "I wanted to come down to Lester's, but Raider said—" She broke off, coloring uncomfortably.

Leslie could just imagine what Raider had told her. It was a wonder he hadn't tacked up a quarantine sign on the house!

"How did you hurt your ankle?" Molly asked quickly.

"Miss Farraday has made it her mission in life to get into trouble on the Danduroo Station," Raider remarked, dumping her unceremoniously on the double bed in the charming guest room.

"Don't let my brother upset you," Molly said consolingly. "We had a fight this morning, and I can see he isn't over it yet."

"We didn't have a fight, it was a discussion—which is now closed," he stated grimly, his face looking like it was carved from stone.

Molly stood her ground, looking squarely into her towering brother's eyes. "That's what you think!" It was clear that she wasn't intimidated by him.

They were so much alike as they stared at each other, two fiery, independent spirits, neither willing to give an inch. Leslie was fascinated yet embarrassed, feeling like an interloper. She started to edge unobtrusively off the bed with no clear idea of where to go.

Her slight movement caught Raider's attention, breaking the tension between brother and sister. "Where do you think you're going?" he asked.

"I . . . well, I thought I'd turn down the spread." He had dumped her, blanket and all, on top of the pretty quilted green and white spread.

"I'll do that," Molly offered. As the blanket fell to the floor she exclaimed, "Your clothes! They're all torn and dirty."

Leslie looked ruefully down at herself. "Yes, I'm a real mess."

"But I thought you just sprained your ankle," Molly said. "How did all that happen?"

"I tripped someplace in the middle of the woods, and when I found I couldn't walk I tried to crawl on all fours. That didn't work too well, so I used a tree branch for a crutch. I made it, but it took hours and I'm afraid I fell down a lot." Leslie was very conscious of Raider standing silently by, listening to the full story of her idiocy. Now more than ever he would be convinced that she was hopeless.

At least Molly was sympathetic. "You poor little thing," she said. "Here, let me fix the bed for you."

"I don't want to be a bother," Leslie protested, reaching for the headboard to steady herself. It was probably delayed reaction, but she suddenly felt wobbly.

"Don't be silly. You're no trouble at all," Molly said, plumping up the pillows.

The room seemed very warm after the chill outside. Leslie unzipped her jacket, trying to shrug out of it while standing on one foot and holding on to the bed. It was a feat for a contortionist.

Raider was at her side instantly, holding her around the waist with a steadying arm and gently easing the jacket off.

"Thank you," she murmured, her eyes on the carpet.

"Where is your nightgown?" Molly asked. "I'll help you into it."

"I don't have any. I mean, everything happened so fast that I didn't bring anything." She braced herself with both hands on Raider's muscular forearms, wondering why he didn't let go of her.

"No problem," Molly assured her. "I'll get you one of mine."

"You didn't tell me you went through all that," Raider said after she left the room.

"I didn't want to give you further evidence of my clumsiness." Leslie shrugged.

"Or your courage," he said softly, an unreadable expression in his eyes.

"Okay, Raider, out!" Molly ordered. She was back carrying a beautiful pale blue chiffon nightgown with embroidered flowers across the low-cut bodice. Displaying it for their inspection, she said, "How's this? It's brand new. I was thinking of saving it for my trousseau, but since it's unlikely that I'll ever meet anyone to marry, stuck way out here, it might as well be put to good use."

With a strangled exclamation of annoyance, Raider stalked out the door, slamming it behind him.

Leslie looked at the wispy nightdress. "Oh, Molly, it's lovely, but I wouldn't think of wearing it. Especially if you're saving it . . ." Her voice trailed off. Wasn't she rather young to be assembling a trousseau? How old had Gordon, the bartender, said she was—seventeen?

Molly laughed. "Don't worry, I just said that to aggravate Raider. I succeeded, too, didn't I?" she asked cheerfully.

"Rather well." Leslie nodded. "I admire your courage. It's something like rattling the cage of a sleeping tiger and hoping the bars don't break."

"Oh, Raider isn't violent." Molly chuckled. "Actually, he's a marshmallow inside. It's just that he has this tremendous sense of *duty*. He promised Dad he'd take care of me, which is fine except I was little at the time and he hasn't noticed I've grown up."

"I guess brothers always feel protective. Mine is younger than I am, and he still acts that way on occasion. Maybe it's the male ego. They like to think they know more about the world than we poor, weak females."

They grinned at each other, recognizing the common male failing. Then Molly's smile faded. "The trouble with Raider is that he has too doggone much authority. Everyone hops to it when he raises one eyebrow." Having seen it among the station hands, Leslie silently agreed. "Even his women roll over obediently," Molly continued disgustedly. "So naturally he's gotten into the habit of thinking he's omnipotent."

"A case of power corrupting?" Leslie asked with amusement.

"And absolute power corrupting absolutely," Molly finished, nodding her head vehemently. "And you know who I blame? Women! If my dear brother ever got the put-down he deserves, it might crack that supreme confidence a little."

"Hasn't he ever?"

"Not so far. That's probably why he has such an unflattering opinion of women. Just because the ones he deigns to notice fall into bed on command, he thinks we all do. I don't think he even trusts *me!"* Molly crossed her long legs Indian fashion on the bed. She leaned forward, her lovely smooth face flushed with earnestness. "Do you know he won't let me go out with Marshall Goodwin—a boy I went to kindergarten with!—because he runs with a crowd that Raider considers unsuitable."

"In what way?"

"Well, they drink a little."

Because of something evasive in her manner, Leslie asked, "Is that all?"

"Well . . . maybe they smoke a little pot."

Leslie didn't quite know what to say. If she were critical, the girl would close up like a clam. For the first time Leslie felt sympathy for Raider. Raising this beautiful, spirited child couldn't have been any picnic. Choosing her words carefully, she said, "If you and this Marshall are really fond of each other, perhaps you could work something out with your brother, maybe go on dates without the others."

"Marshall Goodwin is a nerd," Molly declared disdainfully. "I don't care two pins about him. It's just the principle of the thing—the fact that Raider thinks I'd be stupid enough to do any of those things."

Leslie blinked. "But if you don't really like him, wouldn't you be penalizing yourself by dating him just to spite Raider?"

Molly smiled smugly. "Marshall is part of my overall plan. If I can get brother dear stirred up enough about old wimpy Marshall, he'll let me go away to college. *That's* what our real battles are about."

"I see," Leslie murmured.

"Raider thinks I want to go away just to get out from under his thumb, but that isn't it at all. I love him and I'd miss him like crazy, but I want to get out and meet people, all kinds of people. I want to be like you. You came five thousand miles by yourself and nothing very terrible happened. I've never even been to Sydney alone," she finished passionately.

"Surely if you explained your reasons," Leslie said gently.

Molly sighed. "I've tried. But then he gets that autocratic look on his face and my fur stands up, and first thing you know we're in a battle royal."

"Maybe he'll change his mind," Leslie said consolingly, not believing it for a minute. It was the only thing she could think to say.

Before Molly could answer there was a tap at the door. Clara entered carrying a tray. "Raider said you didn't have any dinner, so I brought you a little something."

Leslie pushed herself up on the pillows. "That was awfully kind of you. I feel terrible causing you all this extra work."

"Nonsense. I've been after Raider to bring you up here to dinner ever since you got here." Turning to

Molly, the housekeeper said, "Have you finished your homework?"

Molly rolled her eyes toward the ceiling. "What did I tell you?" she asked Leslie. "You see how they treat me?"

"Save the back talk for your brother, young lady," Clara said. "It doesn't go down with me." Indicating the tray, she said to Leslie, "Just put it on the floor when you've finished. I'll get it in the morning."

After she had left, Molly laughed. "We're a houseful of characters, as you can see. Clara is an angel, though. She's another of those crusty-only-on-the-outside ones."

"Is there a Mr. Brandt?" Leslie wondered aloud.

"There is, but that's another story. I'll tell it to you some other time." Molly vanished out the door with a wag of her fingers.

Left to herself, Leslie felt slightly bewildered. They were indeed a memorable household. Raider, strong as he was, evidently had his hands full keeping those two under control.

The meal was delicious, but by this time Leslie was too exhausted to eat much. She was just gathering her strength to lift the tray down when Raider came in.

Eyeing the uneaten food, he said, "Don't you feel well? Is your ankle painful?"

"No, I . . . it's not too bad." Actually it was bothering her a lot.

He disappeared into the bathroom, returning with a glass of water and a bottle of pills. Shaking two into his palm, he offered them to her. "Take these."

"Thank you, but I don't need them."

A gleam of amusement lit his gray eyes. "Still think I'm trying to do away with you?"

She clutched nervously at the sheet. "No, of course not. It's just that I don't take pills."

"You'll take these." His mouth twisted mockingly. "You've proved you're a big, brave girl. It isn't going to add to your stature to lie awake all night in pain."

She took the tablets unwillingly, swallowing them because she didn't have any choice. He stood there watching her until she did.

"See how easy it is when you do as I say?" His smile was suddenly genuine. "Good night, Leslie. Sleep well." Picking up the tray, he left the room.

Leslie didn't fall asleep immediately, in spite of the pills. Her mind was in too much of a turmoil. What a strange paradox Raider Mackenzie was. He could be downright cruel and then turn around and be surprisingly gentle.

Molly had given her some insight into his character, yet it wasn't anything she couldn't have guessed at. The compliance of his numerous women, for one thing. That had made him contemptuous of them, but it hadn't stopped him from accepting their favors.

He was exactly the kind of male chauvinist she detested, Leslie told herself. It was too bad she had to be beholden to him. It seemed he was always snatching her out of one disaster or another. Gazing dreamily out the window, Leslie's last coherent thought was induced by the pills she had taken. She wondered what it would be like to be in Raider's arms for a different reason.

Chapter Five

Leslie was still in a good deal of pain the next morning. She attempted to hide the fact when Molly hurried in to say a brief hello before going off to school.

"Can I bring you anything when I come home this afternoon?" Molly asked.

"If you'd stop at the house and get me some clothes, I'd appreciate it," Leslie said. "Just a shirt and another pair of jeans. I'll be going home this afternoon, but I need something clean."

"You're not leaving so soon? We just got acquainted!"

"You can come down to Lester's to visit," Leslie told her. "I won't be going anywhere for a while."

"But it won't be the same. I want you *here!* Oh, Leslie, you don't know how good it is to have another woman my age to talk to for a change."

Leslie was careful not to smile, both at the notion of

the lovely, coltish Molly as a woman and her feeling that they were in the same age bracket. "Well, we'll see. Bring me the clothes, anyway. Gorgeous as this nightgown is, I can't spend my life in it."

Molly brightened up, leaving with assurances that she would stop by Lester's house on her way home.

As it happened, she didn't have to. Raider did it for her. He came into Leslie's room about an hour later carrying a small suitcase. "How are you feeling this morning?" he asked.

"Much better." But when he reached for her ankle Leslie couldn't help flinching.

Raider's eyes narrowed. "Still playing brave little soldier?"

"I'm not trying to impress you, if that's what you mean . . . unlike your many women friends," she couldn't help adding.

"What do you know about my women?" A look of comprehension followed by amusement warmed his gray eyes. "Oh, I see. Molly. What tall tales has my little sister been regaling you with?"

"She didn't mention you except in a general way." To change the subject, Leslie said, "I asked her to bring me some clothes."

"I already did." He indicated the suitcase. "Can you get into them alone, or do you need some help?" When Leslie looked up indignantly she met a mocking smile. "I could call Clara."

"Don't bother, I can manage by myself," she said coldly, annoyed that she had let him bait her. Raider knew very well what conclusions she would leap to.

"Suit yourself." He shrugged, depositing the suitcase on the bed.

He had included panties and bras along with jeans,

several shirts and one of her baby doll nighties. Leslie knew it was foolish, but it embarrassed her slightly to think of those strong, long-fingered hands rummaging through her intimate things.

Soon after she had struggled into her clothes, Raider reappeared carrying a huge, furry slipper. "I think this will be big enough," he said.

"What's that for?"

"I don't want you to catch cold on top of everything else or I'll never get rid of you," he said derisively. Kneeling beside her, he slid the slipper gently on her injured foot.

"You're all heart," she said dryly, looking down at his bent head and experiencing the strangest desire to run her fingers through that crisp dark hair. Leslie took a deep breath. "Will you say good-bye to Molly for me?" She hadn't expected to be hustled out quite this fast.

He glanced up from his task and she could see the thick, sun-tipped eyelashes that fringed his gray eyes. "You're not going anyplace—or at least you are, but you're coming back here. I'm taking you to the doctor."

He cut off her protests, carrying her down the stairs and into the pickup truck. Instead of going back the way they had come and out of the Danduroo, Raider drove in the opposite direction. A short time later, much to Leslie's amazement, they came on a small airstrip. A red single-engine plane, looking much like a child's toy, stood on the field. There was also a helicopter.

Raider laughed at her expression. "It's the only way to get around in this country. The skies don't need to be paved."

Raider buckled her in securely, but when he slid into

the bucket seat beside her, Leslie gasped. "Are *you* going to fly this thing?"

"Nobody else." He chuckled wickedly. "What's the matter? Are you afraid I'll tip you out?"

The engine fired, exploding into sound and preventing her from the necessity of a reply. As the small aircraft danced down the runway, Leslie clutched the seat so tightly that her knuckles were white. Unlike a jet plane, they were airborne in a matter of seconds, flying just above the treetops, or so it seemed.

The Danduroo was spread out beneath them, and when Leslie got up the courage to look down she was fascinated. In the distance was the forest where she'd had her mishap, and far to the right was a meandering stream, like a blue satin ribbon threading through the green pastureland. Black and white dots were cows, and the racing specks around them were dogs. Farther on, the herds thinned out and the land looked empty. Suddenly Leslie saw movement near a small grove of trees.

She grabbed Raider's arm, excitedly mouthing the word "Kangaroos?"

He nodded, swooping down so she could get a better look. The rather ungainly animals ran from the shadow of the plane, covering the distance to the trees in giant leaps of more than twenty feet. Leslie was fascinated, both by their speed and by their method of flight. From her bird's-eye view she could see the way they held their short forepaws and long tails high, bouncing like rubber balls on powerful back legs and elongated feet. It was a strange yet effective performance.

After they left the Danduroo, Raider followed the narrow road into town. It stretched like a straight tan line, empty except for a very occasional vehicle.

The small town appeared bigger than it actually was

after the isolation of the Danduroo. The collection of stores, a movie theater and traffic lights made it seem almost cosmopolitan.

After her ankle had been X-rayed, Leslie was delighted to discover that Raider's diagnosis was correct. It wasn't broken. It turned out to be a bad sprain coupled with torn ligaments.

"You'll have to stay off of it for about a week," the doctor warned.

Raider's face was expressionless, but Leslie knew what he was thinking. He was afraid he was going to be stuck with her for that long. "I don't have to stay in bed, though?" she pleaded. "I can hobble around with a cane?"

The doctor shook his head. "Maybe crutches. But I wouldn't overdo it or you'll be laid up a lot longer."

On the way back to the plane Leslie renewed her plea to be taken back to Lester's house, only to have her request curtly denied. His implacable expression told her it was useless to argue, and she knew it was because of the doctor's warning. It was fortunate that the noise of the plane precluded further conversation. Raider looked preoccupied, and Leslie was uncomfortable knowing what was bothering him.

When they were in the pickup truck once more she tentatively broached a subject that had occurred to her on the way home. "How do people get to a hospital in an emergency if they don't have a plane?"

"We have an outfit called the Royal Flying Doctor Service," he told her. "They take care of people on the isolated stations. In an emergency they come in a flying ambulance and take the patient back to a hospital if they can't treat him on the spot."

"How about simpler things that just need some

pills?" Leslie asked curiously. "In a city you call your doctor and he has the pharmacy send out a prescription. Surely the service doesn't fly a doctor out with a bottle of cough syrup?"

"They don't have to. Every bush station has a home treatment kit—sedatives, antibiotics, you name it—all in numbered bottles. The doctor prescribes by two-way radio. There are also phone-in clinics every morning and afternoon."

"What an ingenious system," Leslie marveled.

"Who knows, maybe doctors in the city will eventually get around to our method instead of saying, 'Take two aspirins and call me in the morning.'" He grinned.

When they arrived at the house, Leslie reached hastily for her crutches before Raider could lift her down. "I have to get used to them," she said. She was finding it vaguely disturbing to be in his arms.

Never having used them before, Leslie found crutches incredibly difficult to manage. The strain on her shoulders and arms was tremendous. After watching her awkward attempts for a few moments Raider uttered a muffled sound of impatience. Sweeping her off her feet, he carried her into the house.

When he started toward the stairs, Leslie said plaintively, "Couldn't I stay down here? Maybe I could help Clara in the kitchen."

Before Raider could refuse, the housekeeper came down the hall. "Well, what's the verdict?"

"Just a sprain," Leslie told her.

Raider raised an eyebrow. "And some torn ligaments."

"Well, yes, but that doesn't make me an invalid. Is there anything I can do to help, Clara?"

"Sure, you can shell the peas for me."

After Raider had deposited her in a chair and returned with her crutches he left them alone. Leslie gave a sigh of relief that didn't go unnoticed by Clara.

"Did Raider give you a bad time?" She chuckled.

"No. It was very good of him to take all the time off to fly me into town."

"But he reminded you of it, going and coming, is that it?"

"Not really. It's just that Raider doesn't want me here," Leslie said in a little rush.

"Why wouldn't he? There's plenty of room."

"We . . . uh . . . got off to a bad start at our first meeting, and things have gone downhill since. He thinks I'm almost criminally useless."

"That must mean you can't cook," Clara said dryly. "According to Raider, women have two places: in the kitchen and in the bedroom."

Leslie drew an indignant breath. "As a woman, doesn't that bother you?"

"He makes a few exceptions, and I'm one of them." Molly shrugged. "Don't waste your time getting upset about Raider. He had definite opinions even as a teenager, so I doubt if he's going to change now."

"Have you known him that long?" Leslie asked curiously.

Clara nodded. "I was twenty-four when I first came to the Danduroo, and Raider was fifteen. Molly was a newborn baby then." She reached inside the large refrigerator for something, her voice muffled. "Mrs. Mackenzie had had a number of miscarriages and it was a difficult birth. Poor soul, I guess she shouldn't have had any more children; she died just a few years later."

"So Molly doesn't even remember her mother?"

"No, I pretty much brought her up. I came originally as a sort of mother's helper and then I stayed on as housekeeper." Clara laughed suddenly. "I always tell her she was such a handful she discouraged me from having any of my own." Her expression softened. "It isn't true, though. She's the sweetest child you'd ever want to meet. Not a devious bone in her body."

Leslie had felt the same way, even on short acquaintance. "It's strange how different she and Raider are. Not that I meant he's devious," she added hastily.

"No, I know what you mean. Actually they're a lot alike in many ways. That's why they argue so much. Like this college thing. I'm sure she told you about it last night. I wish they'd get it settled already."

"Wouldn't you miss her terribly if she went away to school?" Leslie asked.

"Of course I would; and Raider would too, but not as much," she said dryly. "He has compensations."

Leslie wondered why Clara didn't feel she had the same compensations. She had corrected Leslie when she addressed her as Miss that first night; where was her husband? "Molly feels he doesn't trust her," Leslie said slowly.

"That's nonsense. He knows she wouldn't do anything she shouldn't. More likely he's afraid she'll meet someone who will take her away from us. Raider holds on to whatever's his. He'd like her to marry someone from the Danduroo like I did."

Leslie was momentarily diverted. "I met some of the men the day after I arrived, but I didn't pay attention to their last names. I wonder if I met your husband?"

"He isn't here right now," Clara said shortly. In a transparent attempt to change the subject she said, "I wonder where Molly is. She ought to be home by now."

"I'm afraid that's my fault. I asked her to stop at Lester's house and bring me some clothes, not knowing Raider was going to do it," Leslie explained.

"Did I hear my name mentioned?" Molly appeared in the doorway. "I put the things you asked for in your room," she told Leslie. "And I brought this too," she said, holding up a long jade velvet hostess coat. It had wide, graceful sleeves and gold braided frogs closing the low-cut neckline. It had been a present from Leslie's Aunt Laura. "It's so pretty, I thought maybe you'd like to wear it to dinner tonight."

"Since when do we get that gussied up?" Clara demanded.

"Well, this *is* sort of an event, Leslie's first dinner here. I thought we'd make an occasion of it."

Clara gave her a penetrating look. "Just what are you up to, young lady? If you're trying to cook up something with your brother, you're not doing Leslie any favor. She'd be a lot safer in a wrestling match with a giant kangaroo."

"Raider's not so bad," Molly laughed. "At least Allison and the others don't think so."

"Maybe you ought to ask Leslie before you plan any fun and games for her," Clara said dryly.

Leslie could have told both of them that it wouldn't matter what they planned. Raider disliked her intensely, and the feeling was returned in kind. "I think Clara's right about the dress," she told Molly.

"Oh, all right." The younger girl gave in cheerfully. "At least let me fix your hair, though. You have such gorgeous hair. It's exactly the color of—"

"Why don't you two go in the other room so I can get on with dinner," Clara cut in smoothly.

When they were seated in the comfortable living room, Molly gave a happy sigh. "This is super, just like having a sister. I mean, Raider is a nifty brother and Clara has always been like my mother, but it isn't the same as having someone you can really talk to."

"Clara was telling me about your mother," Leslie said sympathetically. "It's sad that you never knew her."

Molly nodded. "I was lucky that I had Clara, though, and luckier yet that she married Jody. Otherwise there would probably have been a succession of housekeepers while I was growing up. The Danduroo is pretty isolated, as you've noticed, although there *are* a lot of handsome young men for compensation." She grinned.

"Is her husband . . ." Leslie paused delicately. "Clara said he isn't here."

"Is that all she said? Yes, I guess it would be. She's not a chatterbox like me." Molly laughed. "Still, it isn't any secret. Clara and Jody are separated."

"And he left the station?"

"That's really the reason. Jody's brother had a small spread near here. He died recently, and Jody felt he had to go and run it for his sister-in-law. He wanted Clara to come with him and she wouldn't."

"Because of you and Raider?" Leslie asked.

"Only partly. Clara and her sister-in-law don't get along. She couldn't see them all sharing a house together, and she's probably right. They had a big fight about it and Jody went off in a huff. The trouble is that they're both too independent, and now there's pride involved. Raider could settle the whole thing, but of course they won't let him."

"How could he do that?" Leslie asked, curious.

"He'd send over one of his men to keep the place running until the widow decided if she wanted to sell or else looked for a competent foreman. Raider would keep an eye on it, too, just to be sure everything was going okay. That's the kind of person he is."

"Maybe Jody really wanted his own spread," Leslie pointed out.

"No, that's the funny thing. He hated to leave the Danduroo. He's just one of those macho men who feels he's not going to let his wife dictate to him even if she's right. And after they both said a lot of things they didn't mean, there was no backing down. I know Clara feels awful about it, even though she would never admit it. It's a mess," Molly sighed.

"What is?" Raider's big frame filled the doorway.

"Raider!" Molly uncoiled herself from the couch and flew across the room to plant a kiss on his cheek, standing on tiptoe. "I didn't expect you so soon."

"I got through early." He ruffled her hair fondly. "Have you been behaving yourself?"

"Do I have to?" she asked mischievously. Raider aimed a swat at her bottom which she avoided deftly as she ran from the room calling, "I'll tell Clara you're home."

His smile faded as he turned to Leslie and she experienced a pang. He could make her feel unwanted without even saying a word.

"Have you been staying off your feet?" he asked.

"Yes, I . . . I was helping Clara in the kitchen," she said, disgusted with herself because it sounded like she was trying to make Brownie points.

"That must have been a new experience for you," he said unpleasantly.

"Not at all. I'm a very good cook," she flared, regretting it immediately when she remembered Clara's statement that Raider thought women belonged in only two places. Well, he wouldn't discover how well she performed in *either!*

"A woman of many talents, is that it?" he asked sardonically.

"You might say that. At least I haven't had any complaints," Leslie was goaded into saying.

His slow, insolent gaze traveled up her slender body, pausing at her curved breasts. "I can believe that, anyway. In fact, if things were different, I wouldn't be averse to finding out myself."

"You flatter yourself, Mr. Mackenzie. You don't happen to be my type."

His smile was slow and confident. "Are you sure about that?" Sauntering lazily over to the chair she was occupying, he leaned over, putting both hands on the arms and penning her in. "That's a challenge no man could refuse."

"I didn't mean it to be," she gasped.

"Nevertheless, you've flung down the gauntlet and I accept."

His big hand stroked her cheek, the fingers trailing down her neck and over her collarbone in a suggestive pattern. One hand fastened at her waist, the palm making a slow upward circle until it was just below the curve of her upthrust breast. His long forefinger traced the shape of her mouth, pulling the full lower lip down slightly so he could touch the warm moistness within.

Leslie drew in her breath sharply, sitting back in her chair and pushing his hands away. "Stop it this minute!" she commanded.

His hands curled around hers, drawing them in back of her and pulling her forward so their faces were just inches apart. "Are you sure that's what you want?" he murmured, dancing lights making his gray eyes luminous.

"Of course it is," she gasped.

"Really?" His mouth touched hers so lightly that it was like a butterfly's caress as it slid lightly back and forth, exploring rather than possessing. His tongue traced the line of her tightly closed lips, probing delicately, tantalizingly, while his hands moved to her face, the fingers stroking the sensitive spot in back of her ear.

A sensuous feeling of weakness overcame Leslie. She tried to resist, but his practiced male onslaught made it impossible. Her lips parted of their own accord, allowing him the access he demanded. As Raider explored the warm inner recess, her hands touched his shoulders tentatively, cupping around the strong column of his bronzed neck.

He lifted her into his arms, his hands traveling down her back to press her hips closer to his. All of Leslie's senses responded to his masculinity as they never had with any man before. They were locked in an embrace that wed their bodies together, his hard loins moving against hers, promising an ecstasy she had never known. Leslie's surrender was complete. He aroused every erotic area, destroying her will to resist. All Leslie could think of was the necessity to respond to this man. She wound her arms around his neck, returning his kiss with passionate abandon.

"Tell me again that I'm not your type," his mocking voice said in her ear.

Leslie's eyes flew open, her face flaming as reality returned. "You . . . you're detestable!" she cried.

He dropped her back into the chair. "That was even easier than I expected," he said sarcastically.

How could Leslie tell him that she had never met a man like him before? Had never been subjected to such a practiced assault on her emotions. He would never believe it. Raider was convinced for some reason that she was promiscuous, and her reaction to him wasn't calculated to change his opinion. Well, what difference did it make what he thought? The main thing was to see that it never happened again.

"Now that you've satisfied yourself with my morals, I hope you'll leave me alone," she said icily.

"You can count on it, lady," he answered grimly.

"Dinner's ready," Molly said coming into the room. "Help Leslie with her crutches, Raider."

"I can manage," Leslie said hastily, struggling to her feet.

The dinner was delicious, but Leslie was too upset to eat. Her nerve ends were still twitching after that shattering encounter with Raider. Fortunately the others didn't notice. In the relaxed manner of Australia, Clara had dinner with the family. Or perhaps it was because she was considered part of it by now instead of merely a housekeeper.

The talk around the table concerned happenings on the Danduroo of which Leslie was ignorant, so she kept her head down, concentrating on pushing a bit of meat from one side of her plate to the other.

Molly soon brought her into the conversation. "This can't be much fun for Leslie. We ought to talk about something she's interested in."

"You have your choice of men or money," Raider said disparagingly.

"Raider!" Molly looked at him uncertainly.

"Sorry, honey." His eyes softened as he gazed at his little sister. "Just a bum joke that didn't quite come off."

Molly seemed to believe his explanation, even though Leslie knew it for what it was. "Tell us about California," Molly said to Leslie. "I've always wanted to go there."

"You've always wanted to go *everywhere,*" Raider said fondly.

"I'll settle for Sydney," she said quickly.

Raider sighed. "Not tonight, Molly. I've had a hard day."

"I wouldn't mind seeing California myself," Clara said. "Although I don't know if I could take all the noise—and that smog."

"We do have it," Leslie admitted. "I never knew how clean air could be until I came here. Or how beautiful open country is without high-rises and automobiles cluttering it up."

"Is that your subtle little way of saying you're contemplating staying?" Raider asked dangerously.

Since her accident, he hadn't mentioned the sale of Lester's house, yet it was obviously very much on his mind.

"For a while," she told him, lifting her chin defiantly.

"Isn't that super?" Molly crowed.

"It must be nice to come and go as you please," Clara commented.

"Well, actually I can't. I'll have to be home by the end of August. I'm a teacher, and school starts early in September."

Raider's eyebrows had risen in surprise. "Shall I ask what you teach?" he asked mockingly.

"Kindergarten children," she said succinctly. "They give me the ones who are too young to corrupt."

"I was thinking of becoming a teacher," Molly said seriously. "Either that or a ballerina, except I think teaching is more realistic." She laughed.

"There are more of us," Leslie agreed with a smile.

"You need a lot of college, though, don't you?" Molly asked, her eyes swiveling around to her brother.

"You can take as much as you want after you get your degree," Leslie told her. "If you're really serious, I would advise you to go for a doctorate. That's what I wish I'd done. My aunt got her Ph.D., and now she's teaching college. Actually she's on a year's sabbatical in Egypt right this minute. Doesn't that sound glamorous? Imagine being paid for traveling around foreign countries!"

"Fantastic!" Molly's sparkling eyes met an answering gleam in Leslie's.

"I would appreciate it if you didn't put wild ideas into my sister's head," Raider said coldly.

"What's so wild about it?" Molly cried. "I think it's the most exciting thing I ever heard."

"And if she told you she had an aunt who's an astronaut you would want to be that too," Raider said with grim amusement.

Molly's temper erupted. "Will you stop treating me like a child?"

"If you'll stop acting like one."

"What's so childish about wanting to be a teacher?"

"Nothing, if that's what you *really* wanted. What caught your imagination was all that nonsense about traveling around the world."

"It's scarcely nonsense," Leslie said tartly. "My aunt is a recognized authority in her field of anthropology."

"I know all about the females in your family, Miss Farraday. They're all liberated women, aren't they?" he sneered.

"Is there something wrong with that?" Leslie asked, clenching her teeth.

"Nothing, if that's what turns you on," he said negligently. "Does this paragon aunt of yours have a husband whom she leaves while she traipses around the globe?"

"No, she's single," Leslie snapped.

"I'm not surprised," he answered.

"Being married isn't the end-all and be-all of life," Molly cried passionately. "Even though you men seem to think so."

"I'd say it's time we all simmered down," Clara said. "Clear the table, Molly, while I get dessert."

When they were alone, Leslie looked directly at Raider. "I'm sure you realize that I hate having to ask you for anything, but I would appreciate it if you took me back to my place after dinner."

"You're staying here," he said firmly.

"Why? So you can insult me some more?"

"So I can keep an eye on you."

"What do you think I'm going to do with a sprained ankle?" she cried.

"Lady, you could get into trouble with a broken leg," he said grimly.

"Oh!" Leslie's soft mouth thinned in frustration. "I wish you'd just left me where you found me!"

"I'm beginning to wish that myself."

They were glaring at each other when Clara carried in the dessert.

The rest of dinner was not comfortable. Molly and Clara did their best, but Raider was uncooperative and Leslie was too upset to be of much help. It was a relief when they were all free to go about their business.

"I have an awful lot of homework. I'd better get right at it," Molly declared, pushing her chair back.

Clara said there was a program she wanted to listen to and beat a hasty retreat into the kitchen, leaving Leslie and Raider alone once more.

"I'm going out, so I'll have to take you upstairs now," he said distantly.

Leslie wanted to refuse, yet she didn't know how she would manage the stairs herself. It would only provoke

Raider's ready anger again anyway. With a sense of resignation, she allowed herself to be hoisted into his arms once more, vowing to pretend her ankle was all better the next day whether it was or not.

She held herself rigid, seeking the least possible contact with his muscled chest. She clasped her hands tightly together instead of balancing her body with one arm around his wide shoulders. It was an uncomfortable position.

A glint of amusement lightened his grim expression. "If I dropped you now, you'd break."

"I'm sure you're tempted," she said caustically.

They had reached her room, and he dumped her on the bed, looking down with somber eyes. "That's the whole damn trouble. I *am* tempted. You're everything I despise in a woman. You're selfish and greedy and scheming. So why do I still want you?" His hand trailed down her neck to curve around one full breast. "You use this beautiful body to get whatever you want out of a man. What is it you want from me, Leslie, more money?" His hand tightened, the thumb making slow circles over the peak, which became taut against her will.

"No!" she gasped, pushing his hand away.

His mouth curved cruelly. "Maybe I'm wrong in this instance. Maybe you just need a man. Wasn't Marty enough?" He dipped a long forefinger inside the widened V of her shirt, slowly unfastening the first button.

"Stop it!" She grabbed for his tormenting hand. "You're wrong!"

"What am I wrong about, Leslie? Can you deny that you'd like me to make love to you right now?"

"Yes! I mean no! Oh, leave me alone," she cried, huddling back against the headboard and clutching her shirt closed.

"I suppose that's good advice." He straightened up, towering over her while he looked down sternly. "Women like you can get into a man's blood like a virus." A muscle bunched at the point of his strong jaw. "But not mine. Understand this, Leslie Farraday: You're not going to disrupt my life. I won't let you spread your poison here. I want you off the Danduroo." His eyes were as cold as winter. "And I'm warning you. I always get what I want." Turning on his heel, he stalked out of the room.

The door closed and Leslie started to tremble, folding her arms around herself as though for protection. Raider's implacable enmity had left her bruised and shaken. Never in her short life had anyone disliked her so. It was distressing, yet was that really what was bothering her? Or was it the fact that it was a man who had an irrational, devastating effect on her? How could her body quicken every time he touched it?

Leslie was deeply ashamed. Raider was everything *she* detested in a *man*. How could she even now long to feel that firm mouth on hers, to experience the wild, pagan sensation that turned her liquid when his hands caressed her? Was it merely the fact that she was so inexperienced, in spite of what he thought? Biting her lip without even feeling the pain, Leslie prayed that was the reason.

Chapter Six

Leslie's fears about having to face Raider the next morning were groundless. He left early and didn't come home for dinner. Molly explained that he had flown to a distant part of the station.

"When he does that, he usually stays overnight," she said. "It's lonesome out there with only a radio for company, so he usually stops to visit with the foreman."

"You mean people live on other parts of the Danduroo?" Leslie asked.

"Oh, sure. There are several outposts. The station stretches for more than sixty miles. Raider switches the men around so no one spends too much time out there, but they still welcome company."

That day and the next were very peaceful ones for Leslie. Through a determined effort she put Raider out of her mind, spending her time reading and visiting with Clara, and Molly on her return from school.

When Raider did put in an appearance it wasn't as traumatic as Leslie had feared. To her relief he was coolly polite, not ignoring her, yet not singling her out for any of his biting sarcasm either. The whole household breathed a collective sigh of relief.

As the days went on, Leslie was dismayed to discover that she wasn't healing as fast as she expected. While her ankle was a lot better, the torn ligaments still pained a great deal when she tried to walk. At least she could manage the steps, though, with Molly or Clara to help. After she made it clear to Raider that she neither needed nor wanted his assistance, he allowed the others to take over, watching her slow, ungainly efforts with an unpleasant smile.

Although his silent disapproval made her uncomfortable, Molly's delight in her presence was compensation. Every afternoon she sought Leslie out and they spent hours talking. Leslie discovered that in some ways the young girl was wise beyond her years. In others she was a typical teenager.

"Guess what? Mary Jane Bennett is having a party tonight," she said, exploding into Leslie's room one late afternoon.

"Is that such an event?" Leslie smiled. "From what you've told me, you go to lots of parties."

"Not like this! Mary Jane's brother is on leave from his ship. He's in the navy. Oh, Les, you should just *see* him in his uniform." She flopped on the bed, arms outstretched. "He's *gorgeous!*"

Leslie watched her in amusement. "Does this paragon have a name, or do you just salute and address him as sir?"

Molly sat up, crossing her legs and clasping her ankles. "His name is Clive," she breathed. "Isn't that romantic? Like Clive of India."

"Very romantic," Leslie agreed. "What are you going to wear?"

The next hour was given up to the pressing problem as Molly selected and discarded dresses, turning to Leslie for her opinion. When the weighty question was settled to both their satisfactions, Molly started the laborious process of getting ready. Ordinarily she wore a minimum of makeup and let her soft hair hang loose, but since this was a special occasion heroic measures were called for. It took longer to look older.

"After I wash my hair, I think I'll try one of those tricky chignons," Molly said reflectively. "Do you think that would be more sophisticated than piling it up on top?"

After giving her opinion Leslie prepared to leave. "Do you want me to tell Clara you won't be home for dinner?" she asked.

"Oh, would you, Les? I forgot all about it."

Molly helped Leslie down the stairs, leaving her at the bottom in her rush to get back to the important things. A rush of affection engulfed Leslie as she watched the younger girl's rapid progress. Molly was such a darling! She hoped that young man tonight would pay a lot of attention to her.

Leslie made her way to the kitchen, stopping on the threshold in shock. Clara was standing with her back to the door, leaning her forehead against the wall. One hand was resting on the wall telephone as though she had just hung up.

"Clara, what is it? Have you had bad news?" Leslie cried.

The older woman turned slowly. Her cheeks were very pink, and there were tears in her eyes. "No, not bad news. Good news—the very best." Her voice broke on the words.

"I see," Leslie said slowly, not really seeing at all. It was somehow shocking to find Clara like this. She who was always so crisp and efficient, handling Raider's and Molly's eruptions in a calm, no-nonsense manner that smoothed the troubled waters. In spite of her disclaimer, something terrible must have happened to have wrought this change.

"No, of course you don't understand." Clara wiped her eyes and pulled out a chair. "Come sit down." When Leslie had hobbled to the chair, Clara took the one opposite. "I know Molly told you about Jody and me." Leslie made a halfhearted protest which Clara waved aside. "It's all right. It isn't exactly a secret around here."

"We weren't talking about you," Leslie said anxiously.

"I'm sure you weren't, but knowing Molly, I know she told you the whole sorry mess."

"Only because she's concerned about you," Leslie said, since it would be foolish to deny it.

"I'm aware of that." Clara smiled. "Anyway, that was Jody on the phone just now. Today is our anniversary and he called to ask me out to dinner. We've both been a couple of stiff-necked fools. I'm ashamed to say that I was worse than he. I can't tell you how often I wanted to call him only I let pride stand in my way."

"Does it matter now?" Leslie asked softly. "He called you."

"Yes, and I'll never forget it. I'm going to make it up to that man," she vowed fiercely.

"I'm so happy for you, Clara." Leslie leaned across and squeezed her hand impulsively. "I don't have to tell you to have a wonderful evening."

The older woman colored like a young girl. "I

imagine Jody will see to that," she said dryly, with a return to her old manner. "Can you and Molly manage alone? Raider won't be home, so it will be just the two of you. I fixed some—"

"Go make yourself beautiful and stop worrying about us," Leslie interrupted.

"I would like time to do something about my nails," Clara said wistfully.

"Then why are you sitting here? Go!"

After she had left, Leslie sat on at the kitchen table, smiling as she imagined their reunion. She didn't know Jody, but he must be truly special to have a woman like Clara in love with him. Today was a lucky day. Romance seemed to be in the very air. Both of the women in the house were going out to meet the men of their dreams, even though in Molly's case it was probably a temporary vision.

Leslie felt like Cinderella sending her stepsisters to the ball, except that in reality they were her dear friends. She hoped with all her heart that the evening would turn out well for both of them.

Her smile faded as she thought of Raider. Thank heaven he wasn't coming home to dinner. No amount of magic in the air would change his attitude, and it would have been horrible to try and force down a meal alone with him.

Leslie didn't intend to tell Molly or Clara that the other was going out, not wanting them to fuss about her being alone. She only hoped they wouldn't discover it for themselves. Fortunately they didn't.

Clara left first, sticking her head inside Leslie's door. "I'm going now. Will you say good-bye to Molly for me?" She gave a self-conscious little laugh. "I don't want to answer her thousand and one questions or sit through all her well-meaning advice."

"You go ahead, I'll take care of it," Leslie said reassuringly. "And have a gorgeous time."

"I intend to." Clara smiled shyly.

Molly's leave-taking was more prolonged. She bounced into Leslie's room a dozen times for advice and approval. Her hair and the pretty dress she had chosen were perfect, yet she needed confirmation. When she was finally satisfied with the result and ready to leave, Leslie gazed at her fondly.

"You look very chic," she said, knowing that would please her. "Have fun, honey."

"Oh, I will. I feel it in my bones!" Molly threw her arms around Leslie. "I'll tell you all about it when I get back."

The house seemed very quiet after she had left. Leslie read for a while, but the book failed to hold her interest. She felt vaguely restless. Maybe I'm hungry, she thought.

Getting downstairs by herself was going to be a challenge. After some contemplation she made her way to the staircase, easing herself gingerly to the top step. She slid her crutches down, watching with satisfaction while they bounced their way to the ground. So far so good. Holding her injured leg up, Leslie managed to scoot on her posterior from one step to another, pulling herself up at the bottom by the newel-post.

This certainly proved that she could get around by herself. If Raider weren't so darn stubborn, he'd admit it. He was just keeping her here because he knew she didn't want to stay. Well, maybe she wouldn't bother to ask him. Perhaps she'd just take off on her own. It was a notion that pleased her by its defiance even while she knew it to be impractical. How would she travel the distance to Lester's house if Raider didn't take her?

Dismissing him from her mind, she opened the

well-stocked refrigerator. Leslie examined the contents, discovering that she didn't feel like cooking for herself. She wasn't that hungry after all. Maybe some scrambled eggs.

As she was reaching for the carton a sound from the hall made her eyes widen. Had that been the front door opening? Everyone was out for the evening and any visitor would ring. Leslie stood in a tense listening pose. When the only sound was her own heart beating, she relaxed. Then there was the measured tread of footsteps and her mouth went dry.

She was staring at the door in icy fear when Raider appeared. He took in her terrified face and rigid body. She was grasping the crutches so hard that her knuckles stood out whitely.

"What the devil is the matter with you?" He frowned.

The relief was so great that Leslie sagged against the refrigerator. He crossed the floor in a few giant strides, catching her as she was about to fall.

"What's going on here?" Raider asked.

"I thought . . . I thought . . ." Leslie's shaking lips couldn't form the words.

He held her close, stroking her back soothingly. "It's all right, I'm here now. What did you think?"

"I thought you were a burglar," she managed, clinging tightly to his reassuring bulk.

"A what?" He lifted her chin to look at her incredulously. "How would a burglar get in here?"

"I don't know," she said with a question in her voice. "I guess they can get in anywhere." To her dismay, she found she couldn't stop trembling.

Raider picked her up, carrying her over to a chair, where he sat down still holding her. Leslie made a halfhearted attempt to get up, not really wanting to leave the shelter of those capable arms. No matter how much she hated this man, there was no getting away from the fact that he made her feel safe.

"Now what's all this about?" he asked. "What are you doing down here alone at this hour? Where are Clara and Molly?"

"They both went out."

"And left you alone?" He frowned.

"I'm not a child, Raider. I don't have to have someone baby-sit with me." She made a tentative move to get off his lap, but his arms tightened.

"Suppose you tell me exactly what happened," he commanded. "It isn't like either one of them to do a thing like this."

She told him about Molly, and Raider's eyebrows rose cynically. He had evidently been through a lot of her schoolgirl crushes. When she told him about Clara, however, he expressed deep satisfaction.

"It's about time those two came to their senses," he said. "I only hope nothing sets them off again tonight."

"I don't think it will. Clara was like a young girl getting ready for a date." Leslie's dreamy smile faded as her eyes met Raider's, and she realized that her fingers were moving slowly over his shirt. Her cheeks flamed and she pushed herself off of his lap. "I hope they get back together again," she said, not looking at him. "But will that mean she'll leave the Danduroo?"

"I hope not," he said almost absently. His enigmatic gaze was focused on Leslie. "Not for my sake, for hers. However, if that's what she wants, she has my blessing."

"Would it be hard to replace her?" Leslie asked.

"I don't know. Do you have someone in mind?" he asked mockingly.

"No, of course not! I was just making conversation."

"Suppose you tell me instead what you're doing in the kitchen? Didn't you have dinner?"

"Well, I . . . I wasn't hungry. I thought I'd just scramble some eggs." It suddenly occurred to her. "Have you eaten? Would you like me to fix you something?"

"No to both questions," he said. "I'm hungry and I want something more substantial than that. I'll cook dinner for you."

Waving aside her objections, he went to the refrigerator and inspected the contents. After peering into some covered casseroles he rejected them, taking out a huge steak instead.

"That looks like the side of a cow!" she gasped.

"Spoken like a true city girl. This, my untutored urbanite, is exactly the right size for a starving man and a woman who is always watching her figure." He looked critically at her slender body, or what he could see of it in the voluminous green velvet hostess gown. Leslie had put it on tonight because it was warm. And, she figured, what was she saving it for?

"I've never dieted in my life," she protested. "And I should think you'd be glad that I'm skinny, considering the amount you've had to haul me around."

His gaze rested on the white skin visible where the gold braided frogs closed the deep neckline. "I didn't say you were skinny, and I wasn't complaining." A mischievous light lit his eyes. "You don't weigh nearly as much as a dogie, and I've lifted many of those out of a mud hole."

Leslie laughed in spite of herself. "I'm glad I didn't know you were making the comparison every time you picked me up."

Raider's expression changed as he looked at her merry, relaxed face. "I wasn't," he said quietly.

Leslie caught her breath. Raider was so different tonight—almost friendly. Strangely enough, it didn't make him any less disturbing.

He stared at her for a moment longer before turning back to the stove. Leslie couldn't think of anything to say, so she watched his deft movements instead. Without any wasted motions, he went about the task of preparing dinner, scrubbing potatoes and putting them in the microwave oven, taking a head of lettuce out of the refrigerator and putting the steak on the broiler pan.

"You really do know how to cook, don't you?" she exclaimed.

"Anybody in this part of the country better," he answered succinctly. "If you're caught out in the bush, it's either that or starve. Don't any of the men you run around with know how to cook?"

She thought about the men she knew. "Not really," she admitted. "Some of them have one specialty that they make a big deal over like maybe spaghetti, but for the most part I think they regard cooking as . . . well, sort of effeminate."

Looking at Raider moving from stove to sink with catlike grace, Leslie was more than ever aware of his potent masculinity. She stared at the muscular forearms revealed below his rolled-up sleeves, at the big, capable hands that could be cruel and gentle. Leslie shivered. Nothing Raider could do would ever detract from his compelling male image.

"It sounds like your boyfriends have a problem," he said disparagingly.

"Chances to prove your manhood aren't as prevalent in the city," she retorted, annoyed as much by the little ripple that had traveled up her spine as by his implied criticism of her friends.

Raider turned to look at her, a small smile teasing the corners of his firm mouth. "I can think of a couple of ways."

An angry retort sprang to Leslie's lips, but she stifled it. This was no time to reopen the warfare between them. Not when Raider was trying—in his own way—to be nice. Besides, she always got the worst of their encounters.

"Are you sure I can't help you with anything?" she asked, changing the subject.

He looked at the crutches propped next to her. "What do you think you could do?"

"Anything you told me to," she assured him.

"Anything?" he murmured wickedly.

"You know what I mean," she muttered uncomfortably.

Raider laughed. "Okay, you can sit there and toss the salad after I wash the lettuce."

Leslie felt infinitely better having something to do. Watching Raider's long, muscular body moving back and forth was having a disquieting effect.

He got dinner on the table in a remarkably short time, and it was as delicious as she had known it would be. They ate in a companionable silence for a while.

After Raider had taken the edge off his appetite he smiled at her. "Isn't this better than scrambled eggs?"

"Much better," she agreed. "Also, I hate to eat alone."

"You mean any company is better than none?" he asked sardonically.

"No, that's *not* what I meant and you know it! Couldn't we call a truce just for tonight?" she pleaded.

"I thought that's what we were doing. Haven't I fed you handsomely and waited on you hand and foot?"

"You certainly have, and I'm grateful to you." She

leaned forward impulsively, her eyes wide and shining. "You've really done an awful lot for me. I wish there were some way I could repay you."

Raider's face was expressionless, his eyes narrowed on her lovely face. "Maybe there is."

She sat back stiffly in her chair. "I might have known."

"Don't jump to conclusions, Leslie," he drawled. "Delectable though you may be, there is still something standing between us. Once that's settled we can get down to the fun part."

"Let's get one thing straight, Mr. Mackenzie," she cried in outrage. "There isn't going to be any fun, or anything else, between us! I should have recognized this friendly act of yours for exactly what it was: another attempt to steal my property!"

He was unruffled by her wrath. "I'd scarcely call it stealing. I've offered you a great deal more than it's worth."

"That's what you keep saying, but I have only your word for it."

"Would you like to have the property assessed? I'll fly someone in from Sydney."

"Oh, sure! A friend of yours, no doubt!"

Raider relaxed in his chair, one long arm draped over the back. He was amused rather than annoyed by her accusations. "You have a very suspicious mind."

"I never did before. It comes from dealing with you," she flared.

"I've been perfectly honest with you. Your ten acres aren't really important. I just don't like the idea of Danduroo property being in the hands of an outsider." His tone dismissed her as completely as though she had been from outer space.

She *was* an outsider, Leslie realized, yet she had

been accepted into this lovely land by everyone except Raider. She, herself, felt a growing attraction for this beautiful country. Raider had no right to turn her out.

"Lester must have felt I belonged here," she told him defiantly. "From what I hear, he loved this place as much as you, and *he* thought I'd fit in or he wouldn't have left it to me."

Raider's eyes were glacial. "That's because he never met you . . . luckily."

"It wasn't my *fault!*" Leslie cried. "Can't I ever convince you of that?"

His expression remained grim. "It doesn't matter any longer. What's important is the disposition of his property. You say you're not motivated by money? All right, then why won't you sell? All that nonsense about keeping it as a vacation place is just that—nonsense! On a teacher's salary you can scarcely pop over for Easter Week or Washington's Birthday." Deep lines etched themselves beside his straight nose. "Or do you have some other form of income?"

Leslie went up in flames. "Don't you *dare* make those snide accusations! I've never taken anything from anyone in my whole life except a loan from my aunt, which I'm paying back. I worked after school all the time I was in high school and I put myself through college because my father didn't think I was worth it."

Raider looked at her curiously, some of the coldness leaving his face. "That's the first time you've mentioned your father. It sounds like you didn't have a very good relationship."

Leslie immediately regretted her indiscretion. "It doesn't matter," she muttered. "It has nothing to do with you."

"No, but I'm interested."

"Why?" she asked bluntly. "So you can find out that

my own father didn't like me? That ought to please you greatly."

A puzzled frown drew his brows together. "Is it possible—" He broke off, regarding her intently. "Do you have any brothers or sisters, Leslie? I've just realized I know very little about you."

She gave a mirthless laugh. "That's the first time you've admitted it."

"Okay, I plead guilty." He stared at her thoughtfully. "But there's still the letter."

"We're back to that again," Leslie sighed. "I told you. I never received it."

"No, I meant the—Well, never mind for now. Tell me, do you have any other family?"

"Very little. Just my younger brother, Bart. He's a junior at Stanford. And then there's Aunt Laura; she's my father's sister."

Raider nodded. "The college professor. Your father's sister, you say? Do you get along with *her?*"

"I didn't mean to imply that I don't get along with my father," Leslie answered carefully.

"Is your brother working his way through college too?" Raider asked abruptly.

"Well, he . . . no, he isn't."

"I believe you told Molly you went to UCLA. That's a state school, not a private college like Stanford where the tuition is pretty stiff."

"Oh, all right," Leslie sighed. "So my brother is Dad's favorite. Is that what you want me to admit?"

"Tell me about it, Leslie," he said gently.

"I guess it isn't too unusual for a man to prefer a son," she said defensively. "A lot of men are like that." Leslie bit her lip, finding the old sadness still capable of causing pain. She looked very young and very vulnerable.

Raider stared at her for a long moment while he seemed to be wrestling with some problem. Apparently coming to a decision, he reached across the table and took her hand, his long fingers closing over hers. "Keep the property if it makes you happy, Leslie," he said quietly.

She looked at him uncertainly. This was such an unexpected development that it threw her off base. After alternately using threats and seduction to get his way, why was he making this about-face? Leslie didn't trust this man for a minute. There had to be an ulterior motive.

"I can scarcely believe you mean that," she said, watching his face for a reaction.

"No, I can see where you would be suspicious." He chuckled. "I've given you rather a bad time, haven't I?"

"It hasn't always been a barrel of laughs," she admitted.

"I know, and I want to make it up to you. For everything," he added softly.

Suddenly Leslie understood, and her pride was wounded. "I neither need nor want your pity. Maybe my father didn't love me, but a lot of other people do," she said childishly.

"I have no doubt of that." Raider's eyes roamed over the exquisite contours of her flushed face. "And I think you're wrong about your father. I think he loved you very much."

Her long lashes fell. It wasn't true, but it was easier if Raider believed it. "What other reason could you have for changing your mind?" she asked in a low voice.

"Lester wanted you to have it," he said simply.

"You said he wouldn't have if he'd known me."

"I've changed my mind about that, too." A teasing

smile lit his gray eyes. "There is just one thing. If you intend to stick around these parts, you're going to have to learn to ride."

Leslie's suspicions returned. "I suppose you know that's a sure way to get me to sell."

He looked at her appraisingly. "Everything I've seen of you has convinced me that you're not a coward, Leslie. Is there any reason for your tremendous terror of horses?"

Although she told herself it didn't matter what he thought of her, Leslie found she did care. Haltingly she told him about her first experience on horseback.

Raider's face became grim as the sorry story unfolded. Uttering a half-suppressed oath, he said, "It's no wonder! Why didn't you tell me before? Never mind, I know the answer to that. Well, tomorrow we're going to lay all your fears to rest."

Leslie's startled eyes widened. "What do you mean?"

"I'm going to teach you how to ride. The *right* way."

"Oh, no, Raider, I couldn't! Please don't make me!"

His hand covered hers once more, his thumb making little circles on the soft skin of her inner wrist. "Trust me, honey. I won't let anything happen to you."

"I believe you. It's just . . . oh, Raider, I *can't!*"

"You can do anything you put your mind to," he said firmly. "Haven't you already shown me that?"

She knew he was referring to the way she had dragged herself out of the woods. It provided the out she needed. "I can't do it tomorrow. My leg."

"That's right, I forgot for a minute." He frowned. Then his face cleared. "Well, we'll just have to postpone it for a few days."

Leslie breathed a sigh of relief. "Yes, I guess so."

He laughed. "Don't get your hopes up. I'm not going to forget about it."

Knowing Raider, he undoubtedly wouldn't. He had a one-track mind when he was set on an idea. Well, she'd think of something when the time came, Leslie assured herself. In the interim she was going to enjoy this new relationship with him. Her heart felt suddenly light.

"And speaking of that leg, you've been on it too long," he said.

"I've just been sitting here," she protested, not wanting the evening to end.

"For hours. You ought to be in bed with your foot elevated."

Leslie looked at her watch, amazed at the time that had elapsed and how much had happened since she decided to fix herself a snack. "I'll help you clean up first," she said.

"You'll do no such thing. Do I look helpless?" Raider demanded.

He looked anything but. Standing before her with his hands on his hips, Raider looked exactly like what he was: a rugged, virile male who could send any woman's blood pounding through her veins with the promise in that lean, muscular body.

"I could put the dishes in the dishwasher if you cleared the table," she said tentatively.

"Absolutely not!" He took her hands, pulling her upright and swinging her into his arms. "It's upstairs to bed for you."

"You don't have to carry me," she told him. "I would have gotten back up if you hadn't come along."

"But I did," he pointed out. "Fortunately for you."

She made a face at him. "I didn't think it was so lucky. You scared the daylights out of me."

"Silly girl. We don't have burglars on the Danduroo. Where would they come from?"

"I don't know," she said defensively. "What do I know about a cattle station?"

"This country must seem very strange to you, Leslie," he said quietly.

"In a lot of ways," she agreed.

He watched her intently. "If things had been different—between us, for one thing—would you have enjoyed your stay?"

She smiled. "I did anyway."

"How could you? You haven't been anywhere or seen anything."

"That's not true. I flew in a private plane for the first time and saw a whole bunch of kangaroos and shared a cookout with some real live cowboys." She grinned mischievously. "Although maybe I shouldn't bring it up."

"I deserved that." His answering smile was rueful. "What I meant by seeing things was Ayers Rock or the Henley-on-Todd Regatta. If you're still here when it's run, I'll take you to that."

"I've never been to a yacht race," she told him.

"Well, they aren't exactly yachts, and the river doesn't have any water in it." He laughed at her expression. "Every year about the end of August there's a race on the dry Todd River bed. The contestants make contraptions shaped like boats with sails but no bottoms. Each one has an eight-man crew. They get inside, pick it up and run with it."

"You're joking!" When assured that he wasn't, Leslie said, "That would be something to see."

"It is. We'll do Ayers Rock and the Regatta at the same time. They're both up near Alice Springs."

"That's quite a distance from here, isn't it?" she asked.

"Not by plane."

"It must be wonderful to know how to fly." Her face was wistful. "Nothing is beyond reach."

"Would you like to learn?"

"Do you mean it?" she asked incredulously.

He nodded. "You take your medicine on the horse and I'll teach you to fly." He had put her down on the bed and was sitting on the edge beside her.

Leslie wrinkled her nose at him. "I knew there was a catch. How about a substitute for the riding lessons? Couldn't you teach me something else instead?"

Raider traced the curve of her cheek, his finger trailing down the side of her neck. "I might at that," he murmured.

Leslie was incapable of moving, even though alarms were sounding throughout her body. His touch was like a feather, yet it seemed to burn her delicate skin. She looked up at him in mute appeal, her soft mouth trembling.

"Don't be frightened, honey. I won't do anything you don't want me to." His low voice was soothing, seducing her will to resist.

His hand slipped inside the wide neck of her jade gown, caressing her smooth shoulder. Edging the fabric aside, he leaned forward and kissed the ivory skin, moving his lips back and forth sensually. "Mm, you taste delicious. And you smell beautiful, too." The words were muffled by his nearness.

"Raider, please—" She made a halfhearted protest.

"What is it, darling? What would you like me to do?" His hand wandered slowly over the rich fabric, pausing to cup her breast lovingly.

She gasped as a wave of indescribable pleasure followed the movement of his fingers. It took a great effort to say, "You mustn't do that."

Obediently his hand uncurled, sliding down her side instead to stroke her hip and thigh. Leslie shuddered, shifting her body as a cascade of emotion swept through her, driving out everything but the need to be closer to this man.

Raider gave a low cry of triumph deep in his throat. "You want me, don't you, sweetheart?"

Before she could summon up the strength to deny it, his mouth touched hers, gently at first. There was still time to draw back; Raider's passion was carefully leashed. But once he kissed her she was lost. Her lips parted of their own volition and he pulled her close, his tongue eagerly seeking the entry she had provided.

He leaned across her, his hard chest solid against her yielding softness. Wrapping both arms around her, he rolled her into his arms, pressing her body firmly against the length of his. Leslie could feel the strengthening of his loins and she gloried in her ability to excite this man who was giving her so much pleasure in return.

Without relinquishing her mouth, Raider slowly undid the fastenings of her robe, slipping it off her shoulders and down to her waist. Leslie shivered as his hands caressed her body, teasing the tips of her breasts until they turned to tightly curled rosebuds under his experienced touch. When his mouth closed around one and his tongue explored it lingeringly, Leslie arched her body into his, moving her hips to help him remove her gown completely.

Raider raised himself on one elbow to look at her, his eyes smoldering as they devoured every inch of her quivering form. "You're beautiful," he breathed.

Leslie's long eyelashes swept her flushed cheeks and her hands fluttered up to cover her bare breasts, but Raider wouldn't permit it.

Taking both of her hands in his, he held them wide, bending to kiss the soft skin of her stomach.

"I want to see all of you, touch all of you." The words were punctuated by tantalizing kisses that set her aflame. "I want to possess you completely, my love."

Leslie's self-consciousness disappeared. She needed him to touch her. A primitive urge required it. She wanted him to do all he was doing and more. Her fingers tangled in his thick hair as she whispered his name, managing to convey her longing.

He gathered her in his arms, covering her body with his as he started to unbutton his shirt. Leslie's trembling fingers reached up to help him. Their eyes met and held, savoring the exquisite torture of ecstasy delayed, their throbbing bodies at a fever pitch.

"Leslie, I'm home!" Molly's voice called faintly from downstairs.

For a moment it seemed just a maddening intrusion into their private world, then suddenly realization set in. Raider was the first to react. Springing to his feet, he pulled Leslie's gown over her head, guiding her arms into the sleeves with deft hands. When she seemed incapable of doing it herself, he swiftly fastened the gold frogs, running his fingers through her tousled hair to smooth it.

A second before the door opened he took Leslie's chin in his hand and kissed her hard. "You look fine," he murmured reassuringly.

"Leslie, I can't wait to tell—" Molly's impetuous announcement broke off as she noticed her brother. "Oh, hi, Raider. I didn't expect to see you."

"Hi, youngster. Leslie told me you went to a party. Did you have a good time?" he asked.

"Yes, it was super!" Her gaze narrowed on his unbuttoned shirt. "What are you done up for—or should I say undone?"

"It's my new macho image," he said easily. "I was thinking of getting a gold chain, too. What do you think?"

"Oh, Raider, that's passé," Molly said disgustedly. She turned eagerly toward the bed. "I'm so glad you're still up, Les. You'll simply die when you hear what Clive said to me!"

Raider moved to the door. "Something tells me I'm not needed here. I'll leave you to your girl talk." His mouth turned up wryly at one corner as he sought Leslie's eyes. "Good night, Leslie. We'll take up where we left off another time."

"Has that brother of mine been badgering you again?" Molly demanded after the door closed.

The banter between Raider and Molly had given Leslie time to pull herself together. She admired his coolness, reflecting rather bitterly that it was evidently not the first time this had happened to him. It was a new experience for her, however. Although outwardly calm now, Leslie was still shaking inside.

If Molly hadn't come home, Raider would be making love to her right now. Was she glad or sorry? Her body gave one answer, her common sense another. Leslie wasn't the type for casual love affairs, and there was certainly no future for her with Raider. Therefore she was glad, right? It was difficult to convince herself of that at the moment.

Leslie became aware that Molly had repeated her question. "No, we got along surprisingly well," she answered. "Maybe he's getting used to me."

"Well, it's about time!" Dismissing her brother airily, Molly got down to the more important subject of the party, her cheeks pink with animation.

It was late by the time every conversation had been reported, every nuance carefully explored. Some of Molly's effervescence had dampened and she was starting to yawn.

"It sounds like it was a gorgeous party and I enjoyed hearing all about it, but I think it's time you went to bed, pet," Leslie said.

Molly got to her feet, stretching. "I guess you're right." On an impulse she turned back, throwing her arms around Leslie and kissing her on the cheek. "I'm so glad you're here," she said. "I wish you could stay forever."

Alone in the darkness, Leslie thought about Molly's childlike statement. The terrible realization came over her that she was beginning to feel the same way.

Chapter Seven

If Leslie had been nervous about facing Raider in the past, it was a pale imitation of what she was experiencing the next morning. She had to force herself to go down to breakfast. As a result, the others were already assembled.

Raider got up to help her into her chair, his hands lingering on her arms and sending a shock of remembrance through her body. Luckily the others didn't notice, being completely absorbed with their own lives.

Clara's face was softer, her usual air of efficiency missing as she dawdled with a piece of toast. Molly, on the other hand, was her usual bubbly self.

"Clara and Jody are back together again," she announced. "Isn't that great?"

"Oh, Clara, I'm so happy for you," Leslie cried. "Where is Jody? Am I going to get to meet him?"

"Not for a few days." Clara gave a self-conscious

little laugh. "He had to return to his brother's station, but he'll be back as soon as Raider arranges for one of the men from here to take over. That's what we were just talking about."

"It won't be any problem," Raider assured her.

"You're a dinkum gent, Raider," Clara said softly.

Leslie remembered the term being used to describe Lester. If he had been anything like Raider, she was even more sorry not to have known him.

Raider waved aside Clara's appreciation, turning to Leslie with banked fires in his gray eyes. "Did you sleep well?" he asked, examining the delicate contours of her face lingeringly.

"Yes, thank you," she answered politely, staring down at her plate. She couldn't meet his eyes.

"I didn't," he said. "It's strange. Usually I don't have any trouble at all, but last night I kept having this feeling that there was some unfinished business I should be taking care of." There was an undercurrent of laughter in his voice.

Leslie was aware of Clara's suddenly sharpened gaze. Her throat tightened up and she couldn't have uttered a word if her life depended on it. Molly saved her from having to.

"I didn't expect to sleep either after the party and all, but I dropped right off. In fact, I could have slept till noon. It's a good thing today is Friday," she groaned.

"T.G.I.F.," Leslie said, smiling.

"What does that mean?"

"It's an expression we use in the States. It stands for Thank Goodness It's Friday."

"Amen," Molly said feelingly. "Let's hear it for the weekend."

"I'm looking forward to it myself," Raider remarked, giving Leslie a special smile.

"I'll help you with the dishes, Clara," Leslie said in a strangled voice, pushing her chair back.

"That isn't necessary." Clara rose also, starting to carry out the plates. "You can just keep me company in the kitchen."

"I'm really much better this morning," Leslie said. "For the first time there's only a twinge when I put my weight on that leg."

Raider frowned. "I don't want you overdoing it."

"I think that old cane of Dad's is still around. She can use that," Molly said. "I'll hunt it up right now."

When Molly had gone upstairs and Clara had disappeared into the kitchen, Raider came to stand very close to Leslie. He touched her cheek gently. "Take care of yourself," he murmured. "I have plans for us tomorrow." Before she could answer, he kissed her lightly and was out the door.

Clara and Leslie took time for a cup of coffee after the dishes were done. As they were sitting companionably at the kitchen table, Clara remarked casually, "It looks like you and Raider have settled your differences."

"Yes, he . . . uh . . . yes," Leslie finished lamely.

"That's good. You shouldn't let the past interfere with the present."

"We did get off to a pretty rocky start," Leslie said ruefully. "But it wasn't all my fault. If Raider hadn't come on like thunder, I would have agreed to sell him Lester's land immediately. I'm not entitled to it and I know it."

Clara's brows rose. "Not entitled to it?"

"I never knew him," Leslie said simply. Impulsively she asked, "Do you know why he left it to me?"

Clara seemed momentarily at a loss for words. She looked Leslie over intently, from her shining copper hair to her small rounded chin. "Have you asked Raider that question?"

"Yes. He said something to the effect that Lester was a friend of my mother's. I couldn't convince him that he was wrong."

"Are you sure he is?"

"No," Leslie said slowly. "I never heard her mention Lester's name. If they had had any kind of a relationship, wouldn't she have remembered him?"

"Oh, I think she remembered him," Clara said dryly. "That's all water under the dam, though. The important thing is, what are you going to do now?"

"What do you mean?"

"Have you ever considered living here?" Clara asked casually.

"You mean in Lester's house? I'd love to, but I can't afford it. I have to work."

"That wasn't exactly what I meant," Clara said carefully. "I got the impression that maybe you and Raider . . ." She paused delicately.

Leslie flushed, tracing a pattern on the wooden table. "You know better than that, Clara. You must have seen him through dozens of women. I don't want to be merely the next in line."

"How about the last in line? Somehow I think he feels differently about you," Clara said thoughtfully.

The idea made a bubble of happiness well up in Leslie's breast, yet she knew it was only wishful thinking. She shook her head. "We scarcely know each other. It's only recently that we stopped snapping like turtles at each other."

"That doesn't mean anything. Jody and I used to have some terrible battles. It was almost worth it for the fun of making up . . . like last night." Clara smiled reminiscently.

"That's what this is all about," Leslie teased. "You want the whole world to be in love."

Clara's face sobered. "No, I just don't want you two to make the same mistake that—"

When she didn't continue, Leslie felt a strange prickle up her spine. With a flash of intuition she asked, "Did Lester and my mother have a love affair? Did he ever talk to you about her?"

The telephone pealed sharply, startling them both. As Clara picked up the receiver, Leslie wandered outside, wondering what the other woman's answer would have been, or if she really wanted to hear it.

It began to seem more and more as if there really had been something between her mother and Lester, even though all of Leslie's evidence was to the contrary. Had he asked her to marry him and she refused because, at eighteen, the thought of moving to the other side of the world was too frightening? Had she accepted Leslie's father's proposal on the rebound, which accounted for the lovelessness of their marriage? Was that why she had never mentioned Lester's name, not because she didn't remember him but because she couldn't bear to speak of her lost love?

Leslie sighed. If that were the case, it was terribly sad, but it had nothing to do with her and Raider. Lester may have asked her mother to marry him; Raider only wanted to sleep with *her*.

The thought set up a clamor in her body once more. What was she going to do about that? Every instinct urged her to take what he would give her. He was like an eagle, wild and free. No woman could tame him, but oh, the joy he could bring for a brief period! Was she willing to settle for that? Leslie shivered, only partly from the cold. She had until tomorrow to make up her mind.

As it happened, she had longer than that. On Saturday morning early, Raider got a phone call. There was trouble in the north section and he had to go up and take care of it. Leslie was still asleep when he came into her room to tell her.

He woke her with a kiss, gathering her sleep-warm body in his arms. "Did anyone ever tell you that you have the most beautiful eyelashes in the whole world?" he whispered, nuzzling the delicate spot behind her ear.

Leslie wriggled blissfully against him, wrapping her arms around his neck. This was the best dream she had ever had. It was only when Raider pulled the covers down so that he could draw her slim body even closer that Leslie realized it wasn't a dream.

"What are you doing here?" she gasped. "Suppose someone should come in?"

"It's Saturday, everybody's sleeping." He slipped the nightgown off her shoulder, bending his head to kiss the rosy breast that was revealed to his avid eyes. "God, how I'd like to get in that bed with you!"

Leslie's mind was made up for her. She couldn't deny him—or herself. Moving over to make room for him, she curled her arm around his neck, drawing his head down to hers. Raider's kiss was passionate, awakening a response that made little thrills of expectation race through her body. It was with a sense of disbelief that she saw him shake his head regretfully.

"I have to leave. Some of the men are waiting for me to fly them up to the northern quadrant." He explained about the trouble.

"Can't it wait?" Leslie was appalled to hear herself begging.

His firm mouth softened in a tender smile. "Do you think I'd be leaving if it could? I'll be back, sweetheart. Not tonight, damn it, but tomorrow night for sure." His voice deepened to a throaty growl. "I'd like to find you just like this."

In spite of the urgency, he took time for another kiss, invading her mouth with a male purpose that had her arching her body into his with an abandon he found almost irresistible. Raider was breathing heavily when he finally gathered the strength to put her away. With a last hard kiss, he left before he had a chance to change his mind.

Leslie got through the day and night somehow, although she found it difficult to settle down. When anyone spoke to her she looked at them blankly, her mind far away in something called the northern quadrant.

On Sunday morning Molly said impatiently, "What's the matter, Les? You act like you're a million miles from here."

"I'm sorry, Molly. I . . . I guess I was thinking about something."

"You're not bored, are you?" the younger girl asked anxiously. "You're not thinking of cutting your visit short?"

"No." Leslie smiled fondly at her. "Although I will have to go home shortly."

"I don't want to think about it," Molly announced. "What shall we do today? Let's think of something special."

Leslie was touched. "You don't have to entertain me, honey. I'm perfectly content to stay around here and . . . and do nothing." She had stopped herself just in time from saying "and wait for Raider to return."

"You've been doing too much of that. I know!" Molly's face lit up. "How would you like to go fossicking?"

"What on earth is that?"

"Prospecting for opals. There's an old mine in the foothills near here," Molly explained. "It's been pretty much worked out commercially, but you can still find some opals if you're lucky. We'll get a couple of the station hands to lend their muscle and take off after lunch."

"It sounds terribly exciting," Leslie said. The idea of picking jewels out of the earth seemed fascinating and primitive to a city girl who had only seen gems in a jewelry store.

"It is fun, although we might not find anything," Molly warned.

"I don't care," Leslie assured her. "It will still be like a treasure hunt."

"Okay, I'll call down to the bunkhouse and alert the guys."

"Couldn't the two of us go alone?" Leslie asked. "I mean, it *is* Sunday, their day off. I don't like to ask them to give it up."

"They won't mind," Molly said smugly. "I happen to know that Marty likes you, and if I ask Spike it will make his day. He isn't as cute as Clive, but he's fun."

"I'm surprised you don't ask Clive instead. You didn't see him yesterday either, did you?"

"He had to go back to the base early the next morning." A dreamy smile curved Molly's wide mouth. "He'll be back next month, though."

"It's a good thing Spike doesn't know he's only a stand-in for the main event," Leslie commented in amusement. "Which one is he? Do I know him?"

After Molly described him, Leslie remembered the tall, clean-cut youth with the engaging smile.

Molly was correct about the enthusiasm of the two

men. They were waiting impatiently beside an open Land-Rover, which Leslie eyed dubiously. As soon as they left the station and crossed the highway she began to see the wisdom of a four-wheel-drive vehicle. The road to the mine led across rough terrain strewn with rocks, twisted beige balls of tumbleweed called roly-poly, and giant termite mounds.

Leslie exclaimed in wonder when she caught sight of the first one, an irregular mound almost twenty feet high, rising like a monstrous tree stump. "What on earth is that?" she cried.

"A termite mound," Marty said. "Around here they're sometimes called magnetic nests because they always point north and south like the needle on a compass."

When several were clustered together as they were farther on, they looked like twisted markers in a cemetery. Spike explained the intricate workings of the hardened mud "cities" that housed as many as three million inhabitants, if the queen and all her workers could be counted.

After they threaded their way through the mounds, the going got a little easier. It was a bright day out but slightly chilly in the open jeep. Leslie lifted her face gratefully to the wintry sun, feeling a sense of excitement at the adventure ahead.

"I meant to come by and tell you how sorry I was to hear about your accident," Marty said.

She made a rueful face. "Just plain stupidity. I was running after a koala."

"Cute little critters, aren't they?" He grinned.

"I know it's a cliché, but they do look like teddy bears," Leslie said. "Even to the little pink tongue that sticks out like a bit of felt."

"How would you like to hold one? There's an animal preserve not far from here. We could take a ride over one day if you like."

"I'd love it!" she exclaimed.

"Okay, it's a date. I'll take your picture and you can show it to all your friends. It'll be a nice souvenir when you get back home."

Molly had heard the last part of their conversation. She was sitting in the front seat next to Spike, who was driving. Turning around, she frowned at Marty. "Don't talk about Leslie's going home. I don't want her to."

"I don't either, but you have to be realistic." Marty looked at Leslie appraisingly. "Trying to keep her here would be like putting a leash on a lyrebird."

"Why do you say that? Do I stick out like such a sore thumb?" Leslie asked, secretly hurt.

"Far from it," he said admiringly. "It's just that you're a big-city gal. What would you do with yourself way out here?"

Leslie considered it. Yes, she came from a metropolis, but was that really by choice or circumstance? She thought about the night at the Rose and Thistle. It had been like a big party. Those people had welcomed her into their midst instantly, unreservedly making her feel she belonged as no new acquaintances at home had ever done. It wasn't from a lack of sophistication, either. Their small planes put the high spots of Australia within reach: the glittering night life of Sydney; the surfing Edens of the Great Barrier Reef; skiing on Mt. Kosciusko near Canberra, where the snowfields were bigger than those of Switzerland.

They probably went a great many more places than she did in Los Angeles, where there were undenied attractions, most of them too expensive for her anyway.

Leslie was aware that she had skirted around the main attraction here. Raider. Her heart started to pound as she thought of this evening, when he would return.

Molly answered Marty's question for her. "That isn't fair. Les has been laid up, so she hasn't seen all the things Australia has to offer."

"I don't have to." Leslie smiled. "I love it already. But I have to make a living, as I explained to you."

"You can sell Lester's land to Raider and live on the proceeds," Molly said airily, with the oversimplification of the very young and very rich.

They pulled up to the entrance to the mine, distracting Molly from a problem that Leslie knew had no solution.

The cavelike opening was dark, the descent steep and strewn with rocks. "Wait until I bring the light," Marty called. He and Spike were unloading pickaxes and compact electric torches.

Even with the powerful lanterns it looked sort of spooky. Leslie clung to Marty's arm, also using the cane which she had prudently brought along. The narrow passageway widened into a large chamber faced in roughhewn rock that was mainly mustard colored, striated with pink and red. Chunks had been gouged out of the walls, leaving them jagged in places.

"Okay, this is it," Spike said.

"What is?" Leslie looked at him blankly.

"This is where we start prospecting." They all laughed at her expression. "I think Leslie expected to pick opals up from the floor—already polished," he teased.

"Don't be silly," she defended herself. Looking helplessly around the cavern, she said, "Where *do* you find them?"

"You chip away and hope to get lucky," Marty told her, lifting the pickax.

Leslie began to see what Molly had meant by their needing muscle. The two men wielded the heavy tools, tossing over pieces of potential ore for the girls to examine. Time slipped by as they prospected for the elusive gems, eagerly scrutinizing each dusty nugget before reluctantly discarding it in favor of the next one.

"The least you could have done is bring some beer," Spike complained, sitting down to rest for a minute next to Molly. "This is thirsty work."

"I'll give you one when we get home," she promised. "I'm so disappointed that we aren't finding anything for Leslie."

"The big mines are at Coober Pedy," he reminded her.

"I know, but I was hoping we'd at least turn up a little teeny one to give her some idea what they look like in the raw state."

"We still might," Marty consoled her. "I'll keep slogging on."

Molly consulted her wristwatch. "It's getting late," she said dubiously. "We'll have to be starting back soon."

Leslie was amazed at how the afternoon had flown. It didn't matter that they hadn't uncovered any buried treasure. She had been having such a good time that even Raider had been driven from her thoughts. A thrill of anticipation ran through her as he returned to them.

They were almost ready to call it a day when Marty gave an exclamation of triumph. "I think I've got one!"

They all crowded around as he squatted down on the ground and used a chisel to break open a fist-sized rock.

To Leslie it looked like any of the dozens of others they had poured over, but when it was split in two she could see a shining band of blue in the core.

"That's an opal?" she asked curiously. The flat streak of mixed blues bore no resemblance to the rainbow of glowing colors she was expecting.

"That's it," Marty said with satisfaction. "It's small, but it'll make a pretty little ring or pendant when it's polished up. Another souvenir for you to take home."

Molly turned the chunk of ore to the light. "I'll get Raider to take it into town and have it polished for you."

It was cold when they retraced their steps to the surface. The sun was setting, and without its warmth the air was frigid. Leslie zipped up her windbreaker, wishing she had a heavy sheepskin coat like the others. It was even worse once they got started. The chill wind whistled through the open Land-Rover, seeping inside her jacket. They were nearing the Danduroo when Leslie started to shiver uncontrollably. She couldn't stop her teeth from chattering.

"You're freezing!" Marty exclaimed. "Here, I'll give you my coat."

As he started to unfasten it, Leslie protested. "Don't do that. You'll catch cold with nothing on. I'll be all right."

Marty insisted, compromising only when he saw that she was adamant. He put his arm around her shoulders, opening his coat and wrapping half of it around her so that her body was cuddled against his chest. "Okay, then we'll share. I must say I like this way better," he said with a wicked gleam in his eyes.

In spite of the cold she tried to pull away, murmuring, "Please, Marty, what will Molly think?"

"I don't know, we'll ask her," he teased. "Hey, Molly, is it all right with you if I keep Leslie warm? She's freezing to death, but she doesn't want you to think we're making out back here."

Molly's only reaction was remorse. "Oh, Leslie, I should have loaned you a warm jacket."

The heavy sheepskin lining combined with Marty's body heat had stopped Leslie's teeth from chattering. "Don't worry about it," she said. "We'll be home soon."

Even as she said it the words echoed in her mind. Without thinking, she had used the word "home." Was that the way she was starting to think about the Danduroo? It was a disquieting thought.

Marty's arm tightened around her, unaware that her attention had strayed. "See, we have Molly's blessing."

"Is that what you got out of it?" Leslie laughed.

His hand moved caressingly on her shoulder. "I enjoyed today, Leslie. I hope you did too."

"Very much," she said, turning her head to look out at the darkening countryside. Leslie didn't want to give Marty any false ideas about a possible relationship between them. He was much too nice to be misled.

He put his hand around her chin, gently guiding her face back to his. "I feel the same way as Molly. I wish you didn't have to go home."

The Land-Rover stopped in front of the house, saving Leslie the necessity of answering, even though Marty's arm still circled her and he seemed to be waiting for a confirmation of his sentiment. A harsh voice made her pull away hurriedly. In the gathering gloom she hadn't seen Raider on the steps.

"Wouldn't it be better taste to do that sort of thing in private?" he asked tautly.

Molly jumped over the side of the jeep. "Hi, Raider," she cried in pleased surprise. "We didn't expect you back so soon."

"That seems fairly obvious." His eyes raked Leslie with contempt.

She pulled out of Marty's embrace, nervously smoothing her hair. "We . . . uh . . . we went— What do you call it?"

"Fossicking," Marty supplied. The smile he turned on Raider faded as he noticed the bigger man's grim expression. "I think we'd better be getting back now," he told Spike.

"Molly promised me a beer," Spike protested.

"That's right," Molly agreed. "Come in and we'll show Raider the fruits of our labor. Marty really made points with Leslie today," she told her brother.

"I'll just bet he did," Raider said savagely. "And vice versa. Leslie has a potent way of saying thank you."

The two station hands exchanged a furtive look. "I think I'll take a rain check on that beer after all, Molly," Spike said loudly. "There . . . uh . . . I forgot about something I have to do."

The jeep roared off, leaving Molly staring after it. She turned on her brother with her hands on her hips. "I don't know what's eating you, but you didn't have to take it out on them."

A vein throbbed in Raider's forehead. "Go inside, Molly. I want to talk to Leslie alone."

"No! You're probably going to be just as rude to her!"

Leslie forced a smile. She had a feeling he was going to be more than that, and she didn't want Molly to witness it. "It's all right, Molly."

"No, it isn't!" the young girl cried. "You don't know

him. He can be really rotten. I'm not going to leave you alone with him."

Raider's smile was bitter. "It's the other way around. I never should have left you alone with *her.*" He turned to Leslie. "Was that vulgar display really necessary in front of my sister?"

"*What* vulgar display?" Molly demanded before Leslie could answer. "You mean because Marty had his arm around her? How Victorian can you get? She was freezing in that thin jacket and Marty was keeping her warm. Look at her now. She's practically blue!"

Leslie was indeed trembling, as much from the force of Raider's cruel words as from the cold, but they couldn't know that. Grabbing her roughly by the arm, Raider jerked her inside, Molly following indignantly.

"I think you owe Leslie an apology," she said.

"Will you kindly keep out of things that don't concern you?" he grated.

"She is a guest in this house and you insulted her," Molly maintained, sticking her chin out pugnaciously. The family resemblance was very strong at that moment.

"Raider just got the wrong impression, that's all," Leslie said placatingly. She couldn't forgive him either, yet she didn't want to be a source of friction between them.

"If he wasn't always jumping to conclusions that wouldn't happen," Molly said in annoyance. The telephone rang, distracting her attention. She was reluctant to leave the battlefield, but after several rings Molly couldn't resist its siren call.

Raider waited until she was out of the room before rounding on Leslie. "Did Marty take up where I left off?" he asked grimly.

Hot color flooded her face. "That's a disgusting thing

to say!" She turned toward the stairs, keeping her head high to cover the desperate hurt he had inflicted.

He pulled her back, his hand rough on her arm. "Is it?" His eyes raked her, traveling insolently over her body. "I was right about you the first time. Any man will do as long as he's a warm body."

His hand was bruising, but she refused to wince. Looking him straight in the eye she said, "If that's the way you want it."

The pressure on her arm increased until she cried out in spite of her resolve. "You know damn well what I want—or what I *wanted.* I didn't realize I'd have to share you with the whole station."

Her hand came out in a stinging slap that seemed to reverberate in the quiet hall. Raider's face darkened as he started toward her menacingly, reaching out to grasp her slender shoulders.

Molly returned, crying out when she saw the anger in her brother's face. "Will you leave her alone, Raider!"

"I told you to stay out of this," he said furiously. "Leslie doesn't need championing. She knows her way around quite well."

"You're a real judge of character, aren't you?" Molly asked disgustedly.

Raider controlled himself with an effort. "I've had a little more experience than you."

"Then how come it hasn't made you any smarter?" she countered. "You get these irrational ideas in your head that a bulldozer couldn't shake loose. Like Leslie being a bad influence because she let Marty put his arm around her. For crying out loud, *everybody's* a bad influence as far as you're concerned! I can't go away to college because I might get corrupted there. I can't go out with Marshall Goodwin because he's too fast for me. I can't—"

"Was that Marshall on the phone just now?" he demanded.

"What if it was?"

Raider's face was like granite. "I'm not going to tell you again, Molly. You are not to go out with Marshall Goodwin."

"You don't have any right to dictate who my friends should be," she stormed, her cheeks flushed with anger.

"As head of this household I not only have the right, it's my duty."

"You run this house like Captain Bligh ran the *Bounty*," Molly cried. "You're lucky, Leslie, you're not stuck here permanently. How would you like to be a member of *this* crew?"

"Don't bother answering," Raider said cuttingly. "I'm not taking applications."

Leslie was stung into angry speech. "You should be. Your present crew has good cause to mutiny."

"It looks like you're outvoted, Captain," Molly crowed.

Raider uttered a strangled oath. "I don't know why I bothered to come home tonight! If any of the men need me, tell them I've gone back up north." The front door slammed after him with a crash that shook the house.

Raider's departure eased the terrible tension. Leslie felt completely drained, but Molly was still charged with rage. "The *nerve* of him! I'm seventeen years old; I won't be treated like a baby anymore. If he thinks he can go on leading my life for me, he's due for a shock. I won't be dictated to!" In her agitation Molly was pacing up and down the hall.

"Calm down, honey. He's your brother. Raider is only doing what he thinks is best for you," Leslie said reluctantly. It was true. His harshness with Molly was motivated by love—quite different from the emotion he felt for her.

It didn't placate Molly. In fact, it aggravated her further. "That's no reason for him to ride roughshod over everyone like some ruling monarch disciplining the peasants. This time he's gone too far and I won't put up with it."

Leslie eyed the defiant girl apprehensively. "What are you going to do?"

"I'm going out with Marshall tonight."

"Oh, Molly, I don't think that's a very good idea. Why don't you wait until you both cool off and can discuss this sensibly?"

"I *am* being sensible. He's the one who is pigheaded."

When no amount of coaxing would change Molly's mind, Leslie went into the kitchen to enlist Clara's help. She was dismayed to find a note from Clara saying she had gone to join Jody for the night.

What to do now? With a sinking sensation, Leslie realized there was nothing she *could* do. Molly was too much like Raider, implacable when her mind was made up. It was no wonder they clashed. Leslie just hoped her defiant gesture wouldn't be found out. She shuddered to think what Raider would do if he ever discovered that Molly had disobeyed him.

Chapter Eight

Leslie spent a tense evening worrying about Molly. Was Raider right about Marshall? Probably. If only he hadn't been so heavy-handed with his warning. Didn't he realize that was the wrong way to handle a high-spirited girl like Molly? Leslie sighed. He was too autocratic to expect his decisions ever to be questioned. Or his judgment.

Leslie was a case in point. On the basis of the flimsiest evidence, Raider had made up his mind about her, she thought bitterly. Tonight he had been the old Raider, attacking mercilessly. Had she only imagined the tender man who had wakened her with a kiss just yesterday? Leslie began to tremble as she remembered that brief time in his arms, his hands gently caressing her body while his lips promised limitless joys.

Her cheeks burned at the memory of how she had begged him to stay with her. Was that why he thought she was easy? He couldn't know she had never done a thing like that before. Thank heaven he had to leave! There could never be anything between them, and the sooner she removed herself from this house the better. Tomorrow she would go back to Lester's—or maybe it was time to go home.

The telephone broke into this disquieting thought. Leslie stiffened as she heard Raider's voice, the last person she expected to hear from.

"I had to talk to you," he said quietly.

She waited until she could get her breathing under control. "I don't think we have anything more to say to each other."

"Maybe you don't, but I do. Molly was right. I owe you an apology."

"Yes, you do!" she cried, forgetting her intention to stay calm. "How could you accuse me of such things?"

"I have no excuse," he said simply. "I guess it was just disappointment, if that makes any sense. I worked like a dervish up here to get through so I could come back to you, and then you weren't there. When I saw you drive up in Marty's arms, I just saw red."

"It wasn't the way it looked. Molly explained that."

"I know and I'm sorry. Can you forgive me?"

"I suppose so, but I don't want to see you again," she said in a small voice. "In a way I'm glad you called. It gives me a chance to say good-bye."

"Where are you going?" he asked sharply.

"Back to Lester's and then home." Once it was actually spoken the decision was made. This cold, heavy feeling over her heart would go away in time, Leslie assured herself.

"You can't do that," he said tautly.

Suddenly she realized what was disturbing him.

"Don't worry; I'll sign the property over to you before I leave."

He swore briefly under his breath. "We'll talk about it when I get there."

"I won't be here. I'm going to Lester's tomorrow morning."

"I'm coming home tonight," Raider said shortly.

"What! No, you can't! You mustn't do that because of me!"

"Calm down." Raider sounded more relaxed. "That isn't the only reason, although it's the major one. I did a lot of thinking on the way up here. I realized I've been behaving like the wrong end of a horse—and not only with you. Maybe I have been keeping too tight a rein on Molly. Maybe it would do her good to go away to college."

"Yes, she . . . she's really a very level-headed girl," Leslie said faintly.

"I agree, that's why I made the decision. Can I talk to her? I'd like to tell her right away, sort of smooth things over before I get there."

Leslie's mind was racing at top speed. This was a catastrophe! Molly's cherished dream would be over if Raider ever discovered she had defied him. It would be useless to try to explain that he had brought it on himself. Raider's mercurial temper would goad him into taking a stand. Leslie made a lightning decision.

"She . . . uh . . . she can't talk to you right now, Raider; she's washing her hair."

He chuckled. "Translate that as sulking, is that it?"

"No, really, she—"

"It's all right, Leslie. I'll be home in about an hour and a half, and we'll straighten everything out then."

"So soon!" Leslie gasped.

"Just can't wait to see me, can you?" he asked dryly. "Well, I guess I can't blame you." His voice deepened as he murmured softly, "I only hope you and I can straighten everything out too."

Leslie sprang into action the minute she hung up. Flinging on a coat, she dashed out of the house and down to the men's quarters, deciding that it would be quicker than trying to explain things over the phone. Every second counted.

Haste proved to be her downfall. It was a moonless night, and in the stygian darkness Leslie stepped in a rabbit hole. She pitched forward, landing painfully on her knees and the heels of her hands. Small pebbles gouged her delicate skin, but that wasn't the worst of it. A searing poker of pain shot up from the ankle that had been almost healed.

Oh, no, Leslie thought in dismay! Why hadn't she brought a flashlight? Well, it couldn't be helped. At least it was her left leg; she could still drive. Leslie pulled herself to her feet, gritting her teeth with grim determination. She made it to the bunkhouse by the simple expedient of ignoring the pain. Her ankle would just have to wait.

Marty was surprised to see her, to say the least. "What's up, Les? You look like there's a kangaroo chasing you." Taking another look at her shaken face, his grin faded. "Is something wrong?"

She took a moment to catch her breath, carefully shifting her weight to her right leg. "I have a favor to ask of you. I want to borrow a car—a jeep, a truck, anything at all."

He stared at her. "What do you want it for?"

"I can't tell you that. Won't you please trust me?" she pleaded.

His eyes studied her fondly. "Of course I trust you,

honey. I just don't like you running around alone at night. You don't know the countryside. I'll be glad to take you anywhere you want to go."

It was a temptation to accept his offer. Although it was true that she had only a vague idea of how to get into town, Leslie knew it wasn't fair to involve Marty. If her plan failed and she didn't get Molly back before Raider returned, Marty would be accused of being in on the deception. Besides, the fewer people who knew about it the better.

"That's good of you, Marty, but this is something I have to do myself. Please don't ask me any questions."

His hesitation was only momentary. Marty disappeared into the house, returning in a moment with the keys to a small car parked nearby. After explaining how the lights and heater worked, he leaned in and kissed her cheek. "If you need anything, just call me."

She gave him a tremulous smile. "Thanks, Marty, you're a good friend."

He returned her smile with a slightly wistful one. "I guess I'll have to settle for that, at least for now."

The trip into town was dark and slightly scary. Twice, small animals ran across the road, startling her. Added to that was a terrible feeling of isolation. The road stretched ahead in a straight line with not a sign of human habitation, only the night creatures to keep her company. When the lights of the town loomed up ahead Leslie breathed a sigh of relief, just then realizing how tightly she had been gripping the wheel.

Now the problem of locating Molly began. One of the reasons for Raider's disapproval was that Marshall and his crowd thought a big night was to go out drinking. Fortunately there were only three bars in town. The Rose and Thistle could be ruled out because Molly would know that Gordon, her brother's friend, would disapprove of the company she was with almost as much as Raider. That left only two places. Luckily she hit pay dirt in the first one.

The Sundowner was a much more boisterous place than the Rose and Thistle. Raucous laughter spilled into the street, a dubious advertisement for the place. Inside, the lights were subdued, dimly illuminating several couples locked in tight embraces on the dance floor. Leslie stopped at the entrance while her eyes adjusted to the murky light. Her nose wrinkled with distaste at the tacky atmosphere and sour smell of beer from used glasses.

"Well, look what the wind blew in!" A burly cowboy approached, blocking her path. "How about a dance, baby?"

"No, thank you." Leslie started to push by impatiently.

"Aw, come on, be friendly," he said, putting his arm around her waist.

"Take your hands off me!" she demanded in a loud voice.

"Leslie! What are you doing here?"

She whirled around at the sound of Molly's voice. "Thank goodness I found you," Leslie exclaimed. "You've got to come home immediately."

The young girl's eyes darkened with apprehension. "Has something happened to Raider?" she quavered.

"No, it's nothing like that," Leslie hastily reassured her. "I'll explain on the way. Just come with me quickly."

Molly flung her head back. Once her fears had been allayed, rebellion returned. "Did Raider send you to drag me back by the ear?"

"Of course not." Leslie tried to stifle her impatience. "You've got to trust me, Molly; there isn't time to go into it now." When the girl wavered, she gave her a level look. "I thought we were friends."

That did it. "I'll get my coat," Molly said quietly.

"Hey, what's going on?" A young man whose good looks were marred by slightly glassy eyes and a loose mouth joined them, putting his arm around Molly's shoulders. The glass in his hand tilted precariously.

"I have to leave," Molly told him.

"Oh, I get it." His smile was contemptuous. "They sent your governess to bring you back to the nursery all safe and sound."

Molly gave him a look of disgust. "Buzz off, Marshall —permanently."

When they were in the car, Molly turned a rueful face to Leslie before she could say anything. "I don't know how you happened to show up, Les, but I'm sure glad you did. Marshall is a wimp and his friends are worse. I never had such a crummy time in my life."

All of this, and she hadn't even enjoyed herself! "Oh, Molly." Leslie breathed a sigh of resignation.

"I'm not going to admit it to Raider, though," she said defiantly.

"I certainly hope not!" Leslie cried in alarm. "Your brother must never know about tonight." She launched into her explanation swiftly.

Molly's first reaction was sheer bliss. "I'm going away to college!"

"If we can get you home in time," Leslie muttered grimly.

The joy faded from Molly's face. "Raider would change his mind if he ever found out, wouldn't he? He'd think I wasn't trustworthy. Oh, Les, how could I behave like such a brat? If I dished my chances I'll just die!" Tears sprang to her eyes.

Leslie patted her knee. "Don't worry, pet, we'll

make it." Her foot pressed down on the accelerator. "When we get home, you scoot right up to your room. I'll take the car back to Marty and that will be the end of it."

"You're so good to me, Les. If we were truly sisters you couldn't have done any more."

"We women have to stick together." Leslie smiled. "This will be our secret. Something that's just between the two of us."

When there were no cars in front of the house, they both breathed a sigh of relief. Hustling Molly out, Leslie drove away hurriedly. It wasn't until she got to Marty's that her delayed reaction set in and she realized how much pain she was having. Her ankle throbbed like a living thing; it was difficult to put even the slightest pressure on it.

Marty came out while she was hobbling to the door. "What happened?" he exclaimed, coming forward to catch her before she fell.

"I turned my ankle again. It's nothing, it will go away." The pain was so intense she didn't even know what she was saying.

"How could you turn your ankle in the car? Where did you go?"

"I . . . it's . . . I can't explain." Tears swam in her blue eyes, making them shine like sapphires in the headlights.

Marty opened the passenger side of the car. "I'll take you home," he said.

Leslie was so grateful to him for not asking any awkward questions on the short ride back that she reached out and put her hand on his arm. He covered it with his, patting her reassuringly.

She was struggling to get out of the car when Marty

came around and lifted her into his arms. "You're in no condition to walk," he said. "I'll carry you into the house."

Leslie put her arms around his neck, resting her head on his shoulder. "You've been so great, Marty. I just wish I could tell you about it."

His arms tightened. "There's no need." He looked down at her sympathetically.

Suddenly they were impaled in a pitiless light as a pickup truck drove up and stopped with a screech of brakes.

"Oh, no," Leslie groaned under her breath.

Raider was on them like a ravening tiger, his lips drawn back in a feral snarl. "It seems I'm always interrupting you two. Have you ever thought of making love *indoors?"*

Leslie was struggling to get out of Marty's arms. He set her down gently on the steps before turning to the furious man confronting them, his own anger rapidly rising. "I'm getting pretty tired of this, Raider."

"You're getting tired of it? How do you think I feel?"

"I'm beginning to have a fairly good idea, but that doesn't give you any right to insult this lady."

"I have to hand it to you." Raider raised a sardonic eyebrow in Leslie's direction. "You've managed to pull the wool over everyone's eyes but mine. Too bad they don't know you like I do."

"You flaming jackass, you said it yourself!" Marty exploded. "If that's what we were leading up to we wouldn't be doing it in front of your house."

"Maybe you couldn't wait," Raider said tautly. "When Leslie gets eager she can drive everything else out of a man's mind."

She gave a strangled cry, remembering the urgent

way she had clung to Raider, surrendering completely to his sensual caresses. In his anger at her supposed promiscuity he was going to tell the whole world.

Marty doubled up his fists, stepping closer to Raider. "I ought to knock you from here to Darwin for that."

"You could try," Raider said contemptuously, his own hands closing spasmodically.

"No!" Leslie sprang to her feet, trying to insinuate herself between the two men. "Won't you listen to reason, Raider?"

"Stay out of it, Les. He's been asking for this for a long time," Marty grated. "Our beloved leader is starting to think he's a little tin god. A punch in the mouth might make him realize he's human like the rest of us."

Leslie grabbed Marty's arm with both hands. "I don't want anyone to get hurt."

Raider's eyes glittered like gray glass as they narrowed on her appeal to the other man. "Don't worry, I'll try not to mess up your boyfriend too badly."

As she felt Marty's muscles tense, Leslie turned to Raider. She had to stop this somehow. "I wasn't out with Marty tonight," she cried desperately. "I only borrowed his car. He was just bringing me back."

Raider's gaze sharpened. "Where were you?"

"I . . . I had an errand to do."

"You don't have to tell him anything," Marty said.

"Shut up!" Raider commanded. "I asked you where you were," he repeated to Leslie.

What was he thinking now? she wondered wildly. Leslie was caught in a trap from which there was no escape. She couldn't tell him the truth, and her pain-fogged mind was incapable of thinking of a plausible lie. What reason could she have had for going out alone tonight? She stared at him uncertainly, her soft mouth quivering.

"Damn it, will you stop browbeating the poor kid?" Marty burst out.

The front door opened and Molly joined them in her nightgown and robe. "What's going on out here? I could hear the hollering all the way upstairs."

"Go inside, both of you," Raider ordered his sister and Leslie. With Molly's appearance he had gotten a grip on himself. Turning to Marty, he said coldly, "You and I will settle this thing tomorrow."

After shooting a look at the girls, Marty nodded curtly. "That's fine with me." His shoulders were stiff as he walked to the car.

Once they were inside, Molly said, "What was all that about?"

"Go to sleep," Raider told her.

She hesitated. "Didn't you want to talk to me?"

"Not tonight," he said tightly.

Molly looked questioningly at Leslie, who shook her head imperceptibly. If only she had sense enough not to push her brother. The only good thing that had come out of this cataclysmic evening was the fact that Raider didn't know what Molly had done. Suddenly Leslie felt so exhausted that she thought she might faint. She started toward the stairs, being careful not to limp even though every step was torture.

Raider whirled her around with a brutal hand on her wrist. "I want to talk to you."

"What about?" Molly asked instead of Leslie.

"It doesn't concern you." A white line appeared around Raider's mouth. "Go to your room."

"Anything to do with Leslie concerns me," Molly declared passionately.

"Isn't that interesting?" Raider's smile was mirthless. "You've done quite a little snow job on my sister, haven't you?" he asked Leslie. "It's a good thing you decided to leave tomorrow. It saves me the trouble of throwing you out."

Molly's dismayed eyes flew to Leslie's face. "That's not true, is it? You're not leaving?"

Leslie tried to smile. "It's really for the best."

"But why? You don't have to go home yet—back to the States, I mean."

"Perhaps Miss Farraday needs more privacy than we afford her here," Raider said mockingly. "Every time I catch her in Marty's arms I react in—how did you put it?—a Victorian way."

Comprehension dawned on Molly's face. "So that's it! You didn't tell him?" she breathed.

"No," Leslie said quickly.

"Tell me what?" Raider asked dangerously. "Did you know she's been carrying on with Marty? Did she use you to help her set up her little liaisons?"

"What a vile thing to say!" Molly exclaimed. "Leslie hasn't been carrying on with anyone."

"Hasn't she?" he asked unpleasantly. "You don't know very much about your dear friend after all."

"Raider, please!" Leslie begged, her pale cheeks flushing with delicate color.

"Raider, please," he mimicked bitterly. "You have all sorts of meanings for those two words, don't you? Do you also say 'Marty, please'—and 'Harry, please'—and 'Tom, please'?"

"Leave her alone!" Molly shouted. "If you want to know where she was tonight, *I'll* tell you!"

"Molly, *no!*" Leslie commanded sharply.

"Do you think I'm going to let him go on thinking those things about you?" Molly cried.

Leslie took a firm grip on the banister, holding her trembling body erect. "It doesn't matter."

"It does to me!"

"What lie have the two of you cooked up together, and why have you suddenly gotten cold feet?" Raider asked Leslie caustically.

"That does it!" Molly exploded. "She told you the truth. She wasn't with Marty tonight, she was—"

"I forbid you to say another word," Leslie interrupted, the words crackling out.

"Who the hell are you to forbid my sister to do anything?" Raider exclaimed.

Leslie's control suddenly snapped. "And who the hell are you to sit in judgment on me?" she asked, her blue eyes blazing. "I don't have to answer to you for my actions. The only thing I *will* tell you is that I've never done anything that would abuse Molly's trust in me. I wonder if you can say the same thing, Mr. Mackenzie."

With a muttered oath he grabbed her wrist, dragging her toward him. The unexpected action made her stumble forward, putting all her weight on her left leg. Leslie gave a ragged scream of pain, collapsing at Raider's feet as he held onto her limp arm.

"What happened?" Molly rushed forward fearfully.

"I don't know." Raider scooped Leslie up, starting for the stairs. "I'll get her into bed and we'll find out."

He raced up the staircase, with Leslie like a small, yielding bundle in his arms. Her bright hair splayed out over his broad shoulder, falling away from her pale, delicate face. Raider's breathing quickened as he gazed down at her in deep concern.

After he put her gently on the bed, Raider unzipped her jacket while Molly started to take off her shoes. When she touched the injured ankle, Leslie's eyes opened and she cried out, flinching away.

"What is it, Leslie? Where do you hurt?" Raider's hands were gentle on her shoulders as he eased her back against the pillows.

She bit her lip and remained silent, unwilling to look at him.

"You have to tell us so we can do something about it," Molly pleaded.

"It's my ankle," Leslie said reluctantly. "I twisted it again."

Raider's deft fingers went to the injured area. He was startled when he saw the swelling that all but obscured the fragile bones of her ankle. "How did you do this?"

The eyes of the two girls met over Raider's bent head. Leslie signaled a firm negative in answer to Molly's uncertain expression.

As soon as Raider looked up, Leslie's face became apprehensive. A muscle jumped at the point of his jaw. "All right, I won't ask you. Molly, go get me a roll of bandages and a couple of cushions to elevate her foot."

When they were alone, the quiet room seemed to reverberate. Leslie had never known that silence could be so noisy. She turned her head on the pillow, her whole body drooping with misery.

"You should have told me," he said at last. "I'm not a monster, even though you must think I am."

She raised her hand in a helpless gesture, letting it drop back onto the coverlet. "I don't think you're a monster. It's just that we're like matches and gasoline. Every time we get together there's an explosion."

A little smile twitched the corners of his firm mouth. "It isn't always this painful." A long forefinger traced the curve of her cheek.

"Don't!" She shrank away from him. "Maybe it isn't

for you, but it is for me. I've been burned as badly as I care to by you, Raider. I'm throwing in the towel and going home."

"I didn't think you were a quitter," he said softly.

"I didn't either," she sighed. "You've won, though. As soon as you draw up the papers I'll sign them and be out of your life."

"You think that's what I want?"

"You've said so," she answered simply. "In any case, it's what *I* want."

His expression was unreadable. "Too bad you can't have your wish."

"What do you mean?"

He gestured to her foot. "It seems we're back to square one."

"You think I did this on purpose so I could stay here," she said in a low voice. "You really don't trust me, do you?"

"I don't think you did it on purpose." He sighed heavily, pausing before continuing, "As for trusting you, how can I, Leslie, when you won't even tell me where you were tonight? Are you letting me think all kinds of lurid things just to torture me?" he demanded.

"If you trusted me they wouldn't occur to you," she countered.

His eyes grew bleak. "I'm a man, my dear. I know more than a few of the facts of life."

Too bad I don't, Leslie thought bitterly. She might as well have the game since she already had the name.

Molly returned with the things Raider had requested, and the next few minutes were spent making Leslie more comfortable. Raider's hands were exceedingly gentle as he performed the necessary tasks, minimizing her discomfort as much as possible. She couldn't help realizing the care he took, and she tried to convey her gratitude. Raider was forever beyond her reach, yet at least she wanted him to know that she appreciated the kindness he had shown her on more than one occasion.

"Thank you, Raider. I'm sorry for everything and I'll be out of your way by tomorrow."

"You aren't going to let her go, are you?" Molly asked her brother.

"No, I'm not going to let her go," he said firmly, smiling at her disturbed face.

"Why won't either of you believe me?" Leslie cried, helpless tears filling her eyes and spilling down her cheeks.

"I think this is your department," Raider told his sister. "Distraught women leave me helpless." Bending over Leslie briefly, he squeezed her hand in his strong grip. "You'll feel better in the morning," he said reassuringly.

The room continued to pulse with energy even after his departure. Raider left his indelible mark on everything he touched, Leslie thought hopelessly, including herself.

"For once, big brother was right," Molly said wryly. "Everything *will* look better in the morning—except that I'll still feel like a fink. You should have let me tell him, Les."

"Absolutely not!" That was the one thing Leslie was sure of. "What would it prove to have his trust in both of us destroyed?"

"But it isn't fair! I'm the only one who violated it."

"And you're the only one who matters to him, so let it be," Leslie said firmly.

"I'm not so sure." Molly looked thoughtfully at

Leslie's lovely face. "I think the fact that Raider was so livid when he thought you were playing footsie with Marty proves something. He never got that excited about the defection of any of his other girlfriends."

"Were there any defections . . . on their part?" Leslie asked dryly.

"Not many," Molly admitted with a laugh. "But that's not the point." She looked at Leslie with growing excitement on her mobile face. "I think Raider is in love with you!"

"Oh, Molly dear, you couldn't be more wrong. Your brother doesn't even *like* me."

"As I understand it, you can love someone without really liking them," Molly said with a judicious air.

"Well, you're half-right, anyway," Leslie sighed.

Molly was undeterred. Throwing her arms around Leslie's neck, she bubbled, "It's going to be so nice having you in the family. Then we'll really truly be sisters."

Leslie shook her head helplessly at the younger girl. Molly lived in a fairy-tale world where marriage was the inevitable conclusion to love. For all of her protestations of sophistication she was still only a little girl. But what would it accomplish to puncture her rosy dreams? After Leslie was gone she would soon be forgotten in the excitement of Molly's own fulfilling life. Much better to let her weave her fantasies if it made her happy.

Long after Molly had left her, Leslie lay in the dark looking out the window. If only those childish dreams could come true. Leslie could no longer deny her love for Raider, a love that had flourished with very little nourishment and at great odds. She knew that he felt desire for her, but it wasn't enough. And it wouldn't last. He wouldn't remember her any longer than Molly would.

Her punishment for coming here under false pretenses was to go through life looking for a man to take Raider's place in her heart. Tears filled Leslie's eyes as she knew with a terrible certainty that it was going to be an impossibility.

Chapter Nine

Leslie's ankle felt a great deal better the next morning, even if she didn't. After cautiously wiggling it she experienced only twinges instead of stabbing pain. Elevating it must have helped a great deal. The swelling had gone down, she discovered on closer inspection.

A sharp rap at the door made her pull the covers up to her chin. That imperative summons could only have come from Raider. What did he want this early in the morning? Was it a simple courtesy call to see how she was, or did he intend to reopen last night's unpleasantness?

When the knock came again, more imperiously this time, she was forced to call, "Come in."

As she had guessed, it was Raider. He stood framed in the doorway, looking at her without any expression that would give her a clue to his mood. "How do you feel this morning?" he asked.

"I . . . much better." She plucked nervously at the sheet.

His lips twitched in an unwilling smile. "You look like a little girl expecting a well-deserved spanking."

She ran her fingers through the glorious spill of copper-colored hair, conscious of her warm, sleep-tousled appearance. "I don't know what you mean."

His smile disappeared. "Don't you? I was referring to that old expression, 'If you can't be good, be careful.' "

Leslie's anger rose along with the color in her cheeks. "If you're alluding to last night again, it's a closed subject, Mr. Mackenzie. You can think whatever you like. I do not intend to satisfy your prurient curiosity."

"You don't have to. I'm no longer interested, pruriently or otherwise," he said grimly. "I just stopped by to see how your ankle was."

"It's fine."

They glared at each other for a long moment before Raider advanced toward the bed. "Suppose you let me be the judge of that."

She sat up straighter against the headboard. "Aren't you willing to take my word for *anything?"*

He raised a sardonic eyebrow. "Do you really want me to answer that?"

Leslie's breathing was rapid. Why did the smallest thing turn into a confrontation with this aggravating man? "I'm fine, I told you. Luckily my ankle was only twisted. It was the swelling that made it so painful, and that's gone down a lot. The ligaments aren't damaged this time."

"I didn't realize you'd gotten your medical degree," he remarked mockingly.

"It doesn't take a doctor to figure that out." She

regarded him with exasperation. "After all, it is *my* body. I do know something about it."

"How many other people do too?" he asked tautly. Without waiting for an answer, he took the blankets and ripped them down with a savage movement.

Leslie repressed a shiver of anticipation as Raider reached for her ankle, his fingers cool against her hot skin. "There! Are you satisfied now?" she asked.

"It's a lot better than it was last night," he admitted. "I want you to stay in bed all day today, though."

"I told you, I'm leaving this morning."

He gave her a level look. "Are you going to force me to take your clothes away?"

"Why are you being so unreasonable?" Leslie cried, pulling the covers over her trembling body. Raider's look was all too masculine. "You want me gone as much as I want to be. Were you looking forward to ordering me out instead of having me go willingly, is that it?"

"I have to go to work," he said without bothering to answer her question. "Promise me you won't do anything foolish, Leslie."

"Like what?" she asked bitterly. "I think I've exhausted the possibilities."

"Knowing you, you'll think of something else," he said with a kind of grim humor. He paused in the doorway. "I'm going to talk to Molly this morning since I didn't get a chance last night." His impassive gaze told Leslie she shared the blame for that. "Did you tell her I've decided to let her go away to school?"

Leslie's mind spun wildly. Should she say yes or no? Would Molly pretend it was the first time she'd heard it? If only she could have spoken to the girl first. Leslie decided to stick to the truth as much as possible, since they were both in enough trouble now. More lies would only get them in deeper.

"Yes, I told her after you telephoned," she said evenly. "I'm sorry if I spoiled your surprise."

"It doesn't matter." He shrugged. "How did she take it?"

"Like you'd expect." Leslie smiled. "Ecstatically."

Raider grinned. "I'll bet she did."

"I'm sure she'll do an instant replay for you this morning," she assured him.

"Then I'd better not keep her waiting." He turned at the door. "You stay where you are. I'll have Clara bring you up a tray."

Leslie didn't argue. Raider deserved this time alone with his sister. She had gotten herself incredibly involved in their affairs, but they should be allowed to repair the breech in their relationship without a bystander looking on, no matter how interested.

Molly burst into her room a short time later to give her a complete play-by-play account. "Well, it's official!" she crowed. "Raider just gave me the word."

"Oh, Molly, I'm so happy for you. Did . . . did you tell him you already knew?" Leslie asked hesitantly.

"Yes, I said you told me last night after he called. That was all right, wasn't it?" Molly looked anxious.

"Of course," Leslie said quickly. "Did he seem disappointed? I mean, did he act like he wanted to tell you himself?"

"No, he was just pleased that I was so happy." The young girl's face was troubled.

"You *are* happy, aren't you? You're not having second thoughts about leaving home?" Leslie asked.

"No, it's what I've always wanted. Oh, not to leave home. I expect to come back for every holiday, and Christmas vacation, naturally."

"I think your brother has a right to expect that," Leslie agreed.

"Yes, those are family times. But it isn't as though Raider really needed me outside of that," Molly explained earnestly. "He'll be better off not having me around to worry about."

"Do you honestly think he'll stop worrying just because you're out of sight?" Leslie asked dryly.

"I suppose not." Molly laughed. "But he has the station to run and he has his own life to live." She gave a sidelong glance at Leslie. "Maybe once I'm gone he'll get around to thinking of getting married."

Leslie felt a sharp pain between her breasts as a remembered conversation at the Rose and Thistle came back to her. His friends felt that was what Raider was waiting for, too. They were even taking bets on the lucky girl, and Leslie wasn't in the running.

"Be sure and send me an announcement," she told Molly, trying to smile brightly.

"Oh, Les, don't be dense! You know you're the one I want him to marry."

"Settle for what you've got," Leslie told her succinctly. To soften the sharp statement, she asked, "Did you discuss universities?"

"Not yet." Molly tacitly accepted the change of subject. "I guess I was too busy thanking him and telling him how thrilled I am." The troubled look entered her face again.

"What's bothering you, honey?" Leslie asked gently.

"I feel so rotten about last night," Molly said miserably. "Like I'm accepting this under false pretenses. I've never lied to Raider before."

"You didn't exactly lie to him," Leslie said carefully. "It was more a sin of omission."

"You mean he was so busy asking you where *you'd*

been that he didn't think to wonder about *me*. That makes it even worse! How do you think I feel, knowing I let you throw yourself to the wolves?"

"I told you it isn't important, Molly. Raider and I have had our ups and downs; one more misunderstanding isn't going to make any difference."

"I don't agree, but that's not the point. The thing is that it's the first time I've ever deceived him, if you'd rather put it that way. Sure we've battled a lot. It isn't the first time I've defied him, but I always did it to his face."

Leslie regarded the young girl sympathetically. Molly was so innately honest that the present situation was obviously painful. "Maybe you can make it up to him by never doing anything like that again."

Molly wandered around the room picking things up and putting them down, examining objects without even seeing them. "Do you think I ought to tell him about last night?" she asked in a low voice.

Leslie looked at her bent head. "That's entirely up to you."

"He'd change his mind about letting me go, wouldn't he?"

"It's possible." Leslie's tone was carefully neutral.

"Oh, Les, I can't take a chance!" Molly cried passionately. "We both know I'll never do it again, so why should I ruin my whole life by confessing now? It would only hurt him, anyway, don't you agree?"

Leslie shook her head. "This is your decision. I've already meddled more than I should have, no doubt."

Molly flew across the room and threw her arms around Leslie. "Don't say that! You saved my life."

"Not your life, your freedom." Leslie chuckled. "The worst Raider would have done is ground you for six months."

"After a few well-chosen words." Molly grinned. "Or should I make that a few dozen? Well, I'd better be off to school before I'm in for some heat from another direction."

She dashed out, leaving Leslie limp. The Mackenzie family was exhausting.

Clara was her next visitor. She came in a short time later carrying a tray. "Sorry breakfast is late. It took forever to get those two off this morning."

"You don't have to wait on me," Leslie chided. "I was going to come downstairs."

"Raider left instructions that you were to stay in bed."

"Since when do you take orders from him?" Leslie asked cynically.

"When it suits my purpose," Clara acknowledged with a smile. "I was sorry to hear that you hurt your ankle again. How did it happen?"

"Just carelessness," Leslie said vaguely.

"What were you doing?" Clara questioned her curiously. "I asked Raider and he got the funniest look on his face."

"He was probably bored to death with the subject. I am, myself."

Clara didn't take the hint. "What's going on around here? It must have been quite a night last night."

"What do you mean?" Leslie asked warily.

"Marty called early this morning to say he would be in the south pasture whenever Raider wanted to come looking for him, whatever that means. Molly was dancing around like a flea on a dog, waiting for Raider to come out of your room—where, incidentally, he was for quite a while. So I repeat, what's going on?"

Leslie was carefully casual. "None of that sounds too unusual to me."

"Things must be pretty interesting where you come from," Clara remarked dryly.

Leslie ignored that. "You heard about Molly going away to school?"

"Yes, and I'm delighted for her," Clara said warmly.

"Won't you miss her?"

"Of course I will, and Raider will too, but it's the best thing that ever happened to both of them."

"I'm glad you agree." Leslie sighed with relief. It had occurred to her that in her instinctive effort to help Molly, maybe she wasn't doing what was right for her.

"I understand why Raider's been so protective, but it hasn't made either of them any easier to live with. Now maybe we'll have some peace around here."

"I'll contribute to it," Leslie said. "I'm leaving today."

Clara shook her head. "That was another of Raider's instructions. He said I wasn't to let you go."

"How did he propose you stop me?"

Clara looked at her blankly. "I don't know."

"There isn't any way. My mind's made up." Leslie threw back the covers, preparing to get up.

"Where are you going?" Clara asked.

"Back to Lester's to pack up my things, then to Sydney and home."

"Are you going to sell him the property?"

"Of course. That's all that's keeping me here. I'm waiting for Raider to draw up the papers."

"You've told him?"

Leslie nodded. "Last night."

"Another thing that happened last night. I sure missed all the fun." Clara eyed her with interest. "What did Raider say when you told him?"

Leslie thought for a minute and couldn't remember. "It was over the phone. Raider was up at the north quadrant. When he came home we . . . we didn't get around to discussing it."

Clara was silent for a long moment. "That ten acres was an obsession with Raider when you first got here. He badgered you night and day to sell it. Now you're telling me that when you told him it was a deal, he didn't get around to *discussing* it?"

"Well, it . . . uh . . . he was upset about something."

"Something to do with you and Marty?" Clara asked shrewdly.

"How did you know?" The startled exclamation came out before she could stop it.

"It wasn't difficult. Marty was breathing fire when he called this morning. You could smell it over the phone."

"Oh dear," Leslie sighed. "I hoped he—" She stopped abruptly.

"Would you like to tell me about it?"

"I can't. I'd really like to, Clara, but there is someone else involved."

Clara regarded the troubled girl thoughtfully. "Are you trying to play them off against each other?" she asked.

"No! How could you think a thing like that?"

"You'll have to admit it looks very much like it. It seems to be working, too. You've got those two men dangling like fish on a line. They're even fighting between themselves to take the bait."

"You're out of your mind," Leslie said hotly. "Marty is just a good friend, and Raider can't stand the sight of me."

Clara raised her eyebrows. "That's why he's so adamant about keeping you here?"

"Maybe he just wants to be sure I actually sign the

papers." Leslie twisted a lock of red-gold hair around a slim finger. "Who ever knows what Raider's thinking?"

"You're right there," Clara conceded. "But if that's all it was, he could at least let you go back to Lester's."

Leslie's long eyelashes swept down. "He doesn't trust me. He probably thinks I'd skip out."

Clara's expression was a mixture of affection and impatience. "When are you going to stop being such an idiot, Leslie? Just answer me one question. Are you in love with Raider?"

Leslie lifted her head to deny it. Looking into the other woman's sympathetic face, she found that she couldn't. "Yes," she murmured. "What does that have to do with anything?"

"Quite a lot, since I believe he's in love with you too."

"You wouldn't say that if you heard the terrible things he said to me last night."

"Because he was jealous."

Leslie shook her head. "You don't talk that way to someone you care about."

"You do if you're an alpha male like Raider. That's how I know it's love. He was never this possessive of his other women."

"I don't think I could live with his brand of love," Leslie said bitterly.

"I didn't say it would be easy." Clara grinned suddenly. "There are compensations, though. And besides, you probably can't help yourself."

That was true enough. "What do you suggest I do?" she asked hopelessly.

"Stop fighting him and give in. Raider is going to get you anyway. He always gets what he goes after." Clara smiled understandingly at Leslie's forlorn face. "A good breakfast will make you feel better. Yours has gotten cold. Can you hobble downstairs while I heat it up? I could do with a cup of hot coffee myself."

After Leslie assured her that she could get around by herself, Clara left her alone with her chaotic thoughts. Everyone kept insisting that Raider was in love with her when she knew better. Or did she? A thrill of excitement ran up Leslie's spine at the possibility that they might be right. She had never dared allow the thought to enter her mind.

But suppose it was true? What if she stopped striking back at him all the time and showed him how she felt? It would be a terrible risk if she was wrong. Leslie shuddered to think what Raider's reaction would be if all he was after was Lester's property, as she had feared from the beginning. Oh, sure, being a man he'd take everything she offered—and then laugh in her face.

That almost changed her mind. Almost, but not quite. The stakes were too high to back down because of possible humiliation. And the rewards, even if she lost, were something she would remember all of her life.

A growing excitement gripped her as she planned a course of action. Starting that night she would be a different person, or at least she would be the one that everyone else knew, only this time with Raider, too.

After she had made her decision, the day seemed to drag on endlessly, although she spent the last couple of hours of it getting dressed. Leslie had sent Molly down to the little house to bring back her favorite dress, avoiding the avid interest in the girl's eyes.

"As long as I seem fated to stay another day or two I'd like to have something else to wear," she had explained casually. "I'm getting awfully tired of the things I have here."

The dress was a violet print, the color of her eyes

when they were darkened by excitement as they were now. It wasn't overly dressy, yet the simple round neck and full skirt were exceedingly feminine. Leslie pulled her glinting coppery hair up on the sides, letting the back spill down in a cascade of waves and ringlets. It was a deceptively casual hairdo that took ages to achieve. When it was done, however, the effect was worth it.

Her makeup was equally artful—just a touch of eye shadow that looked like the reflection of her own blue eyes, a shimmer of lip gloss to make her mouth rosy, and a mere hint of blusher that blended in to seem natural.

Molly was speechless with admiration when she came to Leslie's room. "You're gorgeous!" she gasped.

"I certainly hope so," Leslie laughed. "I worked over it long enough."

Molly prowled around her, examining Leslie from every angle. "Could you show me how to do my hair that way?" she asked.

"Sure, it's a snap. All it takes is patience. You just pin it up here and here." She lifted Molly's silky hair.

After a perfunctory knock, the door opened to admit Raider. "I came to—" The words stopped as he caught sight of Leslie.

A light flamed in his eyes when she turned toward him, her lips softly parted. The air was suddenly charged with electricity. Leslie felt as though a powerful magnetic current were running between them.

Molly took one look and started for the door, murmuring, "I'll see you downstairs." It's doubtful if they even heard her.

"What have you done to yourself?" Raider asked, walking slowly toward Leslie.

His voice seemed to break the spell. She took a

shuddering breath. "I just sent Molly down for one of my dresses. I got tired of wearing jeans."

For the first time she noticed that Raider was dressed differently than usual, too. He had on dark brown slacks and a brown silk shirt that hugged his narrow waist and wide shoulders. He looked even more handsome than usual, and her heart started to thud erratically.

"I came to carry you downstairs to dinner," Raider said, as though just remembering it.

Leslie swung around on the dressing table stool, holding her arms up to him.

"No argument?" he asked, raising one peaked eyebrow.

She shook her head so the little curls bounced at the base of her white neck. "No more arguments." She smiled.

"What are you up to now?" he asked suspiciously, lifting her into his arms.

Her hand moved caressingly along his neck to rest lightly on his broad shoulder. "Why do you always think I'm up to something?"

"Because I never saw you when you weren't," he said grimly.

"Well, I've turned over a new leaf."

"Why?" he asked bluntly.

"Because I don't want to quarrel with you anymore." She looked up at him appealingly.

A muscle jerked in his jaw as they started down the stairs. "It never bothered you before."

Leslie tilted her head back, her wide eyes looking into his. "Can't we be friends, Raider?"

His arms tightened around her. "No, damn it! I don't want to be friends with you."

A wave of misery swept over her. Here she was in his

arms, so close she could feel the warmth of his body and smell the pungent male scent of him. It was lighting a fire in her veins, but he didn't feel anything except the same hostility. Her long lashes swept down to mask the hurt he was inflicting.

"I'm sorry," she murmured. "I was wrong. Everybody was wrong."

"Leslie, don't you know—"

"Well, I'm finally going to meet you," a light female voice announced. "I've been hearing about you from everyone."

Leslie's startled eyes met those of a tall, beautiful woman standing at the foot of the stairs.

"I'm Allison Trent," she said, extending a slender hand.

Leslie struggled out of Raider's arms, her cheeks very pink. She surveyed the girl's shining black hair and classic features. "How do you do. I've heard a lot about you, too, Miss Trent."

"Do call me Allison and I'll call you Leslie. We don't stand on formality in these parts, as I'm sure you've discovered by now. Have you been enjoying our country, Leslie?"

"Yes, it's very beautiful," Leslie managed past the lump in her throat.

"Why don't you carry her into the den, Raider?" Allison suggested. "Clara says we have time for a drink before dinner."

Leslie clutched the newel-post desperately. "That isn't necessary." Her glance went by Allison. "If you'll just get my cane, Molly, I can manage."

The younger girl's eyes met hers, misery in their depths. "I didn't know she was coming to dinner."

Leslie's smile was brilliant. "Isn't it a lovely surprise? I was hoping I'd get to meet you before I left, Allison."

"Are you going home soon?" the other woman asked.

"Very soon. Raider and I have a little business together, which we both want to conclude as fast as possible."

"Once you get that out of the way, why don't you stay on just for fun?" Allison asked pleasantly.

"Leslie doesn't enjoy our rural-type pleasures," Raider said mockingly.

"That isn't true," she protested. "I enjoyed some of them very much."

Leslie was appalled at the icy look of contempt in his eyes. She had been referring to fossicking and the picnic with the station hands, while he was thinking of something quite different. Well, what difference did it make? Even if it hadn't been for this lovely woman, who was obviously very much at home in his house, Raider had stated his feelings in no uncertain terms.

"Has Raider taken you up Langley's Mountain?" Allison asked. "It's a rugged ride, but it's worth it when you get to the top. The whole countryside is spread out for miles."

"She means it's a rugged *horseback* ride." To Allison he explained, "Leslie is afraid of horses."

He didn't have to say that! It made her look like some kind of freak in this country. To make matters worse, Allison was being kind about it. *I can't even hate her,* Leslie thought despairingly.

"Everybody doesn't have to like horses, Raider," the other woman said, linking her arm with his. "You're just used to Australian girls."

He put his hand over hers, looking down at her admiringly. "The very best kind."

Allison's face flushed with pleasure, but she turned

to include Leslie. "You'll have to excuse Raider; he doesn't even know when he's being rude."

Oh, he knows all right, Leslie thought desolately. "I'm not offended," she said aloud. "I guess everybody ought to stick to their own kind."

"I have yet to discover what your kind is," Raider said bitingly.

Leslie's temper suddenly snapped. She had taken quite enough. "Didn't you know? I like a man who's a good dancer," she said. "One who takes me nice places, the better discos and fancy French restaurants. And of course it's nice if he's handsome, but it's more important that he be rich."

Raider's eyes were frigid. "Yes, the one thing I do know about you is how much you like money."

Hostility crackled between them as Allison looked on puzzled. Fortunately Clara appeared in the doorway to announce dinner.

It wasn't much better at the table. Leslie was ashamed of her outburst and determined not to repeat it, but Raider made it difficult. He sniped away at her with two-edged comments that forced her into saying things she didn't mean. Anyone listening to her would think she hated Australia and everything in it. Molly was a silent lump of misery.

Finally Clara took a hand, directing the conversation away from Leslie. "Where are you two going tonight?" she asked Allison.

"We're flying over to Kalgora to a movie. Would any of you like to join us?" Allison asked politely.

They all declined, although Leslie remarked, "It sounds very glamorous to be flying to a movie."

"Oh, I don't know," Raider drawled. "There's no necking in the back seat."

Leslie bit her lip. She looked down at her plate, close

to tears. Why was he doing this to her? It was worse than last night because she couldn't even fight back.

Raider suddenly threw his napkin down. "We'd better leave if we're going to make that movie. I'll take you upstairs," he said to Leslie.

"That isn't necessary," she said stiffly. "I can manage by myself."

There was steel in his voice. "I said I'd take you."

Leslie knew it was useless to argue, so she and Allison exchanged pleasantries about how nice it had been to meet each other. Then Raider lifted her out of the chair.

"This is so silly!" she couldn't help crying out in frustration. Raider didn't bother to answer.

When he had deposited her on the bed, Leslie looked up at him angrily. "Thanks for nothing! I could have managed without your help."

"So you're fond of telling me." His mouth was set in a straight line. "But ever since you got here I've been bailing you out of one kind of mess or another."

"All right, I never should have come to this country; is that what you want me to say?"

His eyes were bleak as he stared at her. "I never knew before tonight how much you really hated it."

I don't hate it, she wanted to shout. I love it and I love you, but there is no future for me here with either of you. Wouldn't he get a laugh out of that? Well, she wasn't going to oblige him!

"I'm glad you know, because I'm tired of pretending," she told him defiantly. "It's been unmitigated hell and I can't wait to get back where I came from."

"What's stopping you, then?" he asked contemptuously.

"You are. As soon as you draw up those damn papers I'll be out of here so fast all you'll see is a blur."

He jammed his hands in his pockets, turning to stand at the window with his back to her. "You can keep the property."

"Oh, no! I don't want anything that reminds me of this place."

He turned to face her, his face set in stern lines. "Too bad, because I'm not buying it."

"Then I'll *give* it to you!"

"I don't need your charity, Miss Farraday."

"And I don't need yours."

Leslie didn't waver when Raider towered over her menacingly. Finally his shoulders sagged. "Okay, you win. We'll make a fair exchange. Why not? I'll be getting a piece of property and you'll be getting what you want: a great deal of money." His mouth twisted cynically.

A fair exchange. Was that what he thought it was? Hysterical laughter rose in her throat. Well, by his standards it was. He didn't know that her heart would be thrown in for good measure. Then his last words penetrated.

"I'm not going to take your money; at least not a great deal of it," she said sharply. "The first amount you offered will be fine."

"You'll take anything I want to give you," he rasped.

"No, I've been doing that," she said furiously. "If you want to get rid of me, you'll have to meet *my* terms."

"The shoe is on the other foot," he said sarcastically. "You're the one who wants to get out of this 'unmitigated hellhole,' I believe you called it."

"No, I said—oh, what's the use. Let's get this over with."

The door opened and Molly entered, her face anxious. "What's going on up here? I could hear you all the way up the stairs."

"Leslie and I are working out the details of our business arrangement," Raider said coldly.

Molly looked from one to the other. "Isn't this kind of a funny time?"

"It isn't exactly ideal," he conceded. "However, it's the time she chose."

"Because you forced the issue," Leslie flared.

"And if I hadn't, you wouldn't have brought it up?" His raised eyebrows expressed disbelief.

"Certainly not this evening."

"I find that hard to believe." His hard eyes took in the spill of bright curls cascading over her shoulders, then roamed to her breasts and tiny waist. "From the minute I walked in this room tonight I knew something was up. What was that seductive outfit for if not to negotiate the best price?" he asked contemptuously.

Molly made a strangled sound. "Don't you—"

Leslie broke in swiftly. "I might have known you would put your usual interpretation on it."

"Because you never disappoint me. You always act true to form."

They glared at each other while Molly watched helplessly. Leslie was the first to turn away. Clenching her hands tightly for control, she said, "You're right about one thing. This isn't the time. We can conclude our business in the morning. You'll find me at Lester's house."

"Oh, Leslie, no!" Molly protested. "At least stay tonight."

Raider ignored his sister. "It's interesting the way you always refer to it as Lester's house. You never had a feeling of belonging, did you?"

"No," Leslie murmured. How could she, when he made it so obvious that she wasn't welcome?

There was a white line around Raider's tight mouth. "In a way I admire your guts if not your motives. You've hung in here for weeks, hating this country and everything in it."

"That's not true!" Molly put a protective arm around Leslie's shoulders.

Raider's expression was grim. "I'd like to think that at least your feeling for my sister was genuine, but I know I would only be kidding myself."

"You're all wrong about Leslie," Molly said sharply.

He shook his head. "I'm sorry, kid. You're pretty young to be disillusioned, but maybe it's for the best."

"You think you're so smart," Molly said scornfully. "I'm telling you, Les is the best friend I'll ever have."

"It brings to mind that old line about not needing enemies with friends like that," Raider remarked mockingly.

"Would you like to know what she did for me?" Molly demanded.

"Molly, no!" Leslie cried.

The young girl ignored her, the impassioned words tumbling out. "You were so hot to find out where Les was last night and who she was with? Well, I'll tell you. She was with me! I went out with Marshall Goodwin, and she came into town to bring me back."

Raider's eyes narrowed. "You went out with Goodwin after I expressly forbid it?"

"Yes," Molly said defiantly. "Leslie tried to talk me out of it, but I wouldn't listen to her."

"Go on," he said ominously.

"When you called and said you were coming home, Les knew you'd be livid, so she borrowed Marty's car and came after me."

"Is this true?" Raider asked Leslie.

She laughed almost naturally. "You're asking *me* for the truth?"

"Of course it is," Molly said impatiently. "That's how she twisted her ankle—stepping in a rabbit hole in the dark on her way to the bunkhouse."

Raider's expression was unfathomable as he turned to Leslie. "Why did you do this?"

Apprehension made her mouth dry. He had every right to be furious at her interference, well intentioned or not. "You told me on the phone that you had finally decided to let Molly go away to school," she said in a low voice. "I knew you'd be angry and maybe overreact, but it was only a childish act of defiance on her part." Leslie bowed her head, waiting for the explosion.

"I wanted to tell you last night, only Les wouldn't let me," Molly said. "That's the part I'm not proud of. I'm really glad it's out in the open," she sighed. "No matter what you do to me."

Raider's mouth twitched briefly as he looked at his repentant little sister. "I'll deal with you later, young lady. Right now I'd like to talk to Leslie."

"You aren't going to yell at her again?" Molly asked anxiously. "Neither one of us actually lied to you."

"No, I'm not going to yell at her," Raider said. There was silence in the room after Molly left. Raider finally broke it. "Maybe you'd like to yell at *me*. You'd have every right."

Leslie's startled eyes met his. "You're not angry?"

"Only at myself. How could you let me say those things to you without telling me the truth? Don't you care what I think of you?" He waited tautly for her answer.

"Of course I do, but I thought it was more important that you and Molly didn't mess things up between you. You're both so impulsive. You go out on a limb and then saw it off after you," she said, sighing.

Raider moved close, framing her face in his palms, his thumbs gently caressing her cheek. "Do you care that much about the Mackenzie family?" he murmured.

A warmth invaded her body at his touch. It was difficult not to move into his arms and rest her head against his broad shoulder. Lowering her lashes to hide the longing, she said, "I'm very fond of Molly."

His hands fell away. "Well, I guess that's a start."

"Hadn't you better be getting back to Allison?"

"You're right," he said reluctantly. "I'd almost forgotten. You'll stay here tonight, won't you, Leslie? We have to talk."

She shook her head. "I can't."

"Please stay. I know I don't have the right to ask a favor of you, but I want to know you're here."

"What difference can it possibly make?"

He put his hands on her shoulders. "Please?"

It was difficult to deny him anything when he was so close, his eyes warm with a mixture of emotions that she couldn't even separate. "I'll think about it," she said unwillingly.

His smile was twisted. "I guess that's more than I deserve."

After he had gone, Leslie sat by the window for a long time, reviewing the wreckage of her dreams. How could she ever have believed that Raider might be falling in love with her? He didn't even want her friendship! That had really hurt.

Leslie wasn't deceived by the change in his attitude after Molly's confession. That was merely remorse for his brutality. If she was lucky, maybe it would last until she got out of Australia. Leslie didn't think she could survive another set-to with Raider. Perhaps the beautiful Allison would put him in a good mood that would carry over till tomorrow. She got to her feet, resolutely closing her mind to the picture of them standing with linked arms, Raider smiling down at her.

Leslie was so tired that it was an effort to take her clothes off. It seemed a foolish, quixotic gesture to carry out her threat of leaving. What difference did one more night make? She fell into a deep sleep almost as soon as she turned out the light.

Chapter Ten

It was very dark in Leslie's bedroom. She stirred in her sleep, conscious of a presence in the room. Frowning, she tried to surface from the deep slumber enfolding her. Someone murmured her name, trailing cool fingers over her soft cheek.

Leslie turned her head and the hand gently stroked her neck and shoulder. It felt so delightful that she smiled in her sleep, hugging the pillow and drawing her knees up. Her heavy hair was lifted and warm lips caressed the nape of her neck.

Leslie dreamed of Raider. In her dream he was holding out his arms and smiling at her, his gray eyes glowing with the passion she had seen before. But this time there was something more: love was illuminating his face. The open arms were the invitation she had been waiting for all her life.

Leslie turned on her back, her lips softly parted. "Raider," she breathed.

The man kneeling at her bedside said, "Yes, darling."

When she slept on, he leaned forward and kissed her tenderly on the mouth.

Leslie awoke the next morning still in the grip of her wonderful dream. Her face was soft with remembered ecstasy as she struggled against waking, trying to retain the image of Raider as she so desperately wanted him to be. It was no use. The morning light brought reality.

Leslie stayed in bed, trying to summon enough energy to face the day ahead. There was so much to do: packing; the long trip back. With a sigh she stuck one leg out of bed as the door opened and Raider entered.

"Wouldn't it be polite to knock?" she snapped, thrown off balance by his sudden appearance after what she had been dreaming. Her color was high as she pulled the covers up to her chin.

"I'm sorry. I didn't want to wake you if you were still asleep."

Raider was surprisingly meek. Ordinarily, he would have snapped back at her. He was evidently still in the throes of last night's remorse. It augured well for her departure.

"I was just about to get up," Leslie said.

He closed the door and came over to sit on the foot of the bed. "I'd like to talk to you."

She carefully moved her legs so they wouldn't be in contact with him. "I know. If you'll give me a few minutes to get dressed, I'll meet you downstairs."

"I don't mean about business. I want you to change your mind about selling."

"We've been through all that. You're just feeling repentant; you'll be over it by tomorrow," she said cynically.

"I may never get over it." A smile lit his somber face. "You don't want to condemn me to a life of penitence, do you?"

"A little of it wouldn't hurt you," she said dryly.

"That's why I want you to stick around," he teased. "To cut me down to size when I get overly lordly."

That wasn't the reason Leslie wanted. She shook her head. "You'll have to find someone else to be your conscience. I'm going home."

"At least keep the property," Raider urged. "Then you'll have an excuse to come back."

How could she tell him she would never come back? Putting distance between them was her only salvation. "I couldn't afford it. My teacher's salary is my *only* income."

Raider winced. "I deserved that, but it doesn't make it hurt any the less."

She regarded him unsympathetically. "Now you know how it feels."

To her dismay, Raider moved to the head of the bed, taking both of her hands. His hip was pressing against hers. "Leslie, I'm desperate to make it up to you. If I can't talk you out of selling, won't you at least give me a few days to show you something of the country?"

"I think not, Raider. It's best that I leave while we're still on speaking terms. Our truces don't last long."

"One day then—right here on the Danduroo." He held onto her hands when she tried to pull them away. "You've seen just a fraction of it."

"And gotten into trouble every time I ventured out," she said ruefully.

"That's because you didn't go with me. I promise nothing will happen to you this time." He smiled.

What difference did it make? she wondered drearily.

The worst had already happened. "Where did you want to go?" she temporized.

"Would you like to take a flying lesson?"

A tiny smile curved her lips. "I thought there was a condition to that."

"I won't impose it unless you ask me to. Do you want to learn to ride?" he asked hopefully.

"No, I'd probably be like the man who came to dinner," she laughed. "On the morning of my departure I'd break my leg and have to stay on."

"It's drastic, but it might work," he said thoughtfully.

"I have a better idea. I'll just watch and you can show off for me." Leslie was surprised to hear herself agreeing to spend the day with Raider.

Before she could change her mind, he got to his feet. "I'll wait for you downstairs." At the door he turned. "We'll make it a day to remember, Leslie."

She stared after him for a long moment. Yes, it would be memorable for her—the last time she would be with him. Through the sadness ran an undercurrent of excitement. A whole day alone with Raider!

He drove the Land-Rover with the same ease with which he guided a horse or a truck. Leslie stole a surreptitious look at his long, rangy body sprawled comfortably in the seat, his big hands loosely gripping the wheel.

He glanced over at her and smiled. "Are you warm enough?"

It was a lovely day, but this time Leslie had come prepared. "Yes, I borrowed a heavy jacket from Molly."

His hand covered her jeans-clad knee for a moment. "Too bad. I was looking forward to keeping you warm the way Marty did."

Leslie's eyes were troubled. "Did you and Marty . . ."

"All cleared up," he assured her.

She breathed a sigh of relief. "I'm glad."

"He thinks a lot of you. Everyone on the station does." Raider watched her. "They'll all be sorry to see you go."

Leslie bent her head without answering.

Raider stopped the car at a paddock enclosed by a low split-rail fence. To the right was a stable fronting on an oval track. There were several horses and a foal running free in the pasture, while other horses stuck their heads out of open stalls in the wooden building.

"What is the track for?" Leslie asked curiously. "Do you have races?"

"No, we exercise the horses and perfect their gait. We also teach an occasional child or two to ride." He smiled.

"Oh no, you don't!" Leslie shook her bright head. "I'm not falling for that line about how any child can do it."

"Just thought I'd mention it." He grinned. "Come on, we'll look at the horses in the stable."

Raider vaulted the low fence easily, then helped Leslie over. She was absorbed in an explanation about grooming he was giving her when there was a nickering sound behind them. Turning around, her horrified gaze registered two huge beasts bearing down on them. With a terrified scream she threw her arms around Raider's waist and buried her face in his jacket, burrowing inside so she could feel his reassuring warmth.

She could hear the deep rumble of laughter in his chest as he attempted to fend off the foraging horses while still keeping Leslie in a protective embrace. She clung like a limpet, drawing in a sharp breath when a soft nose bumped against her hip.

"It's your jacket," Raider explained when he could stop laughing. "They recognized it. Molly always keeps sugar in her pocket." He reached inside and drew something out. "Here, this is all they want."

Leslie lifted her head cautiously, not relinquishing her death grip on Raider. A large brown horse with a white patch on his forehead was daintily taking a sugar cube out of Raider's palm. Its big yellowish teeth were far from reassuring, but if he had his mouth full, at least he couldn't bite.

The other horse was investigating the contents of Raider's pocket, and he drew out an apple, offering it to Leslie. "Would you like to give it to him?"

She shook her head. When something bumped the back of her knee she yelped, looking around fearfully. A silky tan colt with a blond mane and great dark eyes was nuzzling her hip, his slender legs splayed out at an awkward angle as he leaned against her.

Leslie promptly released her hold on Raider and sank to her knees, putting her arms around the foal's neck. "Oh, Raider, isn't he adorable? He's like a big toy."

He raised his eyebrows. "Do you know what you're doing, Leslie? That's a horse?"

"Don't be silly! He's just a little baby." She rubbed her cheek against the silken coat.

"That's the way they all start out," he assured her.

It didn't seem possible. Leslie looked up at the two big heads bent almost curiously down at her. Raider put his hand under her arm, lifting her to her feet. When one of the horses shifted his weight and whuffled softly she jerked back nervously.

Raider put his arm around her. "He wants his nose stroked."

She reached out a tentative hand. The horse dipped his head toward her and she gingerly touched his nose, rubbing it gently. It felt smooth and warm. She looked up delightedly at Raider, basking in the approval she saw in his eyes.

"That's a beginning," he said.

Leslie was sure that Raider would now suggest she ride the huge thing. She stiffened in opposition, feeling foolish when he did nothing of the sort. Taking her hand, he led her toward the stables.

They wandered along past the half-open Dutch doors that restrained the horses while allowing them to look out. Raider scratched an ear here, patted a nose there, with obvious affection on both sides. There was a current of understanding that ran between them, and Leslie felt herself longing to share it. She had always loved animals; why couldn't it extend to horses?

Almost at the end of the row there was a fat horse that was much smaller than the rest. It had a red ribbon plaited in its mane and wore a comical look of complacency, almost as though it were proud of its adornment.

"This one must be special," Leslie laughed.

"Yes, Pokey is the pet of the station. Everybody feeds her, as you can see."

Leslie approached much closer than she had to any of the others. "Does anybody ride her?"

"If they can get their legs over that broad back," Raider said deprecatingly. "It isn't much like riding. It's more like sitting in a slow-moving rocker."

Leslie made up her mind suddenly. "I wouldn't mind riding this one."

"You wouldn't enjoy it," Raider told her. "Pokey

lives up to her name. She's so slow it takes her half an hour to get around the track once."

"That sounds perfect," Leslie insisted. "Edmund Hillary didn't start out with Mt. Everest."

"Well, if that's what you want," Raider said, shrugging.

It wasn't until he had led the fat mare out of the stall and helped Leslie up that she became suspicious. "You tricked me into this, didn't you?"

He was smiling up at her, his arm comfortingly around her waist. "It was your ultimate decision. I'm through trying to force you to do anything—more or less."

Leslie looked away, aware of what he was saying.

At first Leslie clutched the reins until her hands ached. But as the placid animal ambled along slowly she started to relax. "How do you make her go faster?" she asked after a time.

Raider laughed. "It takes an act of God."

Leslie didn't believe him. However, when no amount of prodding or urging could speed Pokey up, she said, "Maybe I should try something a little more spirited."

They had made a circuit of the track and were back at the stable. Raider reached up and lifted her down. "Perhaps next time."

His hands stayed at her waist and Leslie was thrillingly aware of his nearness. The sun made a glory of her red-gold hair as she tilted her head to look up at him, still holding on to his wide shoulders.

Raider drew a sharp breath, his grasp tightening for a moment. Then he released her, taking her hand. "That was very good for a first effort. Now we'll go inspect the Danduroo."

It was a beautiful ride through tree-shaded countryside of unbelievable serenity. Small ponds dotted the landscape like silver coins strewn by a benevolent giant. Cattle gathered there to drink, filling the air with their lowing. As they drove deeper into the interior, a flock of rose-breasted galahs chattered overhead, the noise sounding like a dozen people all talking at once.

"Are you hungry?" Raider asked.

Leslie hesitated. "A little, but I don't want to go back yet."

"No need to. I had Clara pack us a picnic hamper." Raider stopped the car near a field of wild flowers, reaching on the floor in back to bring out a wicker basket. "The Boy Scouts aren't the only ones who are prepared." He grinned.

After spreading out a blanket he produced enough food for a whole troop: sandwiches and salads, plus fruit and delicious pastries.

"Who did Clara think she was feeding, the entire station?" Leslie exclaimed.

"Everything is done on a grander scale in Australia." Raider smiled. "Haven't you noticed?"

Leslie nodded. "My little apartment is going to feel claustrophobic after all this wide-open space," she said without thinking. Their eyes met briefly before Leslie looked down to crumble a bit of bread.

Raider swore softly under his breath. "We wasted so much time—and all because of that damn letter!"

"You do believe now that I never got it?" Leslie asked anxiously.

"Not that letter. I was talking about the first one, the one from your aunt."

She stared at him blankly. "My aunt?"

"You said you didn't know how Lester knew about you and I didn't believe you," Raider said gently. "Although, in all fairness I couldn't be blamed for that.

You see, just before Lester's accident he received a letter from an L. Farraday. Naturally I thought it was you. It was only after you mentioned your aunt and I thought about it for a while that I figured it out."

"*Laura* Farraday," Leslie breathed, and he nodded. "But how did she know Lester? Why would she write to him? And why would she think he'd be interested in me?" When Raider hesitated, Leslie said, "He was in love with my mother, wasn't he? I didn't believe you that first day when you intimated as much, but I don't think I can doubt it any longer. Even Clara hinted at it."

"What did she say?" Raider asked warily.

"Not very much. It was just a feeling she gave me. That they were in love with each other. Aunt Laura must have known, that's why she wrote to Lester." Leslie's long eyelashes fell. "My parents didn't have a very happy marriage. And even though Aunt Laura was my father's sister, she was very close to Mother. Is it possible that she thought she could reunite them after all those years?"

"There's no point in conjecture. It's all in the past," he said quietly.

"Except that it spilled over into the present," Leslie said sadly. "You were prepared to hate me before you ever saw me."

"But not after."

"How can you say that? You were furious the minute you set eyes on me." Would she ever forget those arms like steel bands around her?

"Only because I was afraid you were going to get killed. You were like a slender daffodil about to be crushed. I was scared stiff!" His voice was awed. "For the first time in my life I was afraid."

Looking at his strong face Leslie could believe it.

This man had never felt fear before. "You didn't sound frightened, you acted like you wanted to wring my neck."

"That was only to cover what I really wanted to do to you." His dark head bent over her bright one. "What I've wanted ever since I saw you." His lips touched hers gently in a kiss that was unbearably sweet.

Leslie struggled against his magnetism. This man had hurt her too often; she mustn't let herself fall prey to him again. She held him off with her hands against his chest. "I don't believe you. You've been beastly to me since the minute I set foot on the Danduroo."

"Not all the time," he teased.

"Yes, every minute," she maintained stubbornly.

Tiny lights flickered in his gray eyes. "I can remember some memorable moments we shared."

Leslie's eyelashes fluttered against her flushed cheeks. "I've forgotten all about those."

"Then I'd better refresh your memory."

He drew her down on the blanket, half covering her body with his as his mouth took possession of hers. Leslie tried not to respond, but he was too experienced for her. He knew the art of seduction too well. When her lips refused to part, his warm mouth slid across her cheek leaving tiny butterfly kisses in its wake. His teeth nipped her earlobe gently, flicking it back and forth with his tongue before exploring the inner contours.

Leslie moved her head restlessly, her breath coming more swiftly. Her hands were at his shoulders, but instead of pushing against them she found herself tracing their width. "Raider, don't do that," she pleaded.

"All right, my darling," he murmured.

Her reprieve was short-lived. Raider transferred his

mouth to the pulse that was beating rapidly in the hollow of her throat. He burrowed inside her jacket, seeking out the shadowed area between her breasts. The indescribable feeling set up a clamor in Leslie's blood that was completely irresistible. When she sighed and put her arms around his neck his mouth covered hers in triumph, parting her lips with ease now. The male invasion was confident. Leslie was his for the taking and he knew it.

He slid the zipper of her jacket down, running his palm slowly over the contours of her body, covered only by the checked cotton shirt. When she shivered at the sensual feeling, he unbuttoned his coat and wrapped it around her, rolling her into his arms. She trembled against him.

"Are you cold, sweetheart?" Raider whispered.

Leslie shook her head and his hand stroked her back, sliding inside the waistband of her jeans and holding her so tightly against the rigid column of his thighs that she was aware of his desire. She moved against him, his hard body lighting a flame inside her that threatened to burn out of control. Leslie had never felt such an aching need.

"You want me too, don't you, my love?" he murmured huskily.

"Yes, oh Raider, yes!" She sighed.

"I want to take you right here in the sunshine where I can see every expression on your beautiful face." His eyes were brilliant as they held hers. "Will you let me do that, Leslie?"

Her softly parted lips gave him the answer and he kissed her fiercely, his hands unsteady as they reached for the buttons on her shirt. Suddenly the sound of dogs barking and the answering shouts of men told them they were no longer alone. They stared at each other in disbelief that anything could intrude on this impassioned moment.

Raider was the first to react. He sat up and swore savagely. Helping Leslie up, he smoothed her hair with an unsteady hand. "Wouldn't you think we could find some privacy in the middle of fifteen thousand acres?"

Her smile was tremulous. "You once warned me against making love out of doors."

His answering smile was reluctant. "That advice wasn't meant to include me."

"It looks like I was saved by the bell," Leslie said lightly, trying to still the urge to throw herself in his arms once more.

"Only for now," he growled.

She picked at an imaginary piece of lint on her jeans. "Now is all we have."

He took her chin in his palm, forcing her to look at him. "You can't still be thinking of leaving?"

"Nothing has changed, Raider."

"How can you say that? You can't pretend you don't feel something for me."

If he only knew! "I'll admit there's a certain physical attraction between us," Leslie said carefully.

"You could hardly deny it," he teased, his fingers tracing a sensual pattern up her leg.

She grabbed hastily for his hand. "I'd have to go home in a short time anyway," she said, her resolve weakening.

"We'll see when the time comes." His lips brushed lightly over hers.

It was no use fighting it. Leslie knew she couldn't leave him until she absolutely had to. "Well, at least we should get our business over with now," she said desperately. If something went wrong between them again, this time she wouldn't have to wait around to sign the papers.

"If you like," he said indifferently, bending his head and deepening the kiss.

A tiny stab of suspicion entered Leslie's mind like a snake. He certainly wasn't putting up any argument now. Had all that reluctance on his part been feigned? Since she had changed her mind a couple of times, did he want to be sure that he had her all wrapped up? Even Clara told her that Lester's ten acres were an obsession with Raider.

Then Leslie's senses took over, silencing the warning her brain was trying to convey. His lips and hands were reducing her to a willing pawn in whatever game he chose to play. What did anything matter as long as her body could come alive like this under his caresses?

"We'll fly to Sydney tomorrow," he murmured against her throat, where his mouth was putting its brand.

"Sydney?" Leslie's response was startled.

"That's where my attorney is."

She moved away slightly. "Isn't that an awfully long way?" Leslie asked doubtfully.

Raider shrugged. "Everything in Australia is a long way. Luckily not by air."

"Maybe I should take along my things. It seems silly to go up and back twice."

"I thought we settled that," he said firmly. "I think you'll enjoy seeing Sydney. We'll stay overnight so we can go to the opera house."

Leslie was momentarily diverted. "I saw it when I flew in and it's fabulous."

"It's even more so inside. Wait and see."

"But staying over and all sounds expensive," she protested. "Wouldn't it be easier if they just mailed the papers?"

"You have to sign them before a notary," Raider told her.

The gnats of suspicion were back, buzzing around her mind in a noxious cloud. Was that really true? Or was Raider so eager to get his property back that he was willing to throw in a little side trip?

"I'll even take you to the Taronga Park Zoo to see a duckbill platypus." He smiled. "Would you like that?"

"Yes, I . . . it sounds very nice."

A horse and rider came out of a grove of trees in the near distance. Raider got to his feet, pulling Leslie up after him. Just before the man reached them he kissed her palm. "I have a feeling it's going to be more than nice," Raider murmured huskily.

Chapter Eleven

The city of Sydney seemed almost as big as New York to Leslie after the peace and quiet of the outback. Actually it was more like San Francisco.

The beautiful harbor was reminiscent of it, as were the hills beyond. The sparkling white opera house, however, was unique in all the world. Leslie was looking forward to spending the promised evening there, inside the spreading curved wings that made the majestic structure look like a giant sculpture by Bufano. That was the first thing she thought of when she flew into Sydney—what was it, a million years ago?

If she had known all that lay ahead, would she have gone through with it? Or would she have turned around and run like a thief for the safety of home? Looking sideways at Raider's handsome profile, Leslie wasn't sure of the answer.

He smiled and took her hand as the cab maneuvered

through the crowded streets. "Are you glad to be back in civilization?"

"Actually I'm a little dazed," she said. The taxi had slammed to a halt to avoid hitting a rash pedestrian and Leslie was thrown against Raider. "This is more dangerous than those wild dingo dogs you warned me about—which never materialized, incidentally. Did you make them up?"

"No, but they're only dangerous to lambs and calves. Were you really frightened?"

She shook her head. "Only of horses, and you taught me not to be."

He lifted her hand, kissing each finger. "I told you there were things I could teach you if you'd let me," he murmured meaningfully.

Leslie's cheeks were still bright with color when they entered the hotel. The Wentworth was quietly elegant, living up to its reputation as one of the finest hotels in Sydney. She looked appreciatively around the red-carpeted lobby before drifting over to glance in the beautiful shop windows while Raider registered for both of them.

Only when she rejoined him at the desk did Leslie have a bad moment. Suppose he hadn't gotten separate rooms? Her fears proved groundless. Their rooms were adjoining, but the door in between was securely locked.

"What do you want to do first?" Raider asked after they were settled.

"Anything you'd like," she answered.

"What I'd *like* to do and what we're *going* to do are two different things," he said dryly. "I promised to show you the town, and I think we should start where it all began, at a place called The Rocks. That's where the first colonials and convicts built houses and barracks."

"Is it true that Australia was settled by British

convicts?" Leslie asked curiously as they strolled out of the downtown area toward the water.

"In large part. You Yanks were responsible for that."

"How could that be?" she exclaimed.

"In the old days, England used to dump her convicted criminals in the colonies, mainly Maryland and Virginia. When the revolution came along, the prisons in Britain got so overcrowded that they had to find another place, so they sent them to Australia."

"And after they served their sentences they stayed on?"

"In reality very few of them spent much time behind bars. They were too busy building housing and learning to raise food. The best-behaved ones were pardoned and given plots of land. They became the hardy pioneers. Some even became famous. Francis Greenway is still considered by many people to be Australia's greatest architect. His picture is on the ten-dollar bill. Not bad for a man convicted of forgery."

The streets grew narrow and hilly as they reached the old part of town. It had been built near the harbor and the first buildings were undoubtedly crude. They had been replaced, however, with tall stone dwellings called terrace houses, which were decorated with delicate and lacy wrought-iron balconies, almost in the style of New Orleans. Only the facade of the old prison remained, like a brooding stone fortress.

From there they wandered along the Circular Quay, watching the busy water. Ferry boats nosed in and out of the many piers transporting passengers to the numerous suburbs. There were sightseeing boats also, plus freighters, pleasure craft, and luxury liners waiting to take people to all parts of the world. It was a very bustling harbor.

"We'll save the opera house until tonight," Raider told her. "There is something I want to do in town."

"Of course! We have to go to your attorney's office." Leslie was so fascinated with the sights she had almost forgotten.

"It can wait until tomorrow." He shrugged.

"No, Raider, let's get it over with."

"You sound like it's a dose of medicine." He looked at her thoughtfully. "Are you having second thoughts?"

Did he sound displeased or was she being hypersensitive again? Lester's property had been the beginning of all this, and now it was to be the end. But what would the conclusion be? Leslie couldn't bear to think that Raider had made love to her solely to get it. She couldn't wait to sign it over to him. His behavior after that would tell the story.

The thorny doubts in Leslie's mind were destined to go unresolved for a while longer. Raider led her into a jewelry shop instead of an office building.

"What are we doing here?" she asked blankly.

"Don't women always like to look at jewelry?" he countered. "This is the finest store in town."

She could readily believe that. The interior had the hushed atmosphere that spoke of money. Deep carpeting cushioned any footsteps, a discreet bell announcing their presence instead. There was a gray velvet couch in the middle of the room and comfortable chairs were drawn up to a long glass showcase containing only a few pieces of jewelry. The ones displayed, however, were dazzling in their opulence.

It was hardly the kind of place one browsed in. "They're going to know we're not customers," Leslie said in a low voice.

A salesman approached. "May I help you?"

"Yes, I'm Raider Mackenzie. I believe you have something for me."

Leslie was embarrassed. It hadn't occurred to her that he actually had business here. Then the full import of it struck her. Who was Raider buying jewelry for? Molly, she hoped, while a desolate feeling in her bones told her that Allison was a more likely recipient.

"Certainly, Mr. Mackenzie, it's all ready," the smiling salesman assured him, unlocking a drawer and taking out a blue velvet box. He snapped it open, holding it out for their inspection. "Isn't it lovely?"

Leslie gasped when she saw the opal ring inside. The large oval stone set in an intricate gold mounting looked like it was on fire. Red and lavender, blue, orange and green glowed in its depths, changing color with every shifting ray of light. It was the most magnificent thing she had ever seen.

Raider was watching her reaction. "Yes, it's very lovely," he said, never taking his eyes from her face. "What do you think, Leslie?"

"It . . . it's . . ." She looked at him helplessly.

"I take it that means you're pleased." He laughed.

"Pleased?" A puzzled frown furrowed her smooth forehead. "I don't understand."

"It's for you," he said simply.

Leslie drew in a sharp breath. "I couldn't possibly accept this."

Raider hesitated, but as she shook her head for emphasis he shrugged. "Tell Marty, don't tell me."

"Are you trying to say *this* is the opal Marty dug up?" she demanded.

"That's the one. Molly gave it to me and asked me to have it polished for you."

"Oh, Raider, it just couldn't be! Marty said it was only a little one."

"Marty is a fine ranch hand but he's no gem expert." His eyes met those of the salesman over Leslie's bright head. "The stone went a lot deeper than he knew."

"I don't know what to say," she murmured.

"I don't think anything is called for," Raider said easily.

"But the setting," she protested. "It must have cost a fortune all by itself."

"That was my contribution," Raider told her. Before she could argue the point any further he said, "Give me your hand."

Leslie reluctantly extended her right hand. After an imperceptible pause he slipped the ring on her third finger.

Leslie had never had anything that beautiful in her whole life. The delight it gave her was outweighing the guilt she felt in allowing Raider to spend so much money on her, even though she knew he could well afford it.

"Thank you," she said shyly. "This was so thoughtful. I won't ever forget you."

"That was the general idea," he said wryly.

Leslie followed him from the shop in a daze. During the short walk down the block to the nearby office building her fascinated eyes scarcely left the ring. She kept turning her hand from side to side watching the changing colors in the sunlight.

As they went up in the elevator Raider chuckled and said, "I think I've created a rival."

The pretty receptionist in the lawyer's office gave him a dazzling smile. "It's so good to see you again, Mr. Mackenzie. You don't visit us often enough."

"That's because I have to wear a necktie and put on my Sunday suit when I come to the big city," he joked.

For all of his pose of being a country bumpkin, Raider could have taken his place at the head of any conference table. His charcoal gray suit was custom tailored to fit his large frame flawlessly, and his shirt and tie looked expensive. He was equally at home in the city or the country, in spite of his preference for the latter.

"Mr. Felton will see you right away," the receptionist assured him.

Gary Felton and Raider were evidently old friends, judging by the hearty greeting he received. They were about the same age. As they shook hands, the attorney's eyes roved appreciatively over Leslie, who had remained in the background.

"I drew up those papers the way you instructed," the lawyer said. "I made it airtight with no loopholes. Too bad the little creep held you up for such a bundle, but I guess it was worth it, whatever you had to do."

The emotion that crossed Raider's face was gone too swiftly to classify. Without losing his poise he said, "I'd like you to meet Leslie Farraday."

There was a pregnant pause. Felton's expression was almost comical. "You're kidding, aren't you? I thought —we both thought—"

"As Miss Farraday informed me when we first met, these unisex names are confusing," Raider said smoothly.

"You said that—" The lawyer pulled himself together with an effort. "I'm very sorry, Miss Farraday. I didn't mean to be insulting."

"I understand. But just to set the record straight, I have no intention of holding Mr. Mackenzie up. What payment does the contract specify?" she asked.

Before Raider could stop him, Felton told her.

"That's ridiculous!" she exclaimed, turning angrily to Raider. "I told you I was accepting your first offer."

"We'll talk about this privately, Leslie," he said evenly.

"No! The land isn't worth that amount, is it?" she demanded of the lawyer.

"Well, it depends," he hedged.

"It isn't and you know it. You both know it. I won't take it!" she cried angrily. "I'm neither an adventuress nor a charity case."

"I'd like to talk to Leslie alone," Raider told the other man.

"You're not going to change my mind," she said when the attorney had beaten a hasty retreat.

"It isn't charity," Raider said quietly. "That property is worth it to me."

"You can have it—at the price we agreed upon."

He shook his head. "I offered more. Would you have me go back on my word? I'd always feel like I took advantage of you."

So it was conscience money. The pain that slashed through her was swift and deadly. Raider had done whatever was necessary to get what he wanted and now he was feeling guilty. He knew she didn't have much money, so paying her off would bring absolution.

Leslie's first impulse was to refuse to sign, but that would only bring them back to square one. She knew she couldn't stand another concerted assault by Raider, brutal or, more especially, otherwise. Arguing never got her anyplace, so Leslie decided to sign over the deed. Let Raider think he had won. When she got home she would send him a check.

Leslie was very quiet after they left the attorney's office. Raider's conciliatory attempts to interest her in the sights around them only made things worse. It just pointed up what she now knew to be true.

That evening, though, she made an effort to enjoy herself. She would never get here again, so she might as well make the most of it. What difference did Raider's motives make? He was being kind and attentive and it really was a very exciting city.

He took her to a beautiful restaurant in the opera house for dinner. It was at the head of a long flight of stairs and completely unexpected in size and elegance. An obsequious headwaiter led them to a choice table by the windows overlooking the harbor.

"It keeps reminding me of San Francisco," Leslie exclaimed. "Although most of the view restaurants there are way up high. This is much more interesting."

"I hoped you would like it," Raider smiled. "It doesn't have the atmosphere of someplace like the Argyle Tavern, for instance, but since we're going to the Drama Theater after, I thought eating right here would give us more time to spend over dinner."

"This is lovely," she assured him. "I don't see how that other place could be any prettier."

"It isn't as attractive, actually. It just has a lot of atmosphere—rough brick walls and candlelight. They're noted for their convict broth and roast beef, and for the community singing. Everybody joins in on the Australian bush ballads."

"Once they got past 'Waltzing Mathilda' I'd have to drop out." Leslie laughed. "And I don't even understand the words to *that.* It seems strange to think they're really talking English."

"A form of it," he corrected her. "In these parts it's called Strine."

"Imagine, a language within a language," she marveled.

"Isn't that what you'd expect from a country where it's cold down south while the north is tropical?" He laughed. "And where you can ski in July and go swimming in one-hundred-degree weather on Christmas Day?"

"That would feel strange," Leslie admitted.

"Something you couldn't get used to?" he asked casually.

"I suppose you can get used to anything," she answered just as offhandedly.

After the play, which Leslie enjoyed thoroughly, Raider took her to King's Cross.

"This is where the action is," he told her. "It's been likened to New York's Greenwich Village or London's Soho district."

It was lively, Leslie had to admit, yet she wasn't sure she cared for it. Loud rock music blared out of numerous night spots and the streets were crowded with people, some of whom looked downright weird. It was like the Fourth of July and New Year's Eve combined. The noise and congestion were giving her a headache.

Noticing her dubious expression, Raider hailed a cab. "I was going to suggest having a drink," he said, "but I gather you'd rather not."

"Well, it *is* a little busy. I was very glad to see it, though," she assured him. "I've heard so much about King's Cross."

"The interesting thing is how different it is during the daytime. Tomorrow these streets will be filled with older people tending their shops and couples having lunch."

Leslie grew silent in the taxi on the way back to the hotel, her head filled with the sights and sounds of Sydney. It had been a wonderful evening and now it was almost over. Everything was. The idyll was drawing to a close.

"Are you tired, honey?" Raider asked, draping a casual arm over her shoulders.

"Not really."

"You're so quiet," he remarked.

"I was just thinking."

"About what?"

Leslie summoned a smile. "Oh, all the things we've seen and done."

"Did you enjoy them?"

"Yes, you've been very kind, Raider."

"I wasn't looking for thanks."

"I know that, but you have been. I wish there were some way I could repay you."

"You already have," he replied with a smile.

Leslie lowered her lashes. So it was out in the open.

As though realizing how that sounded, Raider added, "Your enjoyment is all the thanks I need." The back of his knuckles brushed lightly across her cheek.

A little shiver ran through her. Leslie resisted the urge to put her lips against the smooth column of his neck and inhale the wonderful masculine aroma of him. He could weave a spell almost effortlessly. In spite of everything, today had been a small slice of heaven.

"I'll never forget this day," she said softly. "It's been wonderful."

He was watching her intently. "Quite a change after the Danduroo, isn't it?"

"They're like different countries," she said simply.

Raider removed his arm. "I suppose it would seem that way to someone from a big city."

Did he think she was denigrating the Danduroo? To her own surprise, Leslie found that she was looking foward to returning to it. Sydney was interesting and fun, yet she felt like a visitor here, while the vast station seemed like home. She searched for some way to tell him that without revealing too much.

"Sydney reminds me of Los Angeles, while the outback moves at a different pace," Leslie explained carefully. He didn't take it the way she intended.

"Slow and backward?" Raider asked mockingly.

"Certainly not. That wasn't what I meant at all."

She would have tried to explain, but the cab arrived at the hotel. They were riding up in the elevator when Raider returned to the subject.

"You don't have to worry about hurting my feelings. I realize the outback isn't for everyone. It's too bad your introduction to it was so rocky, though. Everything might have worked out differently." His face was somber.

"It was my fault as much as yours," Leslie said. "After all, I did accept that ticket under false pretenses."

"And you were punished for your sins. Is that the way you look at it?" he asked sardonically.

"No! Why do you persist in taking everything I say the wrong way?"

"Because I think the time has come to stop pretending," he said, opening Leslie's door and handing her the key.

"*You* have, anyway," she said bitterly.

"What do you mean by that?"

"Oh, never mind." She turned away.

Raider took her arm, pulling her back before she could close the door. "No, I think we'd better talk about this."

A couple got off the elevator and started toward them, looking curiously at the tense couple. Raider scowled, pushing Leslie inside the room and closing the door.

"Okay, let's have it," he said. "I've had a feeling all evening that something's been bothering you."

"And you can't imagine what that could be," she remarked stiffly.

He considered it before shaking his head. "No, I can't."

Did he expect her to believe that? Leslie couldn't tell him what was really bothering her, but she could air one complaint. "How would you like to be called a little creep and be accused of the things I was?" Bright flags of color highlighted her cheekbones.

"I'm sorry about that, honey," Raider said with wry amusement. "I explained it all to you. I just never got around to explaining it to Gary."

Despite all her good resolutions, the words tumbled out. "Are you going to answer his question? Are you going to tell him what you *did* have to do?"

Raider frowned. "I don't know what you mean."

Misery engulfed Leslie. Raider had said it was time to stop pretending, and maybe he was right. At least he would know that she wasn't the fool he took her for.

Holding her chin high she said, "I do hope you won't tell him that making love to me was a great hardship."

"What the hell are you talking about?" he grated.

"I suppose I shouldn't complain. Part of it was really quite . . . pleasant."

Raider's eyes narrowed dangerously. "Is that what you would call it?"

She shrugged. "Well, yes, compared to fighting."

He came over to stand so close that she could feel the anger vibrating in that magnificent body. "Are you saying you found my lovemaking merely pleasurable?"

Her nerve ends were sending out warning signals.

Leslie moved away, seeking to make it appear casual. "What's wrong with that? I should think you'd be pleased."

"I'd be more so if you told the truth. I seem to remember your reaction as being a little more—what shall we call it? Abandoned?" he asked mockingly.

She turned her back to hide the wave of color that suffused her ivory skin. "That's just your interpretation."

"You wouldn't describe it that way?"

"Certainly not!"

He moved closer with the silent tread of a stalking tiger. "Not even the morning you put your arms around my neck and begged me not to leave you?" he asked softly.

Leslie started to tremble. If only she could put distance between them, maybe she would be able to keep up a pretense of indifference. As she turned to move away, Leslie discovered to her dismay that she was boxed in between Raider and the bed. To get by she would have to brush against him, something that couldn't be allowed to happen.

Taking a deep breath, she tried to brazen it out. "I will admit that I was a little . . . um . . . stirred."

He laughed outright. "You were a lot more than that, my dear."

"All right, so you're very experienced," she replied angrily. "You know how to turn a woman on."

"You mean that's all there was to it? Sex?"

Leslie avoided his eyes. "Of course. What else?"

"In that case, what are we waiting for?" His hands were at her waist drawing her closer.

"What do you think you're doing?" She held him off desperately.

His eyes were hard. "You've just admitted that I turn you on, and there has never been any secret about my attraction to you. We're two adults; why are we wasting time?"

"No!" His hands had moved up to cup her breasts, and Leslie was having trouble breathing. "You've gotten what you want from me. You can't have it all!"

His lips grazed her cheek. "Oh, but I intend to. And somehow I don't think you're going to stop me," he said softly.

She held herself rigid, turning her head away. Raider's mouth slid down her neck, following the line of her collarbone to the soft hollow at the base of her throat. His warm tongue touched the wildly beating pulse, searing her like a brand.

Leslie's arms were starting to ache from trying to hold him off. "Please stop, Raider," she moaned.

He pulled her against his hard body, running his hands down her back to crush her so tightly against him that she was bruised by his muscular thighs. Heat flamed in her lower limbs as she caught fire from his male desire. Her body became fluid, as though melting to remold itself to his.

"Why should I stop when we both want each other so much?" he murmured, taking her lower lip gently between his teeth.

There had to be a reason, but Leslie was having trouble thinking of it. This man had the power to make her forget everything, even self-respect, in her urgent need for his possession. She was drowning in his seduction, her efforts to save herself becoming feebler.

"That isn't reason enough," she cried desperately.

He chuckled, a dominant male sound deep in his throat. "Can you think of a better one?"

He was slowly undoing the tiny pearl buttons that fastened the front of her dress, pausing to trace the swell of her breasts above the lacy nude-colored bra. His fingers dipped inside, leisurely caressing the sensitive tips until Leslie gasped from the sensual feeling. When he guided her gently down on the bed she didn't have the will to resist.

"This time we've come too far to stop," Raider said in a low voice, lying down beside her. "You know that, don't you?"

"Yes," she sighed, putting her arms around his neck and straining close to him.

His mouth found hers with an almost savage passion. All of his pent-up hunger was expressed in a kiss that seemed to reach for her very soul. His hands wandered restlessly over her, touching, caressing, demanding.

"I've wanted you for so long," he murmured. "You'll never know how often I wanted to come to you in the night, to kiss you awake and make love to you until the sun came up."

His deep, drugging kisses drove away all of Leslie's inhibitions. "Why didn't you, Raider?" she whispered.

"Because I'm a fool," he groaned. "But no more. Tonight I'm going to make you mine over and over again."

He slipped the dress from her shoulders, looking at her slender body with glowing eyes. Leslie's lashes fell as he lifted her tenderly, but she moved her hips to help him remove the silken garment completely. He unclasped her bra slowly, as though savoring each moment and each new glimpse of her pearly skin, trailing long fingertips from her shoulders down to her thighs.

Leslie wanted to touch him in the same way. She unbuttoned his shirt with shaking hands, twining her fingers in the crisp hair that covered his bronze chest. A shudder went through him as her palm glided over his flat stomach, and she gloried in her power over this man who owned her soul and was about to possess her body. He might not love her, but at this moment he was as much in her thrall as she was in his.

Raider left her for just a moment, flinging his clothes off with an impatience that told Leslie anticipation had been replaced by urgency. He removed her last garment, wrapping her in a fierce embrace like none she had ever had with a man before. Her body blazed from the heat of his and she waited for the ultimate embrace.

When he prolonged the moment, bending his head to rain lingering kisses on every sensitive part of her body, Leslie arched herself against him, flinging her arms around his neck and whispering in his ear.

"Yes, my darling," he murmured, parting her legs with his knee and moving her tenderly beneath him.

There was a tiny moment of pain, then Leslie was filled with a sensation so exquisite that she raised her body again and again in a frantic effort to reach an even more ecstatic plane. Raider's arms held her tightly, his body moving in rhythm with hers to some wild dance that promised to end with a burst of celestial music. When Leslie felt she must surely be consumed by the tension within, there was a great release. Giant waves pulsed through her quivering body, breaking and receding, each one growing successively gentler until she was filled with a tremendous sense of peace. Her arms loosened around Raider's neck and she sighed her delight as their heartbeats slowly returned to normal.

"Sweet Leslie," he breathed against her scented throat. "My sweet, adorable Leslie."

She drifted off to sleep in his arms, waking much

later to find him watching her, his expression unreadable in the dark.

"Why aren't you sleeping?" she asked shyly.

"Because I'd rather look at you." He smoothed her tumbled hair gently.

Leslie ran the tip of her tongue over her lower lip, finding it slightly swollen from Raider's kisses. Her lipstick was long gone. "I must look a mess," she murmured.

"Are you fishing for compliments?" he teased. "You look beautiful and you know it."

"Do you tell that to all the girls you make love to?" It was meant as a joke, but as soon as the words were out Leslie would have done anything to recall them. The ugly fact that she was just another girl in his bed was better left unsaid, even though it would return to haunt her in weeks to come.

When she started to move away his arms tightened. "We have to talk, Leslie."

She looked at him with a stricken expression. "Don't say anything, Raider, please. I don't want to hear the answer." Since he wouldn't let her go, Leslie buried her burning face in his shoulder.

Raider tangled his fingers in her bright hair, gently tugging her head back. He kissed her trembling mouth lingeringly. "You little idiot, that wasn't what I was going to talk about," he said fondly.

"I don't want to talk about anything," she managed to say when his lips slid along her jawline to worry the lobe of her ear.

"Neither do I," he murmured, pressing her into the pillows with his weight. "It can wait until morning."

The quickening of his loins told her of Raider's desire, and she was helpless to resist. All reservations vanished the minute he touched her. Leslie's body kindled with liquid fire as he stroked the secret parts he knew to be responsive. Nothing mattered as long as she could follow him once more to that incredible peak of passion where sensation defeated logic and rapture held off pain.

Her breathing quickened as he wrapped her close, carrying her in a dizzy spiral that found her clinging to him and calling out his name. It ended in a shower of sparks and a vibrating descent that left them both totally fulfilled.

Leslie awoke first the next morning, still in Raider's arms. His firm mouth was relaxed in a little smile as though he were dreaming something pleasant. For once she could look at him to her heart's content. Leslie gazed adoringly at the straight nose and high cheekbones feathered by thick, spiky lashes. Her heart swelled with love for this wonderful man who had made her a woman in the fullest sense of the word. Even if last night was all she would ever have, it was worth it.

Raider's eyes opened and he smiled at her. Turning his head slightly, he kissed her warm skin. "Good morning, lovely," he said.

"Good morning," she said shyly. "Did you sleep well?"

"Yes, but it was a waste of time. I should have been making love to you."

She looked up at him provocatively. "You did, don't you remember?"

He rubbed his nose against hers. "If I said no, would you refresh my memory?"

He was teasing, but there was too much truth in it. How long would it take Raider to forget her? Would she blend in with all the others so he would have to remind himself: Oh, yes. She was the one with the copper-colored hair?

His expression sobered as he looked at her downcast face. "You're not having regrets, are you, Leslie?" he asked softly.

"Oh, no," she said quickly. "I'll remember it always. I . . . I didn't know it could be so wonderful, Raider."

"And I didn't know you were a virgin," he said soberly. "Why didn't you tell me, Leslie? I feel like a prize heel."

"But you mustn't. I wanted it as much as you did."

He touched her cheek gently. "That doesn't excuse me. You accused me of taking everything from you, and that's what I've done."

"How can I convince you that you're wrong?" She gave him a wistful little smile. "You didn't take anything; it was a gift, Raider."

He swore softly under his breath, getting out of bed and wandering unselfconsciously over to the dresser to find a cigarette. Leslie looked at his tall, lean body, so perfectly proportioned and blatantly masculine. A familiar warmth stole over her and she breathed a sigh of relief when he reached for his slacks.

Raider sank into a chair, gazing at her somberly. "I can't undo what's done, but perhaps you can consider last night as your wedding night."

Leslie stared at him in confusion. "What do you mean?"

"I'm asking you to marry me," he said quietly.

A rush of blood made her feel dizzy. She couldn't have heard him correctly! Then comprehension dawned, leaving her more miserable than she would have thought possible. Raider considered himself an honorable man. He might be able to square his conscience about abusing her verbally and tricking her into selling him her property, but taking her virginity was more than he could justify. For one crazy moment Leslie was tempted to accept his offer. Then sanity returned and she faced the acting role of her life. Raider must never discover that she was in love with him.

She managed an incredulous tone of voice. "You must be joking. This isn't the Victorian era, Raider. You don't have to marry me."

"I didn't say I *had* to marry you—although that remains to be seen."

For a moment apprehension tugged at Leslie. She couldn't possibly have gotten pregnant, could she? It would be very unlikely, she decided. "All right then, I'll make it easy for you. I don't want to marry *you.*"

Deep lines carved themselves alongside his nose. "Is the thought of living on the Danduroo that distasteful?"

"It has nothing to do with that. Stop trying to make such a big deal out of last night. It happens all the time."

"But not to you. You can scarcely pretend this is an everyday occurrence," he said sardonically.

"Well, maybe I just didn't know what I was missing," Leslie said brightly. "Now that you've introduced me to the joys of sex, my life will take on added color."

He crossed the room in two angry strides, grasping her shoulders and shaking her until she was breathless. "Don't talk like that! You're going to marry me and live on the Danduroo whether you bloody well like it or not!"

Why couldn't he take no for an answer? Why did he

have to keep torturing her with a glimpse of heaven that could only turn to hell when he regretted his quixotic gesture?

"I'm not going to marry you just to salve your misplaced sense of guilt," she cried. "When I do marry it's going to be for love, not because some man happened to appeal to me."

His steely fingers bit into the soft flesh of her arms. "Do you mean that it was only sex between us last night?"

She couldn't meet his angry gray glare. "I'm sorry if I've hurt your feelings."

He took her chin in his hand, jerking it up furiously so he could scan her face. "You might have if I believed you."

"That's up to you." She shrugged, hoping he wouldn't feel the tremor that was going through her. "As far as I'm concerned, last night is over and done with."

"Really?" His voice was softly mocking.

Moving with the lithe grace of a panther, he sat on the edge of the bed and pulled the sheet down, taking her nude body in his arms. Leslie was taken by surprise. When his mouth closed over hers, her lips parted automatically. Raider pressed his advantage, exploring the warm inner recess so sensually that she clung to him mindlessly, anchoring her fingers in this thick dark hair and murmuring his name.

Just as abruptly he pushed her back against the pillows. "So it's over and done with, is it?" he asked contemptuously. "I could take you right now. I could keep you in that bed for a week and you'd still be begging for more."

Leslie looked at him dazedly for a moment, her body chilled without his warmth. Then her cheeks flamed with color and she grabbed for the sheet. "That was a despicable thing to do!" she cried. "Did that restore your macho image? I've already admitted you turn me on; what more do you want?"

"I want to marry you," he said grimly.

What had just happened was a small taste of the humiliation she would suffer if she accepted his offer. He would play with her emotions and leave her dangling somewhere between ecstasy and torment. Better to end it now in one blinding slash of pain.

"I wouldn't marry you under any circumstances, and even in this crazy, upside-down country, you can't make me," she said tautly.

"That's what it's really all about, isn't it, Leslie? History repeating itself?"

Leslie knew she couldn't take much more of this without breaking down. How could she convince him? She searched for the cruelest words she could find. "Yes, that's it. I tried to be polite, but you're just too dense. I hate this country and I hate you. *Now* do you understand?"

Raider's face paled under the deep tan. He stood up slowly, staring down at her from a great height as his eyes grew wintry. "You've finally convinced me. My first instinct about you was right. Too bad I didn't follow it."

Leslie's heart was fracturing in a million pieces. She lowered her head to avoid the scorching look of contempt he was directing at her.

"You have thirty minutes to get ready," Raider said coldly. "I'm leaving then, with or without you." The door slammed with a terrible note of finality.

Leslie could barely drag herself out of bed. Dear Lord, when would this ordeal be over? If only she could leave now and never see Raider again. She considered it for a moment, rejecting the idea reluctantly. Even if she were willing to leave her things behind, her plane ticket was back at the Danduroo and the rental car had to be returned to the agency.

With a wrenching sigh, Leslie turned on the shower.

Chapter Twelve

The return trip to the Danduroo had been the nightmare Leslie had anticipated. The ride to the airport was accomplished without a word passing between Raider and herself. The flight back was equally painful.

Well, it was all over now, she realized, and she sighed, looking around the dusty living room. The small house that she had cleaned so painstakingly needed a thorough going-over again. For a moment Leslie was tempted to leave it as it was, then a sense of duty took over. You just didn't leave a dirty house behind. Besides, Raider already thought badly enough of her. She had fostered those opinions herself, yet for some perverse reason she didn't want him to think she was sloppy.

Compulsion drove her to leave the little house spotless, even to cleaning the closets she hadn't previously gotten around to. What difference did a few hours make?

The bedroom closet had a deep shelf on top, making it difficult to reach all the way to the back. Leslie teetered precariously on a step stool, groping blindly. As the stool tilted, she grabbed wildly for something to hold on to. She managed to right herself at the last minute, but the box she had pulled forward tumbled to the floor, spilling its contents.

It had been filled with papers. Leslie groaned inwardly as she looked at the mess, then her breath almost stopped. Staring up at her was her own graduation picture! She picked it up with shaking hands. How had Lester gotten this? Turning it over wonderingly, she saw a note on the back in what she recognized as Aunt Laura's handwriting.

It said: "I knew you would want to have Leslie's graduation picture. You can be proud of your daughter, Lester; she's as sweet as she is beautiful."

Leslie sank slowly to the floor, her legs like overcooked spaghetti. It couldn't be true! This was all some monstrous hoax! A man she had never seen or heard of was claiming to be her father. Yet even as her mind rejected the idea frantically, irrefutable facts stared her in the face. It was her own beloved Aunt Laura who'd said it, not Lester.

But how could that possibly be? And why hadn't anyone ever told her? Leslie started to tremble violently as she realized she was beginning to accept the possibility. The full implications left her mouth dry. If it was true, then she was illegitimate! And not only that, but what light did this place her mother in?

She had visited Australia—how long ago? Leslie did rapid calculations, her face turning ashen. Yes, the timing was right. And Raider had intimated from the start that her mother and Lester had engaged in a love affair. Suddenly Leslie knew with a terrible certainty that the story was true. Raider had known from the beginning that she was Lester's child. His only mistake was that because of her name, he thought at first she was Lester's *son.* Even that was proof in a way. Her mother had come as close as possible to naming her after her true father.

With an almost calm fatalism, Leslie reached for the other photographs that had spilled on the floor. A laughing snapshot of Lester gave her all the proof she needed. He was squinting into the sun, a handsome, virile man with hair the color of copper. The exact shade of Leslie's own!

Leslie stared at the photo for a long time before she noticed the one underneath it, a picture of her mother and Lester together. A very young Caroline was gazing adoringly up at the big man who held her as though she were a fragile bit of china. His eyes devoured her, oblivious to the camera or anything else. Their love was too obvious to be hidden, even if they had tried.

Tears blurred Leslie's eyes. She of all people could understand how it had happened. After last night she could be carrying Raider's child herself. It wasn't her own illegitimacy she was blaming them for, nor was she sitting in judgment on their morals. The thing Leslie couldn't forgive either of them for was the deception they had practiced. How could her mother have married anyone else while she was in love with, and pregnant by, another man? And how could Lester have allowed it?

Bitterness rose in Leslie's throat. Her earliest battles with Raider were over the fact that she hadn't come to see Lester when he was dying. Where was he when she was born? How could he stay out of her life all the years that she needed him and then expect her to come running when he decided to acknowledge her existence? That was evidently okay with Raider, as one virile man to another. In his eyes Lester was only doing what came naturally.

For the first time Leslie understood the animosity shown by her father. The man she *thought* was her father, she corrected herself. She could even feel sympathy for him. It must have been a living hell having evidence of his wife's illicit romance under his nose at all times. Why hadn't he divorced her when it became obvious why she had married him?

A vision of her mother abruptly surfaced, so different from the vibrant girl in the snapshot. Some of the ice around Leslie's heart melted. Poor Caroline. She had suffered for her mistake too. Everyone had except Lester. Suddenly Leslie couldn't bear to be in his house any longer. She got to her feet stiffly, feeling as though she had aged fifty years in five minutes.

Leaving everything on the floor where it had fallen, she went into the bedroom. It took a very short time to pack because she just threw everything into her suitcases. In a numbed state, Leslie carried them to the front door and closed it behind her without a backward glance, steeling herself to feel nothing.

The highway unwound in a monotonous strip as the small car ate up the miles. Leslie's foot was pushed almost to the floorboard seeking to outrace her mind. It only worked for a little while. Noxious thoughts returned to swarm around her like the ever-present Australian flies.

Raider wasn't the only one who knew about her uncertain parentage. Leslie recalled the startled look of recognition that Gordon, the bartender at the Rose and

Thistle, had given her, as well as Clara's noncommittal replies to her questions. How many more people knew? And knowing, how could they speak of Lester in such glowing terms? Then there was her Aunt Laura. She was in on the deception too. Leslie's mouth twisted with pain. There wasn't anyone left whom she could trust.

A loud sputtering sound gradually penetrated her consciousness and she braked sharply as a giant shadow appeared on the highway before her. Leslie watched in amazement as a helicopter swooped down, hovering over the road directly in her path. After she brought the car to a halt, it landed on the pavement ahead. While she stared, stupefied, Raider jumped down from the cockpit and came over to the car.

"What are you doing here?" she asked blankly.

Instead of answering, he opened her door. "Get out. You're coming with me."

Leslie snapped back to normal. "I'm not going anywhere with you! Get that thing out of my way."

"We have to talk."

"About what, my father?" she asked bitterly.

"You've had a shock," he said gently.

"You bet I have! Why didn't you tell me, Raider? And how could you spout all that garbage about what a fine man he was and that I'm not fit to live in his house?"

The muscles in Raider's jaw bunched as though he were clenching his teeth. "I never said that, Leslie."

"Well, you said—oh, what's the difference? Just get that thing off the road so I can be on my way."

"Not while you're in this state. I want you to come back to the house with me."

"I wouldn't set foot on the Danduroo again if it

guaranteed my eternal salvation," she flared, putting the car in gear. "If you won't move, I'll just have to go around you."

He turned off the ignition key, removing it and putting it in his pocket. "I realize you're upset," Raider said evenly, "but you're going to come with me if I have to carry you."

Leslie searched the lonely countryside desperately. There wasn't another car or truck, not a single sign of life—or assistance. Looking at Raider's set face, she knew he would do as he threatened. Suddenly an escape occurred to her.

"All right, if you insist. I'll have to meet you back there, though," she said. "I can't just leave the car here."

"Get in the helicopter, Leslie," he said implacably. "I'll drive your car off the road. One of the men will pick it up later."

When they were airborne, she faced him angrily, shouting over the noise of the motor. "You're just being obstinate. What is it that you couldn't tell me back there?"

Raider merely shook his head, refusing to say anything even when they were back at the Danduroo. He landed the chopper in the meadow in front of Lester's house, helping Leslie down and marching her up to the door with a firm grip on her arm.

Leslie tried to pull away. "Why did you bring me here? I thought we were going to your house. I don't ever want to see this place again."

He propelled her inside in spite of her protests. The first thing that met Leslie's eyes was the mess of papers on the floor. All the pain and misery she had been trying to suppress rose up inside her. She turned blindly toward the door, blocked by Raider's solid length.

His arms went around her and his mouth rested on her shining hair. "I know how you must have felt, darling, finding out this way. I blame myself for not telling you, but at first I thought you knew."

She struggled briefly, tears coursing down her pale face. But when Raider's arms continued to enfold her, his hands gently stroking her back, Leslie relaxed against him, sobbing out her grief against his comforting chest. After the storm had subsided to a few shuddering gasps, Raider lifted her chin, smiling into her wet blue eyes.

"Feeling better?" he asked softly.

"I guess so." She took the handkerchief he offered. "You said at first you thought I knew. Why didn't you tell me when you realized I didn't?"

"I didn't know how you would take it," he said simply.

"I can understand your reticence. I suppose nobody is overjoyed to discover they're illegitimate," she said bitterly.

He put his hands on her shoulders. "It's only a word, honey. It doesn't mean anything. The important thing is that your parents loved each other—and loved you."

"At least my mother did."

"And your father, too," he insisted. "You must know that."

"Because he remembered me in his will? A little late, wouldn't you say?"

"Leslie, he—"

"Never mind," she interrupted. "I don't want to hear it. Why did you bring me back here? How did you even know I'd found out?"

"I stopped by, and when I saw that"—he indicated the photos on the floor—"I knew you must have discovered the truth. Your car was missing, so it wasn't difficult to guess where you'd gone."

"How did you happen to come here? We didn't have anything more to say to each other."

He took a piece of paper out of his pocket. "Due to unfortunate circumstances, I never got around to giving you your check." His mouth twisted wryly.

"I don't want it!" She backed away as though it were a snake. "I don't want anything from him."

A puzzled frown creased Raider's forehead. "I don't understand your attitude, Leslie. Surely you can understand the pleasure it gave Lester to do this for you."

Anger flamed through her. "Am I supposed to be grateful? Your wonderful Lester couldn't be bothered marrying my mother," she stormed. "He didn't want a grubby little kid around the house. When I had the measles or needed braces on my teeth, he didn't want to know me. But when I graduated from college and wasn't any trouble, he suddenly remembered he had a child."

He looked at her incredulously. "Didn't you read the letter?"

"What letter?"

"The letter from your Aunt Laura; the one I thought you'd written."

"She was no better than they were," Leslie said tightly. "My father—well, you know who I mean—was her own brother."

Raider took her wrist, dragging her over to the couch. Stooping down, he picked up a thick envelope and thrust it into her hands. "Read that."

"I don't want—".

"Read it," he commanded.

Leslie removed the letter reluctantly. Why was Raider doing this to her? He must hate her a great deal to rub salt in the wound, she thought miserably. After the first few words her eyes were riveted to the page. The letter read:

Dear Lester:

I don't know if you'll remember me after all these years, or how you will feel about what I have to tell you. However, I've wrestled with my conscience and this is something I must do. I was the girl with Caroline Reed on that long-ago trip to the Danduroo. I'm not worried about your remembering Caroline. A man doesn't forget the girl he once asked to marry him. If only you two had eloped right then instead of being reasonable when her father asked you to wait for a year. He was only doing what he thought best; but what none of you knew, including Caro, was that she was pregnant.

I'm sorry to come out with it so badly, but there isn't any other way. You have a daughter, Leslie, twenty-three years old, and I believe you have a right to know about it. You're probably wondering why I'm telling you this instead of Caroline, and why it has taken so long. The answer to that will be another shock, I'm afraid. Caroline is dead. She never wanted you to know about Leslie, and while she was alive I had to respect her wishes even though I thought it was a mistake. You see, by the time Caro discovered you really loved her, she was already married to my brother.

Let me try to explain. When Caroline found out she was pregnant, she telephoned you and was told you were "unavailable." They didn't explain that you were setting up a new camp in the western quadrant and wouldn't return for a couple of weeks. The person she talked to said he would give you a message and then promptly forgot about it, probably. Caroline waited and waited for your call. When it didn't come, she felt it was a brush-off, a summer fling that you wanted to forget about.

She could have gone to a doctor for a discreet operation, but she wanted your baby desperately, even though she was convinced you didn't love her, and even though the consequences for her would have been grave. This was twenty-three years ago, remember, a time when people weren't as liberal. She didn't mind so much for herself, but she worried about the stigma on Leslie. In her distracted state, it was easy for my brother to convince her to marry him. He had been in love with her for years and he offered security and a name for her baby, even though Caroline told him the whole story and warned that she didn't love him.

It was a hasty marriage, of necessity, and when your letter finally came explaining why you hadn't been able to contact her, it was too late. My brother Phillip refused to release her, and she had no grounds for divorce. Please don't think he was a monster. He loved her very much and felt that in time she would come to love him. I don't know if it will give you pleasure or pain, but she never did. Caroline loved you until the day she died.

I hope I've done the right thing in telling you. Leslie knows nothing of this, and if you choose to keep it that way, I'll respect your decision.

Best Wishes,
Laura Farraday

Leslie's eyes were wet when she looked up from the thick letter. "It's so sad," she murmured.

Raider's hand gripped her shoulder hard. "Maybe they're together finally."

"I hope so." Leslie stood up and went to look out of the window. "I'm so ashamed of the things I was thinking," she said in a subdued voice.

"You couldn't know. I didn't myself."

She turned startled blue eyes on him. "But you did."

He shook his head. "Not the whole story. I knew you

were Lester's daughter, that's all. I was there when he read the letter."

"He told you that but not the rest of it?"

"I'm not sure he would even have told me that if he hadn't been so shaken. I had been to town to pick up the mail and we were sitting on the fence together as he read it. Lester gave a kind of strangled gurgle and turned deathly pale. Naturally I insisted on knowing what was the matter. I can still remember his words because it shook me up a little, too. He said, 'I'm a father, Raider. I have a child twenty-three years old.' "

"He just said a child? Not a daughter? Then that's another mystery cleared up," Leslie exclaimed.

Raider nodded. "After that he kind of tottered off to his house in a daze and I started putting two and two together. The trouble is, I came up with the wrong answer, just like you did."

"What do you mean?"

He turned away, shamefaced. "I'm afraid I thought your mother had come out here looking for kicks—a quick tumble with a macho cowboy."

"And you thought the same about me," Leslie said evenly.

"I've been a fool from start to finish," he said savagely.

Leslie was surprisingly calm. "Yes, you have been."

There was pain in Raider's face as he looked at her. "She didn't hate the Danduroo the way you do. She would have given anything to live here with the man she loved."

And I would too, Leslie felt like shouting. She lowered her head to keep the knowledge from him. "I don't hate the Danduroo," Leslie said in a low voice.

He reached out and touched her cheek with gentle fingers. "You don't have to worry any more about hurting my feelings. I deserve it. I've hurt yours all too often."

"I mean it, Raider, I love this place." That much of the truth she owed him. A wistful smile curved her drooping mouth. "I must have a lot of my father in me."

Hope flared in his eyes as he cupped her face in his hands. "Then you'll stay?"

If only he wouldn't touch her. It was hard enough to keep from throwing herself in his arms, pulling that dark head down to hers and clinging to him forever. When he was so close that she could smell the masculine scent of him and be tantalized by that strong rangy body, it became a near impossibility.

Leslie shook her head. "I can't," she whispered.

His hands fell away. "That means it's me you hate."

"No, Raider, I—" She stopped herself in time. Taking a shaky breath, Leslie said, "Listen to me, because it's important that you know why I'm leaving. There have been enough misunderstandings around here. Fortunately ours aren't as tragic as my mother and father's, but I still want you to understand."

Something flared in Raider's eyes. "Do you realize—"

She swept on before he could finish. "Last night was a beautiful experience for me, one I'll always cherish. I know it didn't mean anything to you, that I was just another girl in your bed." She shook her head as he reached for her. "You don't have to deny it; I knew what I was doing, and I don't regret it. The only thing I do regret is giving you the impression that I was just looking for a thrill."

He was watching her intently. "If that wasn't it, why did you let me make love to you?"

Her wide blue eyes darkened with pain. "I'd rather not answer that, if you don't mind."

"Do you realize the same thing could happen to you that happened to your mother?" he demanded. "You could be pregnant."

"I . . . yes, I suppose it's possible," she admitted.

"What would you do about it?" he asked harshly. "A convenient operation, or a willing patsy for a husband?" Before she could answer, his hands fastened like a vise around her arms, bruising her with the intensity of his passion. "No other man is going to raise my child! You're going to marry me if I have to tie you up and drag you to the altar."

"You don't know that I'm pregnant, Raider," she said wonderingly. "Why wouldn't you want to wait and find out?"

He folded her in his arms, holding her so tightly that she felt imprinted with every hard, masculine muscle. "I don't give a damn if you're pregnant or not! Just as long as you marry me," he groaned. "If I have to scare you into it I'll do that, or anything else that's necessary. I love you, Leslie; I can't let you go."

She felt suddenly dizzy, afraid to trust what she was hearing. It must be the rapture of being in his arms that was making her imagine the words she longed to hear.

"You mustn't feel guilty because I was a virgin," she murmured. "No one else could have initiated me so wonderfully."

"No one else is ever going to get a chance," he said savagely, his mouth closing over hers with a male dominance that left her trembling.

Leslie was powerless to resist his onslaught, especially when it was what she wanted so desperately. Her hands moved restlessly inside his shirt, feeling the pounding beat of his heart under the curling black hair. Raider shuddered, holding her hips against his and moving with a deliberate sensuality that awakened memories of his possession.

"You can't deny that we have this," he muttered, bending his head to kiss the breast that swelled responsively in his hand. "I'll teach you to love me. I'll spend every night bringing you ecstasy like you've never known before."

Happiness enveloped Leslie in a golden cloak. Raider loved her! All the misery dissolved in a rush of joy as she accepted this gift from heaven. Fitting her body to his, she kissed the strong column of his throat.

"There are a lot of things you can teach me," she murmured, "but not how to love you." When he stiffened in her arms, she drew his head down to hers. "I've loved you since the minute you dragged me onto that terrible horse of yours."

Incredulous joy shone in his eyes. "Then you'll marry me? You'll live here on the Danduroo?"

Leslie didn't bother to answer such a foolish question. Lifting her face to his, she gave him the answer with her lips.

Much later Raider stirred in her arms, brushing back her glorious hair so he could look possessively at the delicate contours of her face. She smiled tremulously up at him. "It's still hard to believe you really love me," she whispered.

He drew her closer, his voice a low growl in her ear. "Would you like me to prove it again?"

"In a little while." She colored adorably. Raider still had the power to make her feel shy. "First I'd like you to tell me something."

"Anything." His fingers trailed lingeringly over her breast.

"Please, Raider!" She captured his hand. "I can't think when you do that."

"Do you really want to?" he murmured, kissing the corner of her mouth.

"Yes!" she gasped, putting him firmly away. "There is something I have to know."

Raider let her go reluctantly. "All right, darling, what is it?"

"That night I told you I wanted to be friends, you said you didn't want my friendship." The hurt still showed in Leslie's voice.

He nodded. "You were driving me right out of my mind. I was in love with you and I couldn't get past first base. I knew I could make you respond to me, yet every time I turned my back, you ran off with Marty."

"Raider, it wasn't—"

He put a gentle finger on her lips. "I know, but that's how it looked. The night you got all done up in that sexy dress was the last straw. I wanted to carry you off to bed and make love to you for a week. And then you came out with that prissy little speech about wanting to be *friends!* I was about to tell you I didn't want to be your friend, I wanted to be your husband and lover, when Allison interrupted us."

Leslie's pleasure at his explanation was marred by the remembrance of Raider's beautiful girlfriend. "I wanted to die when I saw her. Why did you bring her to the house, Raider?" she asked in a low voice.

He kissed her trembling mouth. "A lot of reasons. The hope of making you jealous was the real one, but I told myself that once I saw you together, I'd realize you couldn't measure up to Allison."

"I didn't." Leslie's face was troubled. "She's everything you want in a woman."

"No, sweetheart, *you* are." His smile faded. "You don't know how it tore me up to think you hated it here."

"It was a defense mechanism," she sighed. "I couldn't let you know how I really felt. From the beginning I thought your only interest in me was Lester's property." Leslie bent her head, one finger smoothing the dark hair on his broad chest. "Even that day you made love to me in the meadow—you *did* give in rather easily when I suggested signing the papers."

"I wanted you to have the money, and I knew you'd never take it from me any other way. As for Lester's property, I was going to give it back to you as a wedding present—or a going-away present, if the worst happened." His arms closed convulsively around her. "You don't know the agony *that* thought gave me!"

Leslie snuggled closer to him. Raider's love was all the gift she needed. Something occurred to her. "My beautiful opal ring! I think I knew at the time that it wasn't the little thing Marty had dug up. Was that supposed to be a going-away present too?"

Raider smiled and shook his head. "It was intended as an engagement ring. I wanted to put it on your left hand, but I couldn't take a chance in front of the salesman."

"Oh, Raider, if you only had! The thought of having to leave here almost killed me."

He looked at her as though he couldn't quite believe it. "You really love the Danduroo? You won't be lonely or bored living here?"

Leslie's smile had the quality of the Mona Lisa's. "I understand that taking care of a baby keeps one very busy."

Something flamed in Raider's eyes as he reached for her. "That's very true, but you don't know that you're pregnant."

Leslie put her arms around his waist, moving seductively against his quickened loins. "I'm sure you can do something about that," she murmured.